Escape to Starshine Cove

Debbie Johnson

Storm

Copyright © Debbie Johnson, 2023

The moral right of the author has been asserted.

Ebook ISBN: 978-1-80508-124-1
Paperback ISBN: 978-1-80508-142-5

Cover design: Rose Cooper
Cover images: Shutterstock

Published by Storm Publishing.
For further information, visit:
www.stormpublishing.co

Also by Debbie Johnson

Part One

Happy Talk

Chapter One

Have you ever tried to meditate? And if so, did you find it nigh on impossible? I don't know why it's so hard, because it seems pretty simple on the surface: sit still, breathe deeply, clear your mind. In reality, you might as well ask me to design and assemble a NASA space rocket from scratch – I think I'd find it easier.

I have been coming to these sessions for months now, and I wonder if they know I am a complete fraud – that while everyone else is serenely finding their inner peace, I am sitting here, cross-legged, pondering everything from what I need to buy from the supermarket to the leak in the downstairs loo to the fact that I'm overdue for my smear test. My mind is like an endless spin-cycle on a washing machine, my thoughts churning and tumbling, any hints of calm drowned out of existence.

We've been told not to expect to have clear minds – that most of us might struggle to turn our mental landscape into a blank canvas. Thoughts are normal, we're told – but when they start to intrude, just gently swat them away like you would a curious butterfly that gets too close to your face.

Except my thoughts aren't curious butterflies – they're murder hornets.

I suspect I have been wasting my time, and that I should have been doing something more productive instead, like eating a cake or watching Netflix or sleeping. Except...well, I have trouble even enjoying those things these days. Hence the alleged meditation.

I am, truth be told, a bit of a mess right now. I hide it well: I manage a demanding job, I live in a swish house with a swish man, and nothing about the way I look screams 'disaster zone on legs'. Inside, it's a different story – murder hornets all the way.

I open my eyes a tiny crack, and glance around the room. Everyone else looks pretty blissed out, and I wonder if it's just me who is feeling this way – just me who comes to a meditation class in search of calm and ends up feeling like a big fat failure of a woman who can't even sit still properly. In fact, I find these classes stressful, which is pretty ironic really. I might be the only person who comes out with higher blood pressure than I started with.

I see the big clock on the wall at the front of the room, and feel a sense of relief when I realise that this self-enforced torture has almost finished.

The instructor tells us to think about who we are, to be grateful, to fill ourselves with love. I do my very best: I am Ella Farrell. I love my life. I love my job. I love my partner. I love myself. I repeat it over and over in my mind, but it's hard to maintain a lie you're telling yourself – in truth, I'm not sure I love any of those things any more. I'm not sure I have loved them for a long time. And I don't feel grateful, I just feel empty.

The course leader moves on to the one part of the sessions I really enjoy, telling us all to go to our happy place. I have no idea what everyone else's happy place is, but mine is easy – it's a coastline. Wild and beautiful and free, with dazzling blue waves and soft sand beneath my feet and endless views of the edge of the world. I can almost feel the sunlight warming my skin, smell the salt in the air, hear the hiss of the water rolling into land. For those few moments, I almost fool myself – I am almost happy. I have found my nearly-happy place.

We finish up, roll mats, nod goodbyes. I see small clutches of women chatting, maybe planning to go for coffee, sharing stories and laughter and friendship. I just keep my head down, grab my backpack, and leave. I want to try and stay in my happy place for however many minutes my mind will let me.

I walk out of the building, still imagining that sand beneath my feet, that warmth against my skin, and emerge into reality.

I am in inner-city London. It is raining, and it is loud. I lurk by the edge of the pavement, momentarily stunned by the assault on my senses. A big red double decker bus whooshes past, splashing me with filthy gutter water. Two pigeons are fighting over a discarded sausage roll, and I notice that one of them only has one leg. I can hear sirens, and shouts, and am immediately approached by a man who could be anywhere between 30 and 90. His front teeth are missing, and he tells me he needs some change to pay for a night in a hostel.

I hand him a fiver and walk away before he can talk to me any more. I know I am being rude, that a few minutes of my time would be more compassionate than the cash. I can't find it in myself to care, and I stride briskly ahead, avoiding eye contact with every other living creature around me – human, pigeon, even the big fake smiling faces on billboard ads.

My happy place is gone. I'm left with this – my actual place.

I need to go to work. I have a night shift at a drop-in health centre, and I have my clothes in my bag. I need to make my way there, shower, and put on my game face. Transform myself into a caring professional who can help people in their hour of need.

Except, I realise, as I narrowly avoid stepping into a pile of vomit on the pavement, that I don't think I can. I don't think I can help anyone any more. I don't think I have anything left to give.

I stand still for a moment, frozen in time and space, the raucous rhythms of the city moving around me, people jostling me out of their way, the sound of a drill on a building site burying itself deep into my brain.

I have to go home, I think, hailing a black cab. I have to go home, and escape the murder hornets before it's too late.

Chapter Two

I stand outside the house I live in and stare at it. The cab driver leans his head out of the window, his sparse grey hair getting flattened by the incessant rain of our glorious English summer.

"You all right, love?" he asks, frowning.

"Perfect," I reply, forcing a smile onto my rain-soaked face. "Never been better."

He shakes his head, and I suspect he's seen stranger things – cabbies have seen it all, haven't they? The history of human existence should be written by Hackney drivers, I suspect.

He performs an impressive three-point turn and disappears in a cloud of diesel. I heft my bag onto my shoulder and get my keys ready. It is, quite obviously, very wet out here, and it will be much nicer inside four walls. Somehow, though, I still can't quite face it.

I have lived here for eight years, and yet I still don't think of it as home. It is a grand house on the outskirts of Regent's Park, its façade a picture of Georgian grandeur, the inside all mod-cons and cool interior design. There are apple trees in the small garden, and a roof terrace that overlooks the park, and four double bedrooms. It is far too big for the two of us, I've always thought. Far too easy for distance to creep in when you have so much space to retreat to.

Mark's Mercedes is parked in the drive, and I can picture him inside: crashed out on the sofa, maybe watching football, a glass of expensive wine in his hand. It's always wasted on me, the good stuff; I'm a wine philistine.

It's Friday, and he will be trying to decompress from a busy week at the bank where he works as a fund manager. He makes a lot of money, and works very hard, and he thrives on the pressure of it all. I could never afford to live in a place like this on my NHS salary, and it is yet another thing I know I should feel grateful for.

And yet, I realise as I make my way to the front door, I am not. It is a house, not a home, and part of me yearns for our younger days, when we were low on funds but high on love. The Mark and Ella we were back then feel like strangers now, distant memories, versions of ourselves that have been buried by all the layers of years and experience.

I am, I decide, being ridiculous, and I close the door behind me with new resolve to find that version of myself again. I must still be there, somewhere. I just need to send out a search party.

I pause in the hallway, listening out for the expected sounds of the TV but not finding them. I frown, dump my stuff, and stroll through to the kitchen. It is a grand affair, marble surfaces and a barely used six-ring hob for people who live on takeaways, restaurant food and microwaveable ready-meals. I see two wine glasses, half empty, and absent-mindedly I tip out the contents and put them in the dishwasher. He must have gone for a nap, and is probably dreaming dreams of spreadsheets and balances and return on investments.

I sit down on the couch in the perfectly decorated living room, and stare around me. I have the strangest sensation that I have never been here before, that I am a visitor in my own life. I see the framed pictures of the two of us over the years – me and

Mark on holiday in Santorini, me and Mark at Wimbledon, me and Mark with his parents at their home in Scotland. The photos are proof that it all happened, but it still feels unreal. Removed. Maybe, I think, I have finally cracked this meditation lark – and I have meditated my way out of existence.

I remember an elderly patient I saw recently, struggling with memory loss. She described to me how she could vividly remember her early years – her childhood, her pregnancies, her wedding – but struggled to recall what she had for tea the day before. I feel a little like that right now – I know I have travelled with Mark, built a life with him, but none of it seems as bright in my mind as the stuff I did before I even knew him.

My childhood, my university years, the wild summer of backpacking my way around Europe with a group of friends I now barely see. They've all moved on, become Facebook friends more than real friends. They all have children, husbands, their posts filled with pictures of adorable family scenes and dog walks and nights out with school-gate pals. Their lives are not the same as mine, and yet I still have those memories – four girls gone feral in France, in our early 20s and our futures stretching out before us.

I shake off the melancholy, and decide I need that shower. That I need to wash the sad away. I've already messaged work to say I am sick, and it didn't even feel like a lie. I work for an agency that provides locum doctors, and I know they'll be able to replace me. I'm not that important.

I walk slowly up the stairs, as quietly as I can so that I don't wake Mark up. Partly because I don't want to disturb him, partly because I don't want to have to talk to him.

As I reach the landing, I hear a low murmur of conversation, no clear words but the distinct sounds of people talking and laughing. I freeze, momentarily scared that we have been broken into. I soon realise that it seems unlikely that burglars would be sitting in the spare room having a chat, and wonder instead if a radio has been left on. Even though, you know, we don't have a radio in that room.

I pause, hear more giggling, and push the door open. I see Mark, the man who has been my partner for the last 13 years, lying naked on the bed. I see Kim, his PA, in the process of doing some kind of mock-burlesque strip-tease in front of him, teasing off her bra and whirling it around her head. She lets it fly, and a whisper of black lace gets tangled in the dangling light fitting.

I see both of them turn at the sound I make, my gasp of complete disbelief. The looks on their faces would have been comedic if this was a TV show, but it's not – it's my actual life. It's pain and betrayal and hurt and shock, and beneath all of that, perhaps this scene is also not entirely unexpected. It seems to click naturally into place with the rest of my day.

I stare at them both, incapable of forming words, then back away, closing the door behind me. I find that I'm blinking rapidly, that my knees are weak, and I place my hands on the wall as I stagger along, like a mime artist. I am only down a corridor from the master bedroom, but it feels like a million miles away, the space stretching ahead of me, warped into something psychedelic and trippy. My house has turned into Willy Wonka's Chocolate Factory.

I finally reach the room, falling inside its temporary refuge. At least I didn't find them in the bed we share – a small mercy, but a mercy all the same. He may be a cheater, but he's a considerate cheater at least.

I collapse onto the mattress, puffing in air and staring around me, trying to make sense of it all. I stay upright, my hands grasping my knees to keep myself steady.

I'm not sure how long I sit like that, frozen and broken and veering between fight and flight, but eventually I manage to stand up, my legs weak and my breath coming way too fast, teetering into the en-suite. I splash water onto my face, scrubbing at my eyes and kneading my knuckles hard into my sockets until they are sore.

It doesn't help. I can't wash away that scene; I cannot unsee it. Mark, Kim, all of that bare flesh. Even worse, maybe, the laughter, the giggles, the strip-tease – the fun they were having together. That hurts more than the sex, and I think I will remember the giggles for even longer than the boobs.

I lean against the tiled wall and slide unsteadily to the floor. I gaze around, at the signs of our life together – the toothbrushes next to each other in a glass; the little tray filled with his cuff-links and my ear-rings; the laundry basket where our clothes are mingled together more intimately than we are.

None of it feels real. Seeing them together doesn't feel real, the betrayal doesn't feel real. This life we apparently lead doesn't feel real. Only the pain of it feels real – the sting of my eyes, the blood on my lip as I bite it, the cold sense of numbness that is spreading through my body.

I am in shock, I tell myself. I am understandably in shock, and I need to move, or I will freeze here, immobile and forever trapped on a bathroom floor. I will become a statue, like a person from Pompeii trapped in the ashes of my old world.

I hear footsteps on the stairs, the slamming of the front door. I scramble up, make my way back into the bedroom.

Mark walks in, dressed in a slapdash version of his work clothes – trousers on but belt not buckled, shirt on but not buttoned all the way up, his feet bare. His expensive haircut is a disaster zone, dark strands sticking out in distress. He holds his hands out towards me in a gesture that reminds me of someone trying to tame a wild animal, taking hesitant steps in my direction as though scared I might leap up and tear out his jugular with my teeth.

I don't have the energy for that. I don't have the energy for anything.

"Babe..." he says, standing tentatively beside me, ready to flee. "I'm so sorry. I didn't want you to see that."

"Really?" I say, gazing into the blue eyes I know so well. Or thought I did. "You didn't want me to see it, so you thought the best place to bring your other woman was our home?"

"You were *supposed* to be at work!" he replies, his voice plaintive and almost peeved – as though I've somehow messed up here. Somehow failed to stick to his plan. That pushes me over the edge into anger, and I finally find some fury.

"And you're *supposed* to be able to keep your dick in your pants, Mark, so I guess we're both a bit disappointed right now, aren't we?"

He recoils at my tone, and I see him visibly deflate. I see him turn it all over in his mind, can almost visualise the mental cogs turning, the arguments he is formulating, the plan he is making to explain, to justify, to mollify. As I said, he thrives under pressure.

"Don't bother," I say quietly, my anger fizzling out as fast as it came. "Don't bother with the excuses, or the explanations, or the apologies. Don't bother because you know what, Mark, I don't really care."

I am walking towards the wardrobe, fumbling with the handles. My fingers seem to have become disconnected from my mind.

"What do you mean, you don't care?" he asks, clearly confused at having control of this scenario wrenched from him. "Let me explain, at least!"

I turn towards him, and smile. It is a twisted thing, devoid of any pleasure, but it is all I have to offer him. That and the truth – the truth that we have both been hiding from for way too long, the truth that will either kill us or set us free. The truth that I can't avoid even a single day longer. No amount of self-care or yoga or meditation classes are ever going to fix this, to fix me –

because I don't want them to. None of this is right, none of this is working – and now I don't even have to pretend it is.

"No, Mark, let *me* explain," I say, with more calm than I've felt for years. "You don't love me any more. And no, don't argue – it's fine. I don't love you either. Kim isn't causing this – the state of us caused Kim. We've not so much drifted apart as moved to opposite hemispheres. When's the last time we actually genuinely felt right together? It's a serious question – when?"

He gazes at the window, frowning, as I wait for his answer.

"When we were in Barbados," he says finally, not even meeting my eyes.

I nod. It's exactly what I would have said as well. January 2020 – before lockdown, before working from home, before I volunteered at an A&E ward. Before everything changed – before we lost so much, both of us.

The thought of that loss, the thought of how far it has driven us apart, fills me with a new sadness. I reach out, take his hand in mine. He grips my fingers in a way that feels so familiar, that once would have felt comforting – but you can't find comfort in the person who is hurting you. We can't go back; we can only go forward.

"It's over, Mark. It's been over for a long time. I can't carry on pretending to be all hashtag blessed when all I feel, I don't know about you, is hashtag knackered."

He smiles. I am gently poking fun at his Instagram account, which presents a picture-perfect view of our lives – of the lives we seem to have from the outside looking in.

"I'm now feeling very hashtag sad," he replies, turning to look at me. I see tears in his eyes, and mine respond in kind. There is a lot of history between us, between me and this man. A lot of love in days gone by, a lot of laughter – but none of that exists any more. It's time we faced up to that.

"Are you sure?" he asks. "Isn't there some way we could...
try again? Go to Barbados maybe?"

That, in all honesty, is Mark all over – thinking that if he
wants something enough, that if he throws enough money at a
problem, he will be able to solve the unsolvable.

"Take Kim to Barbados," I answer. "Though she'll have to
take her ID to get served in the bars."

He grimaces slightly, and I know I have hit home with that
one. Kim is in fact in her early 20s, but he is 40. He won't
appreciate being reminded that he has become a walking cliché.

"What are you going to do?" he says. "Do you want to...I
don't know, sell the house or something?"

The tone of his voice makes me laugh out loud – he loves
this house, possibly more than he has ever loved anything. He
came from a working-class background, and this place is more
than a building to him – it's a symbol of everything he has
worked for, everything he has achieved. I have the sneaking
suspicion that losing the house would be harder for him than
losing me, which just about sums up exactly why I'm the
emotional equivalent of the walking dead, and he's shagging his
secretary.

I manage to open the wardrobe door, look in at the racks of
dresses and skirts and jackets. I don't feel like any of it belongs
to me. I don't feel like I have ever been the woman who these
clothes have fitted.

"No. I don't want that, Mark," I reply, grabbing a few items
from their hangers. "We can sort that stuff out later. It's not
important, really. As for what I'm going to do, well..."

I glance around at the trendy silver-grey walls, the walk-in
wardrobes, the en-suite with its heated towel rail and rainforest
shower. I see it all, in its shiny perfection, and wonder if I could
turn my back on all of this – ask myself if I need it, or want it.
Will I miss any of it, including the handsome man standing next
to me, if I leave? I don't know, but I think I have to try. I cannot

stay here, with him, in this house I have never loved, haunted by the memory of what has happened here.

"I think," I say slowly, leaning forward to give him a quick kiss on the cheek, "that I'm going to find my happy place. And I'm taking your car."

Part Two

Happy Accident

Chapter Three

One month later

I get out of the car and kick its tyres. Every single one of them. It doesn't make the engine start, but it does make me feel a bit better.

I gaze up at the sky – a merciless blue – and squint against the sun that seems to have decided that England is the new Mediterranean. It's been like this ever since I left London, and at first I took it as a good omen – a sign that things were looking up.

I'd taken myself off the books at the agency, packed the bare minimum, and left the very same day that I found another woman in bed with my boyfriend. I had no plan, no aim, no destination in mind – which turned out to be something of a mistake, as I ended up spending the first night in a Travelodge near Watford wondering why I'd forgotten my toothbrush but remembered a photo album from almost 20 years ago.

As I'd flicked through the pages, though, it had given me the seeds of an idea – I decided that I would go and visit my old friends. That I would reconnect, rediscover the spark of fun and camaraderie that we shared at university, and during that mad trip to Europe. We'd been so close, shared so much – surely it wasn't too late for us? I would tell them about my life, about the events that had cast their shadow over it. About Mark, and London, and my job. I would tell them everything, and they would understand, and they would help – and in return I would finally get to meet their children, see their homes, be present in their worlds again.

It was definitely the seed of an idea – but it hadn't blossomed into much at all. Two of them, Katie and Priya, were away on holiday themselves, it turned out. Which, you know, makes sense during the summer. The third, Lucy, had moved to Ireland without telling me, which I only found out as I stood on the doorstep of her old house on the outskirts of Manchester, feeling like a fool as the new residents explained, and invited me in for a cup of tea. I must have looked as crestfallen as I felt.

So now, a month later, I am here – somewhere in Dorset on the south-west coast of the country. I have no idea why, because I still don't have a plan. I have spent the last few weeks travelling aimlessly from place to place, going where the wind blows me. Some of it has been stressful, and boring, and pointless – unless you count eating in every service station in the land as a win. But some of it has been amazing – a night spent in a yurt overlooking Lake Windermere; walking the Long Mynd in Shropshire; a crazy day out doing Beatles tours in Liverpool that ended up with a karaoke session with complete strangers. 'You're So Vain', in case you're wondering.

Mainly, though, it's been...lonely. I left Mark because I felt alone even when I was with him, and because I couldn't keep up the pretence of being one half of a fake-perfect couple. Now I don't have to pretend – but I'm still lonely. There are only so many beautiful sunsets you can watch in isolation before you start to avoid them; only so many times you can keep a jaunty tone in your voice as you say 'Yes, just a table for one, please'; only so many photos you can store on your phone when you have nobody to show them to.

I thought, maybe, I just needed time to adjust. I have been in a couple for a long time, and perhaps it was too optimistic to expect to just find my happy place straight away. I suspect that your happy place has to be earned, and I haven't put my time in yet. It was probably always unlikely that I could just dump my old life and walk right into a new and better one – but I was determined to keep trying.

I had some vague concept of heading for Cornwall, where I'd spent a few holidays as a child. Happy holidays that I remember being full of rock-pooling and falling off surf boards and eating creamy scones. My parents moved to Portugal when I was 23, and although I've obviously seen them plenty of times since then, we don't have that kind of relationship where we keep up daily chats or share the intimate details of everyday life. In fact, I haven't even told them that I've left London, left Mark, left my career. Maybe it's because I don't want to worry them – but maybe it's because I don't want to get told off by my mum and dad when I'm staring 40 in the face. I'm way too old to be told to sit on the naughty step.

The car, though, had other ideas – it really didn't want to go to Cornwall. It absolutely hated the idea, and has made its feelings known by simply refusing to drive any further. I'm not a damsel in distress, and know the basics of car care – but this is a flashy modern Mercedes that has more in common with an AI overlord than the Renault Clio I drove when I was younger.

I've actually been sleeping in it for the last few nights, so maybe it objected to being turned into an Airbnb on wheels. I'd just had enough of hotels, and of people looking at me with curiosity, and of the conversation issue. The conversation issue has become a bit of a thing with me – I have found myself sitting in hotel bars or pubs or cafés many times in the last few weeks, and sometimes I want to speak to people, to engage in the world around me. Sometimes I want to remain alone and isolated, left with my thoughts.

The problem is that nobody on the outside can tell which mood I'm in from looking, which is fair enough. It never seems to work out right, and I get complete strangers trying to chat to me when I'm feeling silent, and when I'm looking for someone to talk to, everyone else is busy with their own crowd. Because the weather has been so fair, I'd decided there were worse things to do than to recline the seats and just stay in the car instead. It made sense at the time, which is perhaps a worrying thing – my concept of what makes sense is becoming ever more elastic.

Right now, though, as I sit myself down on a patch of grass at the side of the road, nothing makes sense. Without the car's aircon, I am hot. I am tired. I need a shower. I ran out of water a few miles back, and all I have to eat is a packet of crisps I got as part of a meal deal in some services a few days ago.

As soon as the car showed signs of becoming moody, I pulled away from the busy highway that flows along the county, and turned off at the first opportunity. Now I am stuck on what appears to be a completely abandoned B-road, with no phone signal, in blazing sunshine. It is a very pretty place, for a road – the grassy patch I am draped across is backed by hedgerows in full summer bloom, pink and white flowers tangled into the greenery, the hum of bees in the air. The woodland behind is dense, oaks and hawthorns, the ground carpeted with forget-me-nots and bright pink foxgloves. Probably lots of other things but my spotting skills are rusty after living in London for so long. In parts of London, an especially mouldy abandoned kebab counts as wildlife.

The road runs down the side of a very steep hill, and at the bottom, I can see the sea. It looks amazing, even in my foul mood – sunlight sparkling on a rolling blanket of turquoise. The kind of sea you immediately want to jump into.

"Ha," I say out loud – this is another thing I've noticed I do a lot of these days – "at least if I die out here, I'm spending my last moments somewhere beautiful."

I don't really think I'm going to die – I'm a doctor after all; I'd spot the signs. But in this weather, with no water, I am at least running the risk of sunstroke or dehydration, neither of which is a whole lot of fun. I know I'm going to have to get up and walk at some point, find civilisation or at least some phone reception, but right now I don't have it in me. I will sit for five minutes, first, eat my crisps, and decompress from my angry tyre-kicking tantrum.

As I take a few deep breaths and try to give myself a pep talk, I hear a rustling sound in the hedgerow next to me. I resist the urge to jump up and run – there is unlikely to be anything aggressive in an English hedgerow – and instead stay very still, scanning the roots and branches beside me.

Eventually, I see a face. A very small, very furry, very scared-looking face. At first I'm not at all sure what it actually is – cat, ferret, woodland sprite, a previously undiscovered species of hedgehog. It even looks a bit like E.T. at a glance. I freeze, sensing that any sudden movements I make will scare it away. I see brown eyes peering at me from a fringe of matted fur, and a pink tongue hanging out of its tiny mouth, panting.

It is, I realise, a dog. A very small, very dirty, very worried dog. I haven't had a dog since I was 15, and that one was an insanely fat black Lab who regularly got scared by its own radioactive farts and loved every living creature it ever met, including cats, squirrels and postmen.

This one looks terrified, and even jumps at the crinkling sound of the crisp bag. I pull one out, and hold it gently in the direction of the furry face. It recoils a little, then the nose starts to twitch, and eventually it makes a swift snatch and grab.

We repeat this action a few more times, and bit by bit, I place the crisps closer to me. By the time I have one resting on my leg, the dog is confident enough to wriggle itself entirely out of the hedgerow, standing and staring at me, eyes flicking between me and the ultra-desirable crisp.

"Yeah, that's the spirit," I say gently, patting my knee. "You can do it, boy. Girl. Whatever you are – I don't feel like we know each other well enough for me to check just yet..."

Step by shaky step, the dog approaches. When it gets close, it stares up at me with baleful eyes, and obviously comes to a decision. It picks the crisp up, and crawls onto my lap, where it curls up in a smelly ball. I lay a very cautious hand on its back, and stroke it. I feel a tremor go through its body, but it stays where it is.

I'm more accustomed to examining human bodies than canine, but once it seems settled, I slowly run my fingers over its body. Beneath all that tangled grey-white fur, I can feel too-sharp ribs, and when I reach its front legs it whimpers.

I mutter some soothing words, and peer at its right paw. I see a thorn embedded in its pad, dried blood around it.

"Ah, you poor thing – what a curse to not have hands, eh?" I say. "Now, this might be scary, but you've just got to trust me, okay? It's better out than in."

I've spent years removing foreign objects from places they're not supposed to be; some of them you really don't want to know about. Here, I don't have gloves or a sterile environment or tweezers, but I still have technique. I keep a firmer hand on its back, and manage to snag the end of the thorn between my nails. I quickly pull it out, making the sad creature yelp, but I give it another crisp straight away to placate it.

Once the crisp is demolished, it licks its paw, and gives a weedy twitch of its tail. For some reason, it's that twitch that makes me cry – the way this poor, broken creature still has enough hope to try and show some happiness. The way it seems to trust me. The way it is lying here, in my arms, letting me comfort it, one broken creature to another.

I lean down to give its head a quick kiss, immediately regretting it.

"Whoah there!" I say, wiping the tears from my cheeks. "You are one pungent dog! Then again, I'm probably not much better after three nights sleeping in a car and getting baked for the last hour... What do you say, pal, shall we go in search of help? Or at least a bowl of water for you, and an ice cream for me?"

He – my examination has revealed that it is indeed a he – looks up at me, head angled slightly to one side.

"What? You want to do it the other way round? Whatever you say, boy..."

I place him down onto the grass and hoist myself up, brushing leaves off my backside. I have a moment where I wonder if he might just scamper off back into the wood, but he stays at my side as I get my backpack out of the car and gaze down the hill towards the sea.

"Come on then," I say, striding forward down the side of the road. "It looks nice down there. Maybe there'll be a hotel with a swanky spa, eh? One for dogs as well, of course. And then maybe we can find out where you came from – someone must be missing you."

Even as I say it, I wonder if it's true. I've disappeared from my own life with alarming ease. Mark has been in touch about some practical issues, and the agency has said it'll get me work as soon as I'm ready, but beyond that...nothing. Nobody is missing me at all, and in return I am missing not a soul. Depending on my mood, I see this as either a blessing of liberation or proof that I will die alone surrounded by cats that don't even like me.

The dog ambles at my side, still limping a little, his minimonster of a face looking up at me every time I look down at him. It makes me smile, and gives me the boost I need to keep going. The heat is punishing now, even though it's almost 4pm, and there is no breeze at all. Just us, and the fireball in the sky, and a very long road. I feel a bit like an extra in a Mad Max movie, and I suspect I look like one too. My personal grooming has taken a nosedive since I became a nomad.

It takes a while, and I notice that the dog is limping even more now. I realise belatedly that the road is probably really hot on his paws, and I scoop him up into my arms. He weighs next to nothing, and licks my chin to say thank you.

"You're very welcome," I say, narrowing my eyes to try and see where this road to nowhere might be leading us.

Sadly, it looks like 'nowhere' might be the right answer. The tarmac abruptly stops at the bottom of the hill, and turns into a wide dirt track that leads off to the left. I follow it, and we enter another patch of woodland, less dense than that up at the top, trees rooted in sandy soil. Sunlight is dappling through the scattered branches, and there are clear signs that the path is regularly used – but so far, no signs of who uses it, and still no bars on my useless phone.

I am about to despair and turn back when I see a large gate, closed but not locked. There's a sign on it, and I expect it to be one of those usual friendly countryside messages – you know, 'If you leave this gate open you will be shot', or 'Beware: if you enter this field you will be eaten alive by wild vampire pigs', that kind of thing.

Instead, I see a completely charming hand-painted board that looks like it was created by children, or possibly a Turner Prize-winning artist. There is a picture of a bay – blocky stripes of bright yellow sand, blue water – and a smattering of extra images. Ice cream cones, cakes, footballs, teddy bears, a princess's tiara, flying pixies, an animal that looks like a cross between a giraffe and a hippo.

'Welcom to Starshine Cove!' it says, unapologetically missing an 'e'. 'Population: nobody knows!'

I smile, but I also take a photo of it. Old habits die hard, and if I end up getting abducted and burned like a Wicker Woman, I want to leave as many clues as possible. The dog licks my phone as well, so I start to think he does that to everything.

I open the gate, keeping him firmly snuggled in the other arm, and emerge onto yet another path – this one much more narrow, and lined with yet more works of art. There are tiny wooden houses populated by cuddly toys, a little tea set laid out on a miniature picnic blanket, and a small hammock stretching between two shrubs that is filled with plastic dinosaur toys. As we progress, I see colourful pompoms tied to the tree trunks and branches, and a dangling mobile made of intricately perfect fairies with iridescent wings. Amid the shade and the birdsong and the wildflowers all around me, it is really quite magical.

The dog wriggles, and I set him down. It is cooler here, and he seems to want to explore, poking his nose into the leaves that carpet the floor, tail properly wagging now.

"Okay," I say firmly, "that's fine, but don't pee on the dinosaurs, all right?"

He trots away, still unsteady but obviously keen, towards a brook that is living up to its kind's reputation for burbling. The water flows steady and clear, and I am so thirsty I am almost tempted to scoop some up in my hands – but I've treated far too many bacterial infections in my time to do anything so wild. The dog, being a dog and all, has no such concern and throws himself into the stream.

When he emerges, his fur is flat to his body, and I see how skinny he is, the poor thing. He shakes himself right by my legs, spattering my jeans with mud, and we continue to walk.

The next gate has another sign – this one is made out of letters that are covered in stuck-on glitter, and it simply says: 'This way to the beach!'

Okay, so it doesn't say 'this way to the luxury spa', but it is hopeful – somebody painted these signs, made this little trail of whimsy, and if I can find them, they might have something amazing with them, like a chilled can of Diet Coke. Right now, that is the one thing I wish for most in the whole wide world. That and a loo.

We go through the gate, and within seconds we are there – at the end of the world. I stop, unable to take even one more step, completely stunned by the view opening up in front of me. To call it just 'the beach' does it a huge disservice. It is the most perfect beach I have ever seen: a small horseshoe of sand fringing the turquoise sea I spotted from the top of the hill.

There are large rocks that look perfect for sitting on, and the shadows of caves in the red-yellow cliffs, and sunlight that looks as dazzling in its watery reflection as it does in the sky. It is wild and beautiful and free – it is the absolute image of the happy place I have spent so many hours conjuring up in my classes. It's here, and it's real, and somehow, I have found it – my happy place, and a stinky dog that looks like E.T.

There is nobody else here, and I have no idea why – this cove should be full of people; it should be a tourist hotspot. Except…well, as I've just discovered myself, it's not exactly easy to find, and from the main road you'd have no idea it was here at all. Maybe I am even the first person to ever set foot on it…

The dog scampers ahead, and pees on a half-crumbled sand-castle, which disproves my Ella the Explorer theory. Definitely not the first person here.

I stand still facing the sea for a few more minutes, floored by the beauty, by the peace, by the amazing resemblance that this place has to the one I'd imagined.

But soon, I start to be floored by other matters – like thirst, and the need for a loo, and clean clothes. I am not as flexible as the dog when it comes to these issues.

I walk further out into the sand, and gaze around. There are sandcastles, so there must be people. I do a complete circle, and behind me, I spot steps built into the landscape, leading up and away from the beach. They're made of yellow stone, camouflaged by the fact that they are exactly the same shade as the sand.

As I walk up them they widen, and on either side of me there are terraces built from the same pale stone, cleverly designed to flow down the side of the hill to the beach. There are tables and benches and parasols, and the whole place is dripping with hanging baskets and barrels and tubs and troughs full of flowers of every type and shade.

I breathe a sigh of relief as I make my way up the steps, and through the terraces – they must be leading somewhere.

I soon see a single-storey building looming at the top. It is chalet style, all smooth blonde wood and walls of glass – which makes sense with that view on offer. A wooden sign has been planted in the grass, which looks to have been created by the same small hands that paved the way along the woodland – this one features every possible kind of cake, bowls of soup, mugs of hot chocolate with blobby marshmallows on top, and the words 'Cove Café'. That sounds like absolutely the best place on the entire planet right now.

A path leads to the door, either side of it chaperoned by an amazing garden – obviously cultivated but still somehow wild, foxgloves and hollyhocks blending with vibrant buttercups and purple-striped irises. There are more of the little fairies nestled among them, and they look right at home, as though they're about to sip little teacups of nectar and talk to the bees.

When I reach the door, though, I notice something absolutely horrifying – a sign that says 'closed'. I let out a small growl, and decide that it simply can't be closed. Not after all of this. The sign must be wrong, the door must be shut by mistake, and I WILL have my ice-cold Diet Coke even if I have to smash the glass, grab it, and do a runner. I have never considered a life of crime before, but today could be the start of a whole new career.

Before I try anything as deranged as lobbing a terracotta

plant pot through it, I test the door. It slides open on well-oiled tracks, and I feel the remnants of aircon cool against my skin as I step through. Ha, I think, I was right – it was a mistake, and it isn't closed. Except...well, most of the lights are off, and there aren't any customers, and there are no staff, and... Yeah, okay. It's closed.

It's closed, and someone forgot to lock up, and I really shouldn't be here – but that thing has happened now, and there's no arguing with it. You know that thing when you really need a loo, and as soon as you're near one, your body somehow becomes all relieved and happy and then you have to go even more? I glance around, see the door to what has to be the facilities, and half-walk half-jog in their direction.

I do my business, all the time the dog sitting still before me, staring at me as though he's wondering what on earth is happening. Once that blessed moment is done with, I emerge into the washing area, and make a big mistake – I look in the mirror. Frankly, it's terrifying.

I normally have a relatively neat shoulder-length bob, long enough to tie back but not long enough to be a pain. After a month on the road, and a few nights sleeping in a Mercedes, I now look like Neanderthal Woman the morning after her hen party. My naturally dark blonde hair has lightened, it's a few inches beyond my shoulders, and it is wild – which is what happens, I suppose, when you don't bother using a hairbrush. My skin is bare of make-up and has been for some time, and although I have a nice tan, I also have bright red cheeks and am streaked in sweat and dirt. How did I get so dirty? How did I turn into this? One cuddly stray dog and a long trek through the woods, I suppose.

I splash water onto my face, and run my fingers through my hair. They get stuck, which doesn't bode well for the detangling process. I decide that I don't care, flick myself the Vs in the mirror, and head back out into the closed café. I wonder if there is CCTV, if I've triggered some kind of alarm, if the Dorset constabulary are heading this way, sirens blazing, guns and tasers at the ready...except, well, it's Dorset, and they probably don't send SWAT teams to apprehend women who sneak into buildings to use the toilet.

I emerge into the dim café, lit only by streaks of sunshine that land in swathes through the windows, and look around. It is pretty, the blonde wood theme continuing inside, all the accents and soft furnishings in shades of white and pale blue. There are seashells on shelves, and wild flowers in tiny vases on all of the tables, and a scent of sea-salt and lavender and sugar in the air.

There is also, I see, a giant fridge. A giant fridge stocked with all kinds of amazing items – cloudy lemonade, ginger beer, strawberry cordial, and yes – yes! – cans of Diet Coke. I am now faced with a huge moral dilemma, but luckily it only lasts for about three seconds. There is a small order pad and pen on the pale-wood counter, and I scribble on it: 'I'm really sorry but I needed a drink. I am leaving the money and enough for a tip, just like if I'd been here when you were open. Will write a great review on Tripadvisor too!'

I scoop five pound coins from my purse and place them on top of the note, before creeping behind the counter and filling a bowl with water for the dog. He sniffs it suspiciously first, but then laps at it greedily. I open the giant fridge. I reach out and grab my prize. I feel its sweaty, ice-cold exterior, and feel like crying with joy as I crack it open, relishing the fizz and the hiss and the thought of how good this is going to taste.

I am holding the can to my parched lips when the lights behind the counter suddenly go on. I freeze, caught in the act, eyes blinking at the sudden illumination. The dog hides behind my legs, and I guiltily put the can down. Damn it. So near, and yet so far.

"Can I help you?" a woman's voice asks, and I turn around to see a very short, curvy lady looking up at me with her eyebrows raised. She might be tiny, but she looks like one of those people who doesn't take any crap – in fact, with her blonde curls and hands-on-hips pose, I'm getting a distinct Dolly Parton vibe.

"Um...I'm sorry," I say quickly, gesturing to the note and the coins. "I wasn't stealing, honest – my car broke down and I was too hot and I had no water and then I found a dog and then we walked through the fairy woods and then you were...closed. But I wasn't stealing."

She nods, and walks towards me, her eyes taking in the note, the cash, and then the dog. Her eyes light up and she exclaims: "You found the weresheep!"

"Did I?" I ask, confused, as she crouches down and holds her hands out towards him so he can sniff her fingers. He hesitates, looks up at me, and I tell him it's okay. He tentatively licks her outstretched palm. He definitely does that to everything, it seems.

She strokes the dog for a few moments, then stands up tall. Or as tall as it's possible to get when you're under five foot. She glances at the bowl, and smiles.

"You gave him water before you didn't steal the can of Coke?"

I shrug, and she continues: "Well, what are you waiting for? You've paid for it. Might as well enjoy it. It's fine. My name's Connie, by the way. Connie Llewellyn. Look, you've obviously had a rough day – why don't you just sit down for a minute, get your bearings. When you're done, you have two options – leave the way you came, or pop outside at the front and say hello. No pressure, but you'd be very welcome. I'll leave it up to you."

She pats my arm, and I almost recoil. I have not, I realise, been touched by another human being for a while now. It's not just my hair that's gone feral.

Connie gives me a little wave, and walks away, sashaying her way between the tables and chairs to the far end of the room, spilling out of her skinny jeans in a way that says 'I know I'm hot, and I don't care what you think.'

I follow her path, and see there is a mirror image at the other side of the building – walls of glass, a sliding door that she shimmies out of. Beyond it I see what looks like a patio with more tables, and past that a green space. There are people there, and now I focus, I can hear them – laughter and chatter and the sound of children playing, a dog barking, a ball hitting a bat.

I lean against the counter, and feel the dog's reassuring touch as he leans against the back of my legs. I pause, take a deep breath, and finally do it – I drink that can of pop in three gulps, and my Lord, it is possibly the best thing I have ever tasted. Naturally enough, I let out a loud belch afterwards, and laugh as the dog looks at me with what I interpret as disapproval.

"I know," I say, putting the can in the recycling bin, "I'm not very ladylike, am I? Now, what should we do, pal? I can hear another pooch out there. Do you like other dogs, or are you one of those small ones that thinks he's a Rottweiler, eh? Should we stay, or should we go? On the one hand, I'm not sure I feel ready to plunge back into society. But on the other, my car isn't working and I have no place to go. Tricky, isn't it?"

By this point the dog has lost interest, and instead has trotted over to the door at the front and is barking excitedly to be let out. Looks like he's voted with his feet.

Chapter Four

As soon as I step outside, I become so self-conscious I can barely move. Everyone is looking at me, and I try to keep my head up beneath the scrutiny. I cross the patio, and join the small crowd at the edge of what I now see is a very traditional village green.

The green itself is fringed by shops and homes, some thatched, some not, but all of them old and pretty and well-maintained. There are larger buildings, some barely bigger than sheds, some in a small higgledy-piggledy terrace made of warm golden stone. I spot a small shop, what looks like a bakery, and a pub, as well as a grander hall that looks like an old Victorian school. Every single one of them has a lush garden, whether it's a courtyard covered in pots or green lawns or riots of flowers. It's as though a multi-coloured patchwork quilt has been laid down across the whole place. Behind the green and the buildings, the hillside tumbles down, lush and vibrant, dotted with other homes that are perched precariously on the slope, the landscape cocooning the whole village.

Connie stands up, and waves me over. There are too many people for me to take in all at once, and I feel slightly over-whelmed by them all. I grip my phone tight in my hand, and wonder when I'll be able to call for help and get out of this place. I enjoyed the Diet Coke, but this feels a bit too much.

"I told you!" Connie says, laughing, "she found the weresheep!"

I suddenly realise that the gathering of strangers is not, in fact, looking at me at all – they're looking at the dog. Huh. So much for my ego.

The dog is suddenly skittish, planting itself between my legs. I pick him up and join Connie and her friends, holding him steady while he trembles. A little girl with bright red plaits runs over, soon joined by an even smaller one with exactly the same hair.

"Can we see him?" the older one asks, jumping up and down on the spot.

"Let him settle, now, Lilly," an older man says, walking forward and placing a calming hand on her bouncing shoulder. "Poor thing looks scared to death. And hungry. Run over to mine, will you, get some of those gravy bones I keep in the tin in the kitchen?"

As soon as they scamper away, he winks at me, and adds: "I actually keep them in the porch. It'll keep 'em busy looking though, eh? Give you and this fine fella a chance to acclimatise. I'm George, by the way. And this is Lottie."

He points down at the elderly Golden Retriever at his feet. Her eyes are cloudy, and she's sniffing the air to find the other dog she knows is there but can't quite see.

I nod, and smile at George, and find myself lost in the sparkliest blue eyes I've ever seen. He must be 80 if he's a day, but those eyes...well, all I can say is he'd give Daniel Craig a run for his money. He has a thick head of pure white hair, and a weathered face lined with laughter lines.

"This is the bit where you tell me your name too," he goes on. "Unless you want to be all mysterious, like?"

"Oh! No! No, I'm not mysterious, I'm just...tired, I suppose.

My name's Ella. And this is...well, this is the dog with no name."

Connie ushers me over to a chair, and as soon as I sit down, I am provided with a glass of lemonade and a plate filled with raspberry cheesecake. As welcomes go, it's not a bad one.

Within seconds, I am surrounded – there are more children, and two women who look to be in their 70s, and a middle-aged man who looks like Gandalf complete with long beard, and a small gaggle of teenagers, and even more people heading over from the green itself. Some of them are carrying bats, but I assume they're for playing cricket, not beating strangers with.

"So," I say, trying to maintain a confident smile, "what's with the weresheep thing?"

"Ah," replies Connie, wiping cake crumbs from her face, "well, the little ones have been telling us for a while that there's a strange lamb loose in the woods. Plenty of lambs around here, but none of them were missing, so we weren't really sure what they meant. So their dad, Archie, went out with them to look, and got the briefest of glimpses of this creature here – he realised it was a dog, but to be fair, if you were little and had a vivid imagination, it could be a small sheep, couldn't it?"

I glance down at the dog, who is still on my lap but starting to look around with more confidence. We have so much in common.

He is the right colour – a kind of off-white – and he is very fluffy. I suppose I can see what they mean.

"Nobody could get near him," Connie continues, "even when we tried to tempt him out with food, he was just too scared. We've called around local rescues, the police pound in town, checked if anyone has reported him missing in the hope we could find his owners – but sadly not. We were starting to think we'd never be able to help him until you came along. You must have the magic touch."

"I don't know about that," I reply quickly. "I had a bag of crisps, and I got a thorn out of his paw is all."

"There you go then!" George pipes up, nodding wisely from across the table. "It'll be like Androcles and the Lion during ancient Roman times!"

"If you say so," I reply, wondering who Androcles was, and if he also had a bag of crisps.

"Forgive George," Connie says, grinning at him mischievously, "not only did he used to be a teacher, he's actually as old as Androcles…"

George snorts in amusement and calls her a 'cheeky young whipper-snapper'. Connie looks to me like she's in her 50s somewhere, but I suppose to George, she could indeed be classed as a whipper-snapper.

"Try the cake, dear," one of the older ladies says, leaning towards me. "Fresh made this afternoon, it was. I'm Little Betty, by the way."

I obediently try the cake, as it gives me some time to ponder the name. Little Betty is, in fact, very large – I'm guessing she'll be touching six foot when she stands up, and she also looks like a woman who knows her way around a cake. Sitting next to her is, by contrast, a tiny wisp of a woman with a steel-grey pixie haircut.

"And I'm Big Betty," she says, looking amused.

I'm guessing this is a well-rehearsed routine, and I reply: "Nice to meet you, Betties. The cake is amazing, by the way."

"So, how did you end up here, Ella?" Connie says, topping up my lemonade.

"Oh. Well. My car broke down, top of the hill back there. About 20 miles away, it felt like. And I couldn't get a signal on my phone, so I thought I'd head here and try and find civilisation."

"And instead, you found us!" Connie replies, gesturing around her and laughing. "Where were you on your way to?"

"Um...I don't know, really. Nowhere. Maybe Cornwall. Not at all sure. I'm kind of...on a break."

"From what?"

"Everything."

I don't know what I've said, but it triggers a round of exchanged looks that pretty much everyone around me shares. It's like a Mexican wave of eyes and nods and meaningful 'hmmms'.

"In that case," Connie announces, "you've come to the right place. A lot of us were like that when we first landed in Starshine Cove. For me, it was 23 years ago – found it completely by accident and never left. Three kids later, I'm still here."

"Right. Well. I'm sure I won't be here that long," I reply, feeling slightly nervous, unsettled by all their knowing gazes.

"Don't worry, Ella," George tells me, "we're not planning on holding you captive or sacrificing you to some ancient fertility god to ensure a good harvest."

I force a laugh, but he's nailed it – both of those thoughts had indeed flickered across my mind.

"No, we did that last year, when that lone drifter rode into town on a piebald pony..."

I stare at him, and everyone around me bursts into guffaws of laughter. He was joking. Of course he was joking. Crikey, this being around people business takes some getting used to.

The dog shuffles around, and jumps down to the ground. He ambles over towards Lottie, and takes a quick sniff at her hind quarters before sitting down next to her. She licks his ear, and that's that – friends for life, I suspect. If only it was that simple with people.

Just then, the little girls come streaking across the green, pigtails flying, and arrive in a mass of quivering excitement.

"Granddad, you silly!" the older one – Lilly – says. "The treats weren't in the kitchen at all!"

"Oh no, I'm sorry, girls – I must have forgotten," he replies, his face deadpan. "Be gentle with that dog, now, mind – he's not like Lottie, you can't climb on him or roll around with him till he knows you."

They crouch down, and place a bone-shaped biscuit on the ground in front of him. Lottie immediately snaffles it, so they try again, offering it to my dog – who isn't actually mine – directly. He sniffs it, licks it, then takes it, leading to chorus of oohs and aahs. This continues for a few minutes, the dog becoming ever more confident, until they are throwing them in the air for him to catch.

"Can we clean him?" says the younger girl. "He smells bad!"

"I think that's something best left to his mum, don't you?" George replies. I gaze around, and then realise he means me. I have become a dog's mum, it seems.

The girls stare at me, as though seeing me for the first time, and Lilly adds: "Well, can we clean her instead?"

She is so straightforward about it, so matter-of-fact, that it makes me laugh out loud.

"I think I probably need it," I reply, gesturing to my bird's-nest hair. The girls seem to take this as a yes, and immediately produce a small backpack decorated with pictures of ladybirds. From it they produce a tiny hairbrush, a comb, and a pair of scissors. I am about to object when I realise they are those blunt-edged plastic ones that little people use in school.

They drag chairs over to me, and start to examine me, then begin the detox process. It is very strange, but also quite comforting. Everyone around me seems highly amused. A man with thick, shaggy hair and a bushy beard warns them to be nice, that I'm not a doll, and I assume he is their dad. I hope he's the kind of dad whose kids listen to him.

"So," I say, trying to ignore an especially hard tug on a

tangle, "is there anyone who can help with my car? Is there a phone I can use? Mine doesn't seem to be working."

"We do get a signal here, but it's random, comes and goes as it pleases," answers Connie, grinning as my head is pulled from one side to another and the girls squabble over who gets an especially matted strand. "You can use the landline, of course, and in the meantime, Ged will go and tow it back here for you."

"Is he a mechanic?"

"No, but he has a tractor and a tow bar. Best we can do. But nothing's likely to be sorted today, so why don't you stay for the night? You can wash your dog and have a G&T and enjoy a good sleep. Things will look different in the morning."

Things will look different in the morning...she's right, I know. I won't feel as tired, or as dirty, or as desperate. I will be able to sit and watch the sunrise, and spend time on that perfect beach, and rest my weary soul. It is all too tempting.

"Ouch!" I utter as the girls comb my ears instead of my hair. "But where would I stay?"

"At the pub," answers the younger girl, frowning as she experiments with my too-long fringe, "that's where everyone stays."

Her tone implies I am indeed very stupid for not knowing this. Maybe I am.

Connie nods, and says to Gandalf: "Trevor, will you do the honours?"

He nods solemnly and pulls a small device out of one of the many pockets on his patched cargo pants. At first I think it's a phone, but soon realise it's actually a walkie-talkie. I really have fallen down the rabbit hole. He presses a button, and speaks into it: "Druid 1 to Pub Daddy, over."

Nobody else seems to find this strange at all, and maybe it makes sense in a village the size of a dot that has intermittent phone signals.

There's a crackle, then a reply, and some kind of conversation I can barely follow that involves references to lost sheep, mangers, and safe harbour. Connie rolls her eyes, so I suspect there is some extra ham being added to the ham radio.

Eventually he looks up, serious behind his wizard beard, and announces: "The gods are smiling. He was fully booked, but had a cancellation about half an hour ago."

There is a communal smile, and Connie sees my confusion.

"Right about when you arrived," she says smugly. "You see? It was all meant to work out like this."

"If you say so," I reply, not wanting to be rude. I'm a scientist, and don't even read horoscopes. One person's coincidence is another person's act of fate, I suppose.

The girls have finished with my hair, and I must admit it feels better when I run my fingers through it. They don't snap in two, for a start.

"You look pretty," declares the smaller one. "But you need some jewels."

Within seconds, I am draped in plastic beads and bangles, and have a tiara on my head. My usual go-to look for a day at the beach. Their dad smiles and mouths 'sorry!' at me as he gently persuades them to pack up their beauty shop. He looks at them fondly as they do as they're told, but it is a look tinged with sadness.

"The good news is," Connie says, grinning at me across her impressive bosom, "you get to see Mystery Cricket! Come on, everyone, it's Cricket O'Clock!"

She actually claps her hands as she says this, and everyone leaps into action. Frankly, all cricket is mystery cricket to me, but I suspect that anything in this charmingly weird place has an extra element of the unexpected to it.

Sure enough, I watch as people run over to the green, and the dad with the beard groans as he takes up the bat. George approaches a big wooden barrel that's already been laid out, and the others gather in various positions around them.

He reaches into the barrel, and produces a ball. Quicker than you'd ever expect of a man of his age, he takes a small run up, and lobs the ball. The dad whacks it, and it soars high into the blue sky, eventually plummeting down near the Betties. You'd expect Little Betty to be a natural given her height, but it's actually Big Betty who makes a leap to try and catch it. The two collide into each other, and the ball hits the grass to a chorus of moans.

This is repeated a few times with varying degrees of success, and I am starting to wonder where the Mystery is.

"Isn't this just...cricket?" I murmur to Connie, who has wisely decided to spectate rather than participate.

"Oh, no, love. Just wait for it. Archie – he's in bat – knows something's coming, he just doesn't know when...that's the joy of it, see?"

I nod, even though I don't see at all. And then, as George bowls his next ball, I do – it's not a ball at all. It's a water balloon. Archie must see it as well, but fair enough, he still takes a powerful swing, and ends up completely soaked as the impact bursts the balloon's skin. He shakes himself like a dog, and I find myself laughing along with Connie, the girls screeching in hilarity at their dad's fate.

Next there's another normal cricket ball, but after that, I see that the missile isn't quite right. Archie grimaces and takes a wallop, and it explodes, covering him in a substance that looks like the goo they used to dunk people in on kids' TV shows.

"Jelly Bomb!" everyone shouts at once, as Archie picks bright orange chunks out of his beard, his girls clambering over his legs and squealing in delight.

"There's all sorts in there," Connie tells me, nodding towards the barrel. "Bags of flour, feathers, nothing harmful but a lot of fun. Jelly Bomb is the best, though, and that officially ends the match."

"Right...and how often do you play this game?" I ask,

looking on as Lottie ambles over and starts to hunt for any stray bits of jelly.

"Every Sunday until the end of November. There's usually something going on around here – we are small, but we are mighty. There's yoga, and we do cinema nights in the village hall, and there's usually a barbecue every couple of weeks. Oh, and Fridays we have naked karaoke, that's a lot of fun!"

I'm starting to get used to her sense of humour now, and I pull a face that tells her I don't believe a word of it.

"What?" she says in fake horror. "You don't believe me? You'll just have to wait and see what happens next Friday, won't you..."

I smile, and nod, and tell myself that I won't be here by next Friday. I'll be long gone by this time tomorrow, if everything goes to plan. I'll be on the road, and on to the next place, and... on my own again. I'm not sure how I feel about that. This has been a lot – meeting so many new people, adopting a dog, becoming a thief, watching Mystery Cricket – but it has also been fun. A lot more fun than eating up the miles on the motorway with the radio as my only company.

Connie looks at me and gives me a small smile.

"I know," she says quietly. "It's overwhelming, isn't it? That feeling that you just might have found something special, but that you don't quite deserve it? Don't think about it now. Just relax. And I think it's time you met Pub Daddy. He'll be the calm after the storm. He's not been here as long as the rest of us, so he isn't quite as bonkers."

Chapter Five

Leaving the café's patio isn't quite as simple as it sounds – I need to be fed, watered, and introduced to Ged and a million other people before I go.

Ged is a strapping young lad in his early 20s, who looks like every picture-book image of a farmer I've ever seen – big, brawny, hair that looks like corn, green wellies. All you'd need to add is him chewing a piece of grass in the corner of his mouth and he could advertise organic veg.

He takes my keys, finds out where the car is, and says he'll 'take the Druid with him and be back in a jiff.' In the meantime, Archie and the girls are dispatched to retrieve my bags for me – which is a relief. It'll be good to have a change of clothes and some deodorant, quite frankly, for me and everyone else, I suspect.

While they do that, people come and go, introducing themselves, offering sympathy for my plight, patting the dog, and disappearing again. There is absolutely no way I will ever remember any of their names.

Connie whips up a plate of sandwiches and yet more cake, as well as a big jug of the promised G&T, and when Archie comes back hefting my suitcase and telling us he'll leave it at the pub, I'm feeling a lot more mellow. By this time there is only me, Connie and the dog, which is much more my level of sociability. Plus, I'm mildly drunk. What can I say? I've always been a lightweight.

I know I should be doing things – calling a breakdown service, finding a mechanic, charging my phone – but somehow I just don't care about any of them. Those are problems that will all wait for me, that will all be there in the morning. Nothing earth-shattering is going to happen if I just set them aside for one night – and besides, I remind myself, it's not like I have anywhere urgent to be.

I feel peaceful as I sit there, the dog back on my lap, a glass of booze in front of me. It's a beautiful evening, and for the first time in what might actually be years, a smudge of genuine contentment is creeping over me. I can feel it in the looseness of my limbs, the flop of my fingers, the way the skin of my face feels relaxed. I have lived so long feeling pressurised, tense and taut in every part of my body, that I'd forgotten how it feels to just breathe. To just be. It's a revelation – like a low-level migraine finally clearing.

I stifle a yawn, and Connie laughs as she stands up.

"That interesting, am I?" she asks.

"Nothing personal," I reply, grinning. "And has anyone ever told you you look a bit like Dolly Parton?"

"Funnily enough, I used to make my living as a Dolly impersonator..."

"Really?"

"No. God, you're too easy. You know that don't you? Now come on, let's get you set up. You've had a long day."

I've had a long month, I think to myself, as I follow her around the village green, the dog trotting at my feet. He's had a small bowl of Lottie's food, much to her annoyance, and seems to feel a lot better for it.

As we walk, Connie keeps up a running commentary on village life, pointing out the hall, and George's cottage, and Archie's workshop, where he keeps all his gardening gear and woodworking kit. Archie, it turns out, is the gardener – and goodness, he does an amazing job of it.

"Does he build the fairies too?" I ask, having seen even more of them draped around the village – suspended by wires from tree branches, hiding behind plant pots, peeking out from flower beds.

"Oh no, they're real fairies," Connie replies, giving me a nudge. "Most people can't see them – you must be blessed by the fey!"

"Yep, that'll be it. Me and the fairy folk go back a long way. I see you have a butcher, and a baker – what about the candlestick maker?"

"Ah. Funny story that. We used to have one, but one day she met this owl, and this pussycat, and they ended up going to sea in a beautiful pea green boat..."

"Hmm," I answer, "I think you might have mixed up your stories a bit there, Dolly. Is this the pub?"

We are standing outside a handsome two-storey building, made of that gorgeous mellow stone, all mullioned windows and creeping ivy and spectacular hanging baskets cascading with colour. It has a thatched roof, and looks older than some of the other places I've been shown, with a distinctly crooked feel to it that tells of centuries of use. There is a painted sign hanging outside, not one made by the girls this time – this one is simply painted black, with vivid stars of gold and silver sparkling against the backdrop. Silver and gold letters announce that this is the Starshine Inn, which makes my question redundant.

"Pub, hotel, meeting room, headquarters for the annual Twister tournament...and now, your home. For tonight at least."

She pushes open the door and shouts: "Ahoy there!" at the top of her voice. There are several occupied tables, and a few turn around to look at us – none of which seems to bother Connie.

"Now, prepare yourself," she warns in a much quieter tone. "Pub Daddy is quite the shock to the senses."

I have no idea what she means by that, so I busy myself examining my new surroundings. I've been assured that dogs are very welcome here, but I'm glad when I spot a couple with two Springer Spaniels in a window seat.

As I gaze around, I see a picture-perfect countryside pub – all dark wood and oak furniture, velvet drapes, cosy booths, nooks and crannies and snugs. There's a huge open fireplace, and an old-fashioned jukebox in one corner, and a long bar area bearing real ale pumps and a world of optics reflecting against a mirrored backdrop. The walls are as higgledy-piggledy on the inside as the outside, painted in a rich shade of burgundy, and the floor has a distinct tilt to it. History comes at a price, I suppose.

By the time I've done a visual circuit there is also, as I turn around, a drop-dead gorgeous man standing right in front of me. He's tall, lean and broad-shouldered, with thick dark hair and even darker eyes. My heart does a little flip-flop at the sight, and I stare at him for what is probably way too long to be polite. He seems out of place here – even though he's only wearing Levi's and a black T-shirt, something about him feels impossibly glamorous. It's like bumping into George Clooney at the fish counter in Tesco.

The nickname Pub Daddy had conjured up images of a middle-aged bloke with a beer belly sagging over his trousers, and this creature couldn't be more different.

"You must be Ella," he says, a hint of a smile playing on his lips.

"Yes, I must be," I reply, trying to pull myself together. It's not the first time I've met a handsome man. Mark is a handsome man. Some of my colleagues were handsome men. I've met hundreds of them – but this guy is in a different league. I now completely get what Connie was talking about – he is indeed a shock to the senses. He even smells good.

"And this must be the famous weresheep," he adds, crouching down to make friends with the dog. Connie meets my eyes over his head and pulls a 'see-what-I-mean' face.

"I believe you had a last-minute cancellation, Jake," Connie says when he is back with us. "A little bit of Starshine magic for Ella here."

"Well, Connie," he replies, smiling indulgently, "I wouldn't want to argue, but I believe it was as much a toddler with chicken pox as Starshine magic."

He has a quiet and easy way about him; there is none of the larger-than-life bluster of some of the others I've met so far. I find it soothing, to be honest – like he's a real person, not someone from a panto.

"Ha!" she exclaims, pointing at him. "One and the same and you well know it! Anyway, I need to get home and make sure the kids haven't burned the house down. I'll leave Ella in your capable hands. Has Archie dropped the case off?"

"Yep, it's in her room. Ged's going to bring the car around to the car park."

"There's a car park?" I say, confused. "So, like, there's a road here and everything?"

"Yeah," answers Connie, laughing at my expression. "You just came in the back way. If you'd broken down a couple of miles earlier, you'd have been here in minutes. But then you'd have missed out on the fairy woodland, and the weresheep, and burgling my café, wouldn't you?"

"I didn't burgle your café," I point out. "You left the door open. It was...just entering, not breaking."

"Fair point. Anyhow. If you need anything, love, just shout – and by that I mean pop over to my cottage, or use the walkies. Though the best phone signal in the village is here, and you can even get on the internet because Jake has worked some kind of voodoo."

"It's called a dongle, Connie."

"Wash your mouth out with soap, Jacob Hennessy – I'm old enough to be your mother! Anyhow, I'm away for now. Come and find me in the morning, Ella – I'll be at the café from about 7 if you're an early riser."

She gives me a hug before I can dodge her, and she's so short my chin clears the top of her head. It's like being cuddled by a teddy bear.

Once she's gone, flouncing away in a cloud of blonde curls, Jake shakes his head fondly, and turns back to me.

"Are you okay?" he asks. "Or have they completely freaked you out?"

"Both, I think...this place isn't quite normal, is it?"

"Nah. But normal is over-rated, don't you think? Anyway, like I said, your bag's in your room, and I also have some gifts for you."

"Gifts? Who from?"

"Pretty much everyone. Come on, I'll show you up. We can do a proper check-in later. Just give me a minute to shout Miranda through from the back."

Ah. Miranda will undoubtedly be his wife, and she will be an exquisite creation of high cheekbones and creamy skin and casual-yet-effortlessly elegant clothes draping perfectly from her prima ballerina's frame.

As she emerges from a door behind the bar, I see that yet again my imaginings are way off target. Miranda is at most five foot tall, with a plump face and shaggy black hair – she's also wearing a T-shirt that says 'I'm not fat, I'm pregnant'. A quick glance at her build and her wide-legged stance tells me that she is indeed pregnant, despite looking barely old enough to be working in a pub. An irrational thought crosses my mind, and I wonder if she's been taking her pre-natal supplements – occupational hazard I suppose, and also none of my business.

"Hiya," she says brightly, giving me a wave from behind the bar. "Nice to meet you, Ella. Welcome to the madhouse. Want me to watch the bar for a bit, boss?"

Jake nods, and gestures for me to follow him. He leads us down a long crooked corridor, through a door marked 'guests only', and up a set of steep and equally crooked stairs. Every single one of them seems to creak – it's not the kind of place you'd ever be able to sneak out of surreptitiously.

At the end of yet another corridor, Jake uses an old-fashioned key with a wooden fob in the shape of a star to open the door, and stands back to let me enter. I walk through, and find the most wonderful room I've ever seen, especially compared to my recent round of chain motels.

It's large, presumably the family room as there is a small single bed as well as a double, and the whole of it is painted in delicate shades of pastel. Pale green walls are complemented by dark green curtains, and the bed is draped in a candy-striped duvet.

The furniture is mismatched and quirky, but somehow it all works – a chestnut dressing table bearing a vast vase full of sunflowers, a large mahogany wardrobe, an old-fashioned writing desk complete with fountain pen, ink and blotter. The bedstead is brass, and the pillows are topped with fluffy cushions in peach and pale pink. The pretty colours contrast to the antique feel of the place, balancing each other out, and beneath my feet is a thick shagpile carpet that I just know will feel wonderful once I finally get my trainers off.

There's an equally well-presented en-suite with a stand-alone claw-foot bathtub, and a shower that I expect to spend at least an hour in.

The real star of the show, though, is the view – through an authentic sash window and all the way down to the beach. I stand and stare at it for a few moments, watching the sun setting so gloriously that it's hard to tear my eyes away.

"Wow," I murmur, forgetting I'm not alone.

"I know," Jake replies, standing next to me. "Such a show-off, isn't it? I never get tired of seeing that. That's what makes this the best room in the house. I'm originally from the Midlands, then London, and seeing that every night...well, it reminds me why I left. I warn you, it's addictive."

"I'm sure it is," I reply, moving away before I become rooted to the spot. I feel embarrassed by how emotional the sight of the bay is making me – seeing my imaginary happy place made real, and close enough to touch.

I see my suitcase stashed beneath the bed, and next to it is a dog bowl containing a few pouches of food, a bottle of canine shampoo, and some old towels.

"That's from George," he explains. "I think it's for the dog, not you. The Betties sent over some shortbread; Trevor's passed in a pamphlet about the history of Starshine Cove – which I warn you he wrote himself – and Archie and the girls provided the flowers. In the wardrobe you'll also find some dog blankets, and a bottle of wine...that's from me."

I feel my lower lip tremble slightly, and manage only to mutter my thanks. It's too much. Too much beauty, too much kindness, too much of everything I've felt starved of for the last few years.

Jake seems to understand, and quickly retreats. He pauses in the doorway, and says: "Look, you might want to just crash out for the night. Totally understand if you do. But it usually gets quiet downstairs at about nine. If you feel like it, come and join me for a drink. I can fill you in on the Starshine experience, or I can just stay quiet and fill your glass whenever you need it."

I look up, grateful and scared and exhausted all at once, and nod.

Chapter Six

I have done many things in my life, but I have never washed a dog. I have visions of fighting with him, getting soaked, getting bitten, getting humiliated by my inability to wrangle a 10-kilo lump of fur.

In the end, though, it is all rather sweet. I run the bath, not too deep and not too hot, and I perch on the edge of the tub for a few moments with him, letting him sniff and settle. I talk soothingly to him, telling him what a handsome boy he's going to be, and then slowly lower him into the water.

He is shaking, and obviously confused, but is also looking up at me with such trust that my heart breaks a tiny bit. I know he is probably somebody else's dog, and I know I'll need to try and get him back to them, but right now it's hard to imagine ever being able to say goodbye.

I carefully lather up the shampoo, and shield his little face with my hands as I rinse him, and he stands patiently throughout – scared but stoic. He might not look like much, but he has the heart of a warrior, I decide.

The water turns pretty grim pretty quickly, and I make a mental note to remember to give the bath a good scrub later –

this might be a dog-friendly place, but nobody likes a bad houseguest.

I carry him through to the main room wrapped in one of Lottie's old towels, and sit on the carpet with him, rubbing him gently until he is mainly dry. Even then, I stay sitting with him for a few minutes more, before deciding that it is my turn for the detox.

Predictably enough, he follows me through, and looks on in interest as I start the shower. I'm not used to having an audience when I'm naked, but he seems to want to be near me, and I don't like the thought of shutting him in the other room in case he becomes distressed. This dog, I realise as I luxuriate in hot water and lime-scented bodywash, has turned me into a complete wuss.

Once I'm done, I wrap myself in a towel – soft, fluffy, white, yummy – turban up my hair, and crash out on the bed. Predictably, he jumps up to join me, and luckily because it was so predictable, I've already popped one of the dog blankets on top of the covers so he doesn't get them wet or dirty.

I yawn, and stretch out, and enjoy that moment – the moment when you've been really busy, when you're tired, and you finally get to lie still and switch off. I am cool and clean and comfortable, and I have spent most of the last 24 hours as the opposite. It really has been the weirdest of days, but I can't complain about how it's ending.

I've been charging up my phone, and when I pick it up from the cabinet next to me, I see a miraculous bar or two flickering in and out. Looks like Connie was right – this is definitely the place to be for phone service.

For some reason, as soon as I find that I have a patchy wi-fi connection, I start looking up dog breeds. Now he's dried off, I can see that with a trim, he might be something other than a weresheep. I flick through the pictures, and eventually decide that the one he most resembles is a Bedlington – not

100%, but close enough. And they do, actually, look a bit like little sheep.

"Larry the Lamb," I say, stroking his head, "that's what I'll call you. For now at least."

He doesn't object, and we lie contentedly together for a while longer. I'm turning over so many things in my mind – the past, the present, the future. Friends I used to have, lovers I have left behind, a different life where everything took another path. Larry, in the meantime, is sniffing his own arse.

I try to look up local garages, but the signal chooses that moment to drop out again. I'm pretty sure that if Connie was here, she'd tell me it was some kind of sign. I get up, get dressed in blessedly clean clothes, and pace around the room. I inspect the little knick-knacks, and look at the books on the shelves, enjoying the feel of the thick carpet beneath my bare feet.

I dry my hair, rearrange the sunflowers, and eat a piece of shortbread. And then, when I have done as many meaningless things as I possibly can, I do what I always knew I was going to do in the end. I take my purse out of my bag, and I sit on the bed, and I get out the picture.

It's one of several copies, but the one I always keep with me. The one that lives in my heart.

I unfold it, stroke the creases down, and gaze at the black and white image. This is something I do every night, and have done for a very long time now. Sometimes it makes me smile, sometimes it makes me cry, sometimes it is the only thing that makes me feel anything at all. It is part of my ritual, something I have always clung to, taken comfort from – even when it has hurt.

"This," I say quietly to Larry, "is my baby. I didn't know I was pregnant when I started working in the hospital, but when I found out, my friend who was a sonographer said we'd keep a close eye on her, make sure she was doing okay. Well, we didn't know she was a girl then – we found that out a bit later. We were going to call her Elizabeth. Lizzie. She'd have been three this year, and I think she'd have loved you...and this beach, this place. I think she'd have been blonde and chubby and she would have laughed a lot. I wish, more than anything in the whole world, that I'd ever been able to meet her, but that wasn't meant to be. Or maybe it was, and I just messed it all up. I don't know. Anyway. Night night, lovely Lizzie..."

I place a gentle kiss on the picture, the scan photo that was the closest I ever got to my baby girl, and put it back in my purse. Always close, always on my mind, always very real but also impossible. A dream of a thing.

I was pregnant when the pandemic started, without even knowing it, and at that stage nobody knew much about what was going on. All we understood was that it was bad, that it was killing people, that everyone in the NHS needed to play their part. I went back to hospital work, and back to long hours, and back to spending what felt like days on end on my feet.

I know, better than most people, how common miscarriages are – I know the stats, I know the signs, I know the risk factors, and I know the human face of that pain. I've helped countless patients through it. I know it is something that can happen to any woman, no matter how healthy her lifestyle or how wise her choices – it is not something that you can blame someone for, even though they often blame themselves.

If I was my own doctor, I'd tell myself all of those things. I'd tell myself that it wasn't my fault, that these things happen, that there is no reason that it will happen again. That I hadn't contributed to that terrible loss.

But it's far easier to be logical when you're talking about someone else's pain, someone else's suffering. When it's someone else's body who has betrayed them. When it happened to me, none of that made any sense any more – and I did blame myself.

I blamed my work, I blamed the Government, I blamed the

universe. But mostly I blamed myself – I shouldn't have gone back there, no matter how much I was needed. I should have stayed at home and rested, and been careful, and taken better care of the precious life I was growing inside my own body.

Mark never said any of those things to me, but I always suspected he was thinking them. It was his loss too, and I know it cut deep. Despite all of that, he never criticised, never said those words that I'm sure were bubbling beneath the surface. He didn't blame me out loud, but I did it all for him – assumed that I knew what he was thinking, thought I could feel the anger he must be suppressing.

I might have been imagining it. I might have been wrong about all of it – but every now and then, when I was getting ready for work in the aftermath, I'd see a look on his face. A look that said he didn't understand. We had enough money; I didn't need to work – I could have stayed at home. He never asked me to do that, but I convinced myself that's what he thought.

Looking back now, I see that's when we started to lose each other. He was too good a man to show his frustration when I was suffering – if he couldn't say what was eating away at him, he said nothing at all. We both stayed quiet. We retreated into our own little worlds, our own shells, our own cocoons of grief. We got on with life – at least on the surface. I think, though, that a part of us died when we lost Lizzie. On the surface, our relationship survived – but underneath, it was made of fragile honeycomb, hollow, just waiting to be snapped into pieces.

I suppose that's why it was so easy to leave him, and so easy for him to bring another woman into our home. Why it's so easy for us to now have civilised conversations about finances and our separate futures now – because in reality, we'd been living separate futures for a long time. The other stuff was just us playing catch-up to what neither of us had wanted to face.

And now, I am here, sitting in a perfectly pastel room with a weresheep, wondering what to do next – not just right now, but longer term.

I can't live like this forever. I can't wander aimlessly through the next decades. I'm not hurting for cash, but I will need to work at some point, I'll need to settle, to build some stability for myself. I have no idea if I'll ever be able to practice again, or if I'll become a teacher or a bus driver or a barmaid. Probably not a dog groomer, I decide, looking at Larry's overflowing fur.

I feel like I am perfectly poised between a thousand different destinies, and have no idea what path I will take. It's like a game of blind man's buff – I've been blindfolded and spun around until I'm dizzy, and now I am stumbling around in the dark, trying to find a way forward. It's all very confusing.

"Well," I say to the dog, "it's not like I have to make my mind up now, is it? I don't have a deadline. For now, all I need to do is get through the night. And yes, I can see what you're thinking – it's half past nine, and you need a wee, and I need a drink. Do you think I should go downstairs and see if the handsomest man in the world is still around? You do? Oh, okay then...if you insist."

Chapter Seven

I head downstairs, and take Larry for a trot so he can do his business. I see that my car has been retrieved, and sits forlornly in one corner of the small car park. The dog decides to pee on one of its tyres in protest.

By the time we go back inside, the place is about half-full, and a barman is busy serving. I notice the couple with the Springer Spaniels is still here. One of them thumps its tail when it sees us, but other than that there is no dog-based drama.

I spot Jake behind the bar, restocking the fridge with small glass bottles, and he waves me over.

"You look refreshed," he says, giving me a small smile. "Everything okay?"

His tone tells me that he has managed to see beneath the clean hair and new clothes, through to the slightly murkier truth. It is borderline alarming, and I don't want to engage in anything with a depth of more than five centimetres right now.

"Yep! Great. Thought I'd take you up on that offer of a drink, but if you're busy, that's no problem."

"Nothing that can't wait. Go and find a seat and I'll be over in a minute. What's your poison?"

"Surprise me. Anything at all," I reply, then cast my eye over the various pumps and labels. "Though on second thoughts, nothing that has the words 'Wizard's Brew' or 'Crabber's Delight' in its name."

He laughs and says: "Fair enough. Sardine Stout it is then... only kidding. Go on, sit. You look exhausted."

I try not to be offended at that and do as I am told, pausing on the way to look at a huge framed map of this part of Dorset. I see the busy road I was driving along earlier, and I see place names I recognise as not being too far away – Lyme Regis, Burton Bradstock, West Bay. I see the smaller road I ended up walking down, but what I don't see is Starshine Cove – on the map there is nothing but a yellow wedge of colour that indicates the beach. Huh, I think, weird – Starshine Cove does not officially exist. It is entirely possible I am having some kind of extremely lucid dream, in which I've created an alternative universe.

I wave to the Springer Spaniel people – imaginary or not, I don't want to be rude – and then find one of the snug side rooms that only holds one table. It has a view of the beach, still glorious in the now fading light, and it makes me feel safe to be enclosed and cosy. Larry settles at my feet, twirling around three times before curling up in a fluffy ball. I seem to have accidentally found the most laid-back dog in the known world.

Feeling guilty at the thought, I get out my phone, planning to look at any local websites for missing dogs. I can't keep him just because he's filling a hole in my life – he will probably have left one in somebody else's.

I am browsing, very slowly, through Facebook posts when Jake arrives. He has a pint for himself, and a sparkly concoction in a balloon glass for me. The liquid is clear, but threaded through with what looks like glitter.

"Fancy," I say, taking a sniff, "what is it?"

"Starshine Special," he replies grandly. "House cocktail.

Basically a glorified gin and tonic with a few magical secret ingredients."

"Ah. Magical secret ingredients. I'm starting to think that should be this place's motto."

"Well, if you listen to Trevor, that's factually correct. He has this whole theory about ley-lines and star alignments and stone circles. You should ask him about it sometime – if you've got a few days to spare, that is."

I pull a face and sip my drink. It is delicious, and also dangerous – I should definitely not have another one of these. Or at least not another two.

"So, how did you end up here?" I ask, remembering what Connie said earlier, about him not having been in the village for too long. "If you don't mind me asking."

He grins, and it is a knockout grin, lighting up his whole face and chasing away the more reserved man I've seen so far. It is possibly even more dangerous than the Starshine Special.

"I don't mind you asking, but I totally get why you did – and it's refreshing to have someone around who seems to respect personal boundaries..."

"Not Connie's specialist subject, is it?"

"No. I'm...well, I'm slowly getting used to it. I still need time off every now and then, though – make sure I speak to people who don't live here, make sure I actually leave the place every now and then. Still remind myself that I'm an individual, not part of a whole. That makes me a weirdo by Starshine standards."

"Ha! I don't think it's weird. We all have to keep a bit of ourselves tucked away, don't we?"

"We do. In reserve, just in case. That's my theory anyway, but maybe I'm just being bloody-minded... As for how I ended up here, well, that's a funny story – or at least it seems it now. It didn't back then. It was about four years ago, and I was not at a good place in my life. In fact I was in a completely dark place. I won't bore you with the details, but my mum had just died. She's originally from Italy, and went back there when she was older – so she was a long way away and it was all...complicated, let's leave it at that. And while all that was going on, my marriage imploded. I reacted to all the upheaval by throwing myself into work."

"Running a hotel?" I ask, noting how he has skimped over the ins-and-outs of his dark place, and not faulting him for it – I know I hoard my own story as well.

"No, actually, I was a property developer. Buying, doing up, selling on – that kind of thing, but on a large scale. I was making a lot of money, and ticking all the boxes, but I wasn't really feeling it – the money was just a way of keeping score. Of telling myself I was doing something right at least, that I hadn't made a balls of absolutely everything in my life."

I nod, and understand maybe better than he thinks – I saw Mark's ambition and work ethic skyrocket after we lost Lizzie as well. I was the opposite – mine dwindled to nothing. Once we were through the worst of the pandemic, I signed up with the locum agency, and kept everything very low-key and manageable. I could have joined a local surgery, or been based in a big health centre, but I think I needed to keep moving – it was as though I couldn't allow myself the luxury of a full-time base, of close colleagues who might become friends, of patients who I might start to care for a bit too much. Because once you have those things – the friends, the permanence, the people you care about – you can also lose them.

"So," I say, seeing that he has stalled a little – that sharing even this much is still not easy. "Did you drive into Starshine Cove planning to demolish it all and build a holiday village instead? Like in one of those Hallmark movies where the handsome-but-ruthless property mogul discovers he has a heart of gold after all?"

"Handsome? Thank you kindly," he replies, raising his pint glass and quirking one eyebrow at me.

"Oh come on – you must have looked in a mirror!" I answer, laughing. "I'm just stating fact, not flirting. Anyway...go on, what happened next?"

"I got lost. Now, if Connie was here, she'd say I was already lost, and I ended up getting found – because she loves that kind of thing. But the truth is I just got lost – I was heading for this area, to look at a hotel further down the coast. One of those grand old dames that had fallen on hard times – I thought it looked ripe for a cheap offer, a quick spruce up, and hey presto, 'luxury' apartments to sell on. Maybe I wasn't paying attention, maybe I was just blindly following a dodgy satnav – I've no idea. But instead I ended up here. I stopped, saw that this place was also up for sale, and..."

"The rest is history?"

"Not quite. At first I thought I'd do the same thing – buy it up, sell it on. I didn't imagine it was doing well as a hotel, not in a place like this. Thought it'd be another quick profit. Ran into the first problem when George wouldn't sell it to me."

"George?" I repeat in surprise. "George the old guy who was a teacher?"

"The very same. It had been in his family for generations; his sister used to run it. We met up for a drink, and after a chat that lasted all of five minutes, he told me I wasn't the 'right kind of person' for the Starshine Inn.

"I had no idea what he meant, but I suppose it kicked off my competitive instinct – especially when I found out from the agent that he'd also turned down three other buyers for the same mysterious reason. I decided to stay on and convince him. I kept upping the offer, and he kept turning it down, and eventually I realised that he was either the world's best businessman, or it wasn't the money he was interested in. Which, you know, was a completely alien concept to me at the time – everything was about the money."

"What happened? How did you change his mind?" I ask, fascinated, and already halfway through my Starshine Special.

"I made him an offer he couldn't refuse – that I would stay on, that if he agreed to sell, I'd stay as manager and make a success of it. Naïve, really – it was already as successful as anybody wanted it to be. But somehow it convinced him, and I thought I'd won. Had some kind of back-up plan to get the sale through, then cut and run...except, well, that thing happened."

"What thing?"

"That thing that makes it so damn hard to dismiss all of the guffins about magic and leylines and fate. That thing where I just...fell in love with the place. Felt at home for the first time since I was a kid. Felt happy for the first time in years. Felt like I'd finally found the place I was supposed to be."

"All by accident?"

He nods, and I ponder the story.

"So, it's tales like this that had them all oohing and aahing when I turned up – they're half expecting the same is going to happen with me, aren't they? That I'll fall in love with it?"

"I suspect they are, yes. And really, it's a compliment. This place might be tucked away, but it does have visitors, it does have a small tourist industry. The inn is usually booked up, the café is always busy, Trevor has to reprint his history booklet a couple of times a year. Not everybody who visits stays, obviously. You must be special."

"I'm really not, and I have no idea why they think I might be here any longer than it takes for my car to get fixed up..." I reply, thinking out loud.

Jake meets my eyes, and looks suddenly serious. "I could give you my opinion, but it might not be easy to hear."

I bite my lip, and am half tempted to tell him no thank you, please keep your thoughts to yourself. Instead, I nod, and gesture for him to carry on.

"Don't be offended by this, Ella, but you also seem a little lost. Not just geographically. I'm not buying into the mystic quest nonsense, but I can tell you're in some kind of pain. I can see that when you smile, it doesn't quite reach your eyes. I recognise it, too, that look – the one you're using to convince yourself and everyone else that you're fine, when maybe you're not. It was the look I used to see on my own face, every single day."

"You see entirely too much," I snap back defensively. He might be right, but this isn't pleasant – I feel exposed, vulnerable, raw. Like I'm being very gently dissected.

He leans back, and starts to apologise.

"No," I say, interrupting him, "I'm sorry. I shouldn't have snapped. I'm just...well, you're right, obviously. It's complicated, but you're right. I was a doctor. Am a doctor, I suppose. And the last few years have been..."

"Traumatic?"

It sounds like such a dramatic word, but I realise that it is the right one. All of it – the hours, the lack of supplies, the sheer madness of it all – has taken its toll. Even without Lizzie, without Mark, it would have been hard.

"Maybe. I don't know – and I don't want to bleat on about it. Other people lost a lot more than I did. And please don't tell any of the others, all right? I'm just not ready to...to be part of anything yet, if that makes sense? It's tough enough putting up with my own scrutiny, never mind a whole village worth!"

He reaches out, briefly touches my hand – a brush of his fingers against mine – before moving them quickly away when he sees me stiffen.

"I won't, I promise," he replies firmly. "You're fine. You're safe here, even if it's just for a night."

Safe, even just for a night. It sounds so simple, so consoling, and I find myself welling up in response. That makes me angry, and I screw up my eyes and tell myself off. It's quite the rollercoaster.

"Are you ready for a change of subject?" he asks, patting the seat next to him until Larry agrees to jump up and join him.

"More than you can possibly imagine," I reply, laughing and crying at the same time. "Tell me more about the village. Why isn't it on the map? Why isn't it full of tourists? How many people even live here?"

"Right. All good questions. Let me whip up another round first."

I know he is only doing that to give me a break, to allow me the dignity of getting myself back under control, and I am grateful. Larry trots away after him, and I suspect he is on the lookout for crisps.

Sure enough, he returns a few moments later licking his lips, looking very pleased with himself. I see Jake check in with the Springer Spaniels – or possibly their owners – and then head back to the snug with another Starshine Special. This, I tell myself, will definitely be my last one. Tomorrow is going to be challenging enough without a glittering hangover.

"So," Jake says, settling himself down, "I think somewhere in the region of a hundred people live here. There are more houses, set further back from the green, roads that straggle through the woods. Some come and go; others are here all the time. Some, like Trevor and the Betties, have been here all their lives – others are new arrivals. And they still count Connie as new, by the way, even though she's been here a couple of decades.

"As for why it's not on the map, I have no idea. Maybe it didn't exist when the maps were drawn up, and it's never become big enough to make it. Maybe it's deliberate. Maybe we've actually imagined the whole place..."

I laugh loudly, and look at him with delight – a smile that, I think, goes all the way to my eyes.

"I was thinking exactly that a bit ago! What if it's all a hallucination? What if someone spiked my Costa with acid at the last services? What if I'm in a coma and creating my own netherworld?"

"Yeah, what if?" he answers, grinning at me. "Well, all I can say is if that's the case, it's you and me both. But if we work on the assumption – far less likely, I know – that this place is real, then it is a bit of a secret. But not a complete secret – there are families who have been coming here for years, even the grandchildren of people who've been coming here for years. Other people find it by accident, like us. But it never gets rammed, it's never too busy – it's usually just right."

"And the tourists, the business from them, it's enough to support everyone? I mean, I've seen some run-down little seaside towns in my time, but this one is perfect – everything looks in great shape, the gardens are something else, all the shop-fronts are nice, nowhere is boarded up or empty…"

"That's because of the other big secret about Starshine Cove – it's a hotbed of entrepreneurship."

"Really?" I say, trying to imagine a group of people who chuck jelly at each other as corporate masterminds. And failing.

"Really. Don't get me wrong, a lot of the people who live here have ordinary jobs – they commute to the towns or work from home, and there are civil servants and factory workers and farmers and all the usual stuff you'd expect. But there's also the other side of it. Like the Betties."

"What about them?" I ask, calling to mind a pair of healthy but ageing women.

"Well, the Betties don't just bake for the village – their cakes and biscuits are stocked in all your fancy supermarkets, all over the UK. And George might be a retired teacher, but he also has an impressive stock portfolio. Connie…well, yes, she runs a successful café. But before she crash-landed here – and I mean that literally, I'm sure she'll tell you the story – she was a high-flying chef at a restaurant in London. The kind with Michelin stars.

"Every few months, she hosts gourmet nights at the café, charges a fortune, and they're sold out a year in advance. And Daisy – she's away at the moment – uses the rock from the caves to make jewellery and art, and she can't make enough to meet demand. But while they might be making money, there's also a bit of an unofficial socialist vibe – everyone pays a tithe to the village council, which is why everything looks so good, why there are so many facilities, why everyone is so well...looked after, I suppose you'd say."

"What about you?" I ask. "Are you still wheeling and dealing?"

"Little bit," he replies, grinning. "I still own properties, here and elsewhere. I'm just less hands on than I used to be."

The Springer Spaniel couple momentarily interrupt us, telling Jake they're turning in for the night and arranging a time to come down for breakfast. While he makes conversation with them, I ponder what he's told me – and the bit that I still don't understand.

Once they're gone, I ask: "What do you mean? The rock from the caves?"

He is silent for a moment, one corner of his mouth twitching in a mischievous smile.

"Ah. You've not been there. It's probably easier to show you," he eventually replies. "Are you and the dog—"

"Larry," I interject.

"Are you and Larry up for a little walk?"

Chapter Eight

He lends me a fleece that is way too big for me and smells of his aftershave, grabs a large torch, and the three of us head out. I notice that he doesn't lock any doors, and remember that the café was left open too, and wonder what kind of place I have landed in. It ain't London, that's for sure.

The three of us head around the side of the car park, and Jake leads us to a wooden staircase that winds its way down to the beach.

The sun has completely set now, but it still isn't dark – the stars are crystalline jewels in the purple-black sky, and the moon is hanging, almost full, round and pale, admiring its perfect reflection shining in the mirror of the sea. All I can hear is the sound of the waves sucking and hissing onto sand, and the occasional call of an owl in the distant woodland. It is peaceful, calm and still, and utterly magical.

We don't talk as we walk, and that suits me just fine. It would almost feel rude to talk, to interrupt the serenity of the scene. I've never imagined my happy place at night before, and I think I like it even more like this – it feels private, special, like a late-night show being put on for an exclusive audience.

I walk at Jake's side, the moon so bright that we even have shadows, Larry scooting around in zig-zag lines finding interesting smells but never straying too far. After a few minutes, Jake stops, and gestures to the caves I'd spotted on the other side of the horseshoe-shaped cove when I first arrived.

I gaze inside, and feel a twitch of uncertainty. I am in a strange place, with a strange man, being asked to walk inside a dark cavern. It goes against everything I have learned after years of living in the city.

"It's okay," he says, encouragingly, "the tide is coming in, but it won't trap us. I can tell we have a while yet."

That hadn't even been on my mind, but now it is.

"How do you know so much about tide patterns? I thought you said you grew up in the Midlands?"

"I did," he replies, clambering over some loose rocks at the cave mouth, "but I'm a very quick learner!"

Larry has no qualms about following, scampering over sand and pebble and disappearing after Jake – which means, of course, that I now have to go in. Can't have Mama's Little Soldier left all alone.

I take a quick last look at the sea, at the way the moonlight paints it an otherworldly shade of silver, and follow on.

The ground is rough but easy enough to make my way over, especially when Jake shines the beam of the torch down to light my path. I soon catch up with him, see a child-like grin on his face, realise that he is excited to be sharing this with me. The breeze has ruffled his hair, and he looks suddenly younger – more alive.

"Okay," I say, as I stand next to him, "here we are. In a cave. It's all very mysterious, but..."

He lifts the torch up, and shines its beam on the roof of the cave. All I can do is gasp at what I see.

We are completely surrounded by rock that shines and glitters, sparkling in shades of silver and gold, green and blue, deep tones of purple and iridescent black. It is as though someone has studded the whole place with gems.

He slowly moves the torch around, and I see that the walls are the same – a mass of glowing rock that twinkles hypnotically beneath the light. I feel my eyes widen, and I reach out to touch the side of the cave. It feels damp, rough, ordinary – like any other cave. But the way it looks...it's as though I've fallen into a kaleidoscope.

"Oh my God..." I mutter, transfixed by the sight, by the vibrancy, by the unreal gleam of the place. "It's like it's made of multi-coloured diamonds..."

"I know," he replies warmly. "I still remember the first time I saw this. It was...well, it was special. And I hope this is special for you, too."

I meet his gaze, and nod. "It is. Thank you. It's probably the most beautiful thing I've ever seen. What is it?"

He continues to move the torch around, highlighting different sections of the cave, each one completely distinct from the last.

"I don't know. I've heard some people mention mica, or silica, or calcite. Lots of stuff that sounds like it comes from a geology textbook. But on this one, I'm with the locals – I just think it's magic."

I stand still, drinking in the glow, the ethereal shimmer. I can hear the waves creeping in and out on the shoreline, and still hear that owl, and smell the fresh tang of salt. I might be a scientist, but on this occasion all my qualifications count for nothing – I have to agree. It's magic.

Jake is quiet for a few minutes more, seeming to understand my need to drink it all in, to lose myself in the sense of wonder.

"On the right night," he says eventually, "it's even better. When the moon is at the right angle, and shines straight in, when the stars are all aligned, you don't even need a torch. The whole place just...comes to life."

I nod, and think that I'd like to see that. That I will come back here, one day, when the time is as right as the angle of the moon, and I will stand here and come to life myself, among it all.

For now, I have this – this perfect memory, this perfect image, stored in my mind in a room I know I will visit over and over again.

The image of the night I stood with Jake, wrapped up in a blanket of starshine.

Chapter Nine

I wake up the next morning to glorious sunlight flooding through the window, and a dog sitting on my chest, licking my face.

I have slept well, deeply, free of the distressing dreams that I usually battle at night. You know, those ones where you're trying to find a certain door, but when you do it has no handle, or where you need to call someone urgently but your fingers turn into cooked spaghetti as you try to dial?

I stroke Larry to show him I am conscious, and allow myself a few moments of peace, remembering the shimmering lights of the cave. A dream I had while I was wide awake.

I drag myself out of bed, and open one of the dog food sachets for my hungry friend. Then I pull on clothes, check my phone and see that it is after 9. I can't recall the last time I stayed in bed for so long.

I make my way downstairs, see the bar area busy with people eating breakfast, and head outside with Larry. I spot a ridiculously tall teenager loitering by the fire escape; his hair is parted in the centre, with one half bright green and the other half black, like an alt version of Cruella de Vil. He has a vape in his hand, and as soon as he sees me he tries to hide it. Rebellious enough for the hair and the vape, not rebellious enough to want me to see it.

I feel words of warning spring to my lips, but remind myself that he is not my patient, and this is none of my business. He crouches down to play with Larry, and looks about 12 when he grins.

"You're up early," I say, mentally adding 'for a teenager'.

"Yeah, been helping my mum, then thought I'd come and plug myself into the matrix. Can't get wi-fi in my house."

I can only imagine what torture that must be for someone of his age, and nod sympathetically. This, I realise, is probably where all the youths of Starshine Cove hang out, desperate for a glimpse of TikTok or to post on Instagram.

"I'm Dan," he says, offering me his hand to shake in a very grown-up way. "I'm Connie's son. Nice dog."

"He is, isn't he?" I reply, finding myself inappropriately proud. "No idea who he actually belongs to..."

"Kind of looks like he's decided he belongs to you...but I suppose you could take him to the vet, maybe get him scanned?"

"Scanned?" I repeat dumbly, my mind immediately imagining Larry wriggling inside an MRI tube or licking the lube off an ultrasound wand.

"Yeah, you know – for a microchip. Most dogs have them these days. There's a vet in the next town over."

"Oh. Right. That makes a lot of sense. I'll do that, just as soon as I get my car sorted."

"Yours is the Merc, yeah?"

He says this with a touch of an American accent, and I smile inside as I imagine him playing *Grand Theft Auto* or watching repeats of *Strike Back*, all the while living in a speck-sized village on the far coast of England.

"It is. Next on my to-do list is to get it sorted, and then I'll be on my way."

He nods, and starts to walk away. Before he disappears around the corner, he pauses and adds: "It's not so bad here, you know. Even if the wi-fi is non-existent."

Crikey, I think – even the kids are in on it. He slouches away, and I keep an eye on the dog as I pull out my phone. He's right – the reception is stronger here. I find the nearest Mercedes repair shop, and call them to explain my plight. They take the details and the reg number, and promise to be there as soon as they can.

After that task is complete, I wander down the wooden steps to the beach again. It is completely empty, and I take my trainers and socks off so I can stroll along the sand barefoot. It's not too hot as yet, the sky clear, the view stretching out along cliffs of red and gold, the sea disappearing into infinity. Larry is chasing the waves as they retreat, yapping at them and running away when they come back. Simple pleasures. We should all be more Larry.

Inevitably, I arrive at the pale stone steps that lead up to the café. It was only yesterday that I landed here, tired and thirsty, and made my way up the very same path. Weirdly, it feels like I've been here for a lot longer. Maybe I can add 'time-slip' to my crazy theories.

Larry bounds ahead, obviously remembering it as a nice place full of good smells, and dashes straight through the now open door. If Larry is going to stick around, I probably need to get him a lead, I think.

I needn't have worried – by the time I catch up, he is inside, saying hello to Connie, who is feeding him treats out of a big glass jar. I glance around and see a few other people with dogs in here – a giant Old English Sheepdog that looks like he's stepped out of a Dulux ad, and a pair of matching French Bulldogs.

"Good morning!" Connie says, a huge smile on her face. She's wearing cut-off jeans and a pastel-blue gingham shirt that could be fresh out of Dolly's wardrobe. "How did you sleep, like a baby?"

I've never understood that phrase – in my experience babies don't sleep very well at all.

"Great, thanks, Connie. I met your son this morning."

"Oh. Which one? No, hang on, it's got to be Dan – the other is away. I lose track sometimes."

"Umm...yes, it was Dan."

"Ah. Green hair, vape?" She shakes her head and adds: "He thinks we don't know, like all teenagers. We were hoping he'd grow out of it, but there may be need for an intervention. Anyway. Can I get you something to eat? Just had a delivery of some fresh-baked pain au chocolat..."

As soon as she mentions it, my nostrils start to twitch, my mouth waters, and I realise I am ravenous. It's all I can do to contain myself, and not leap over the counter like a ravaging baboon.

"That would be marvellous, thank you," I reply, following her towards the source of the smell. Freshly baked pain au chocolat – possibly the peak of mankind's achievements.

"So, Dan had a good idea," I say, as I perch on a stool at the counter. "He suggested I take Larry – that's what I'm calling him..."

"Larry the Lamb. Yes, I see it!"

"He said I should take him to the vet, get him scanned to see if he has a microchip?"

Connie pauses, hand on hip, looking thoughtful. "That is a good idea. Who'd have thunk it, my little rebel using his brain? I'll call them now. You enjoy your breakfast. Coffee?"

I nod gratefully, and look on in amazement as she does about six things at once. She is using an old-fashioned landline, its long red cord wrapping around her as she moves, while she pours me a filter coffee from a huge pot, passes over a small jug of cream, refills the pot, and then wipes over the already spotless surface. I listen to her end of the conversation, and after a few minutes she hangs up.

"Bugger..." she exclaims, realising that she is now completely entangled in the phone wire, twirling around to unwrap herself. "Happens every time. Anyway. Vet says that's fine, pop over this morning and she'll give him a check over as well."

"Is it walking distance?" I ask. "My car should be fine later today, but at the moment I'm stuck."

She holds up one finger, and picks up the phone again, while at the same time buttering two slices of thick wholemeal toast.

"Sorted. You can take my car. Meet Dan back at the inn, and he'll give you the keys."

I am momentarily dumbstruck by this idea. We are basically strangers, and here she is, offering me her vehicle. I mean, I could drive away into the sunset and never be seen again – she doesn't even know my full name.

She laughs at my expression, and adds: "Don't worry. I trust you."

"But why? I could be spearheading an international car theft ring for all you know..."

"Well, if you are, you'd have to be desperate to take a Fiat 500, wouldn't you? Eat up now. You're all skin and bones."

I am not all skin and bones. I am of a perfectly average build, but Connie is clearly one of those women who shows her affection through food. There are worse flaws.

I do as I'm told, say my goodbyes, and head back around the village green. Various people say hello and wave, offer me a cheery good morning, and it all feels surreal after years of living in London and avoiding eye contact with anyone you don't know personally. Heaven forbid someone might actually try and talk to you.

Dan is already back there when I arrive, slouching against what could only be Connie's car. It is indeed a Fiat 500, but one that is bright pink, and comes complete with spidery eyelashes over the front lights.

"Suits you," I say to Dan, who is wearing baggy jeans, a Nirvana hoodie and Doc Marten boots. "Are you old enough to drive?"

He looks slightly offended and tells me he is 17 and three quarters. Nothing screams maturity like adding the 'three quarters'.

"So, can you give me directions?" I ask, taking the keys and popping Larry on the backseat. He immediately emerges with a half-full packet of Oreos, which I take from him.

"I can come with you, if you like," he replies. "Sophie – that's my twin sister – is helping out at the café later, so I've got nothing else to do."

"Are you bored?" I ask, remembering vividly being his age, and finding everything in the whole world excruciatingly dull.

"Little bit," he replies with a cheeky grin. I gesture for him to get in, and we set off. I soon discover that the road on the other side of the hill is just as steep as the one I walked down, but a lot busier. Dan gives me directions, and tells me about the A-levels he's doing, and I ask him what he wants to be when he's older. Not when he's 'grown up', because that would be an insult.

"Premier league footballer sounds good," he says, as we make our way along the A-road.

"Oh. Do you play a lot of football? Are you in a team?"

"Nah. Fall over my own feet. But you asked what I wanted to be, not what I could be…"

"Fair point. So, what else is there, then?"

"Dunno. I like taking pictures, and drawing."

As he's just told me he's studying Maths, Chemistry and Biology, I'd expected a different answer – wondered if he was looking at medical school, even. It seems like a waste of three tough qualifications to just become a photographer.

Even as I think it, I am annoyed with myself – not everybody has to be a brain surgeon. Not everybody has to pursue a profession, or have a high-flying career. Not everybody has to follow the same path, and who am I to judge, or to say what is important?

"Right. Well, if that makes you happy, maybe that's the way forward..."

"That's what my mum always says. Other people's mums are like, ooh, work hard, go to uni, get a job. She's just all 'do what makes you happy' and shit."

"She sounds truly awful."

He grins a bit, then clamps down on it. "She has her moments. Anyway, you want to turn right here, then left at the ice cream farm and right at the horse trough."

These are directions that could only be given in the countryside, but they are also accurate, and we are soon pulling up outside a small business park. There is a garage, the vet's surgery, and a shop that sells surf boards and flip-flops. The big city.

We clamber out of the car, and head to what the sign tells me is Dr Wong's Veterinary Practice. Dr Wong herself is approximately 700 years old and talks with the most dense West Country accent I've heard since I arrived here as she ushers us in.

She barely speaks to us after that, but is the very picture of gentleness with Larry, as she picks him up and cuddles him and places him on her table. She examines him, looks at his teeth, pokes around in some personal places, and then scans his ears and head with a hand-held device. He endures it all stoically, but I'm sure he looks at me in disgust.

"No chip," she announces, finally seeming to notice us. "Not neutered. Signs of malnutrition but otherwise healthy. Approximately three years old."

"What do you think he is?" I ask curiously.

She gazes at me over her specs, and says: "Well, I'm not entirely sure, but my years of experience tell me he's a dog."

She bursts into laughter at my face, and continues: "Some Bedlington. Some Shih Tzu. Some Maltese perhaps. A bit of everything – the very best kind of dog. I don't think anyone is looking for him. Feed him small amounts several times a day, and book him in for his op."

She gives Larry a little kiss on the nose, and then looks at us as though wondering why we're still here.

"But..." I say, "is there any other way to find out who he belongs to?"

She thinks about it, and replies: "I will make some calls, put out alerts on the missing pet noticeboards. But for now, he needs an owner. Are you not willing to be that?"

She fixes me with a stern glare that reminds me of my old French teacher, and I mutter: "I am, yes. For now."

"Good. Nice dog, deserves better. No charge for now, but come back soon. Leave your number."

She turns her back on us, and it appears we are dismissed. I scribble my details down on a notepad, and we leave.

"Wow," I say, as we return to the car. "That was fun. Did I do something to offend her?"

"Dr Wong? No, she's like that with everyone. Doesn't have much time for people, but she's great with the animals. Can you take me to McDonald's?"

He says the name with great reverence, and it is funny how a child who is probably fed the very finest of food by a former Michelin-starred chef still yearns for the Golden Arches.

"Depends," I reply, fastening my seatbelt. "How far away is it, and will your mum kill me?"

"Just a few miles, and no, as long as she doesn't find out. There's a Marks & Spencer there as well, and a big pet shop…"

I narrow my eyes at him, knowing that I am being played, but unable to resist. He has, after all, said the magic words – Marks & Spencer. I've been washing my clothes on the road, using launderettes or facilities at various hotels, but I am running low now, and the thought of a new multi-pack of knickers fills me with delight.

"It's a deal," I say, starting the engine. "As long as you don't use that vape. Those things are not good for you."

"Better than smoking!"

"Did you ever actually smoke, though? Are you using the vape to wean yourself off a 30-a-day nicotine habit?"

He doesn't reply, just stares out of the window. Thought not.

"What are you, the vape police…" he mutters, a few seconds later than he needed to for it to have any impact. It obviously took him a few moments to come up with.

"Yes, that's me," I answer jauntily, giving him a crisp salute. "Sergeant Ella Farrell, Vape Police, West Dorset branch, reporting for duty!"

He tries not to laugh, but loses the battle. Despite the hair and the vape and the attempts to be surly, this is clearly a kid who has a bedrock of humour.

We carry on with our trip. I stock up on dog food and buy a lead and collar, then leave Larry outside with Dan while he eats his McMuffin and I browse underwear. Not the kind of thing you want to do with a teenage boy in tow, even if Larry had been allowed in.

I buy a few extra T-shirts, and a pair of shorts, and impulse buy a pretty summer dress that is made of layered floaty fabric, a rich cream patterned with tiny pink rosebuds. I have no idea when I will ever wear it, as I don't tend to get invited to many garden parties these days, but in the bag it goes anyway. I tell myself that I now have all that I need to move on. I won't need to ask to use anyone's washing machine, and as soon as the car is sorted, I can leave. I'll stay in the area, move on slowly in case Dr Wong miraculously finds Larry's real mum, but I will take myself away from Starshine Cove.

When I started this journey, I had no real plan, and certainly no intention of settling down anywhere. The cove, for all its charm and beauty, simply has too many people in it to really be my happy place. When I pictured that beach at the end of my wasted meditation sessions, I didn't imagine it came with a whole village full of people who wanted to get to know me. They have been hospitable and kind and accepting, but they have also been overwhelming. Even having Dan in the car – a kid who barely speaks – feels like an intrusion, and I feel the need to be alone again. Apart from Larry, obviously – maybe I have more in common with Dr Wong than I thought.

As we pull into the car park at the inn, I see a man in over-alls packing a bag. He looks up and waves, and I see his van, realising that it is the company I called earlier.

"All sorted," he says, as I approach the car, "fault in the electrics. Car's still under warranty so no problems."

"So I'm good to go?" I ask, trying to ignore the stray strand of disappointment that intrudes on my thoughts.

"You're good to go."

We say our goodbyes, and I stand with Larry, watching as both the van and the bright pink Fiat 500 disappear up the road.

Good to go, I think. Well, Connie can't have it both ways – if we're going to listen to the signs and interpret everything as an act of fate, this is a pretty clear one. This is destiny telling me to take a hike.

I go inside, and find Jake and Miranda chatting behind the

bar. She's wearing a different-coloured T-shirt but with the same slogan, and I suspect she must have bought a batch of them. She smiles and heads through to the back, saying something about refilling the ketchup bottles.

Jake leans forward on the bar, resting his arms on the wood, giving me a nod of greeting. He is back to being sensible Jake now, out of the starshine. Sensible, but still insanely good looking. It makes perfect sense that his mum was Italian – you can see it clearly once you know.

"Morning," he says politely. "Everything okay? The mechanic called in."

"Yeah, I just saw him. The car's sorted. I'm good to go."

"That's...good news? If you want to go, at least. The room was booked out for a week, if you wanted to stay for a few more days..."

It is tempting. The thought of that pretty room, of this kind man, of that beach just on my doorstep. It is tempting, but it is also unsettling, and I suspect that staying any longer will simply make it harder when I have to move on. Better to rip off the plaster, as they don't teach you in medical school but everyone knows.

"Thanks, but I don't think so. I'm a bit scared of staying for a whole week in case there really is naked karaoke on a Friday..."

"Well, I can't speak for what goes on in Connie's own home, but that's not a village-wide event, I promise. But I understand. I really do. And anyway," he adds with a sudden full-wattage grin, "you can always come back if you change your mind."

I nod, and thank him, and ask if I can settle the bill.

"No bill," he says firmly. "First night's on the house."

"Really?" I ask, smiling. "Are you sure you used to be a successful property developer?"

"Yeah. But people can change, can't they?"

I think back to a younger me. To my days at uni. To that backpacking trip with my pals that now feels like it didn't even happen. To a time when I was carefree and passionate and had the world at my feet.

Yes, people can change – but not always for the better.

Chapter Ten

I pack my few belongings quickly, and stand gazing out of the window for a few moments before I leave. It really is a beautiful view, but somehow I know I might be more comfortable with a view of the rear end of a lorry, or a traffic jam. Maybe this is the problem with finding your happy place – even if you find it, you're still stuck being yourself when you get there.

I sneak away without saying goodbye to anyone, which I know is a bit of a dick move, but I can't bear the thought of all the fuss. I know Connie will try and tempt me to stay, offering me cake-based bribes and trying to persuade me to rest up a little longer. I know Larry will curl up with Lottie, and George will twinkle his eyes at me. I know that Jake will give me one of his small smiles and won't apply any pressure at all, which will somehow feel even worse.

I decide, as I set off, that I will write them thank-you notes once I am back in the real world. That is as much as I have to give right now.

Larry seems perfectly happy with the new arrangement, settling down on the backseat of the car, and not even complaining as I sing along to Oasis songs on the radio during a

Britpop special. I have the voice of tone-deaf angel, so I appreciate his tolerance.

We drive around aimlessly, stopping off wherever it seems called for, having rest stops and wee stops and sanity stops along the way. I end up going all the way along the coast and into the next county, Devon, and feel a small thrill as we pass the county sign. For some reason I always get excited when I do that; I think it's a hangover from family holidays, when shouting out that you'd seen a sign or a horse or the sea or a cow was the ultimate triumph.

Part of me just wants to keep going, to drive through the day and the night until I reach Cornwall, until I stand at Land's End and then wonder where to go from there – it is a pretty final destination. But I remind myself that I have Larry now, and that I need to give Dr Wong a day or so to see if she can locate his owners. I make an agreement in my own mind that if I haven't heard from her in the next 24 hours, we are free – I have pulled off the amazing Scruffy Dog Heist, and we will run away together, like Bonnie and Clyde but with less bank jobs and bullets and death.

After a walk along the riverside, we head back in the direction we came from, but keep it fresh by taking different roads. I know, I'm out of control.

We call in at Charmouth beach, where Larry runs around off his lead and I have an ice cream and we totally fail to find any of the fossils which the place is famous for. We stop off at a donkey sanctuary, which doesn't end well as I seem to have accidentally found the one living creature that Larry isn't keen on. We visit a countryside estate that has its own art galleries and jewellery makers and rare-breed pigs, and by evening, we arrive at a pretty little market town called Bridport, where I am hopeful that we'll be able to find somewhere to stay.

My hopes are soon dashed, though – because it is the height of the summer season, and I have a dog these days, which complicates everything. I sit outside in the beer garden of a pub in the evening, calling round various dog-friendly lodgings, repeatedly being told that sadly they are fully booked.

In the end, I give up, and hit the road again. I re-join the busy A-roads, and we battle our way towards the nearest motorway in the hope that we can find a suitable place to rest our heads. In my experience so far, there's always a spare room somewhere near a motorway.

It is dark by the time we reach a new-build hotel down a slip road from the traffic, and the scent of the sea is long gone. It has been replaced by the more familiar odour of exhaust fumes and fast-food wrappers and diesel.

I slip Larry's lead on just in case, and we head to the neon glow of the entrance. A small crowd of people is outside having a smoke, and the cloud whooshes up into the air as the automatic doors open.

Inside, it becomes clear that there is some kind of group staying here – the lobby is full of German teenagers, lounging on the sofas and chattering away giddily. I approach the front desk, and the harassed woman on duty does her best to smile as I stand waiting.

"Do you have a room for one?" I ask, as soon as she's ready. "Well, one person and one dog."

She peers over the counter at Larry, who does his very best 'please take pity on a poor wee mongrel' face. It does make her smile, but it doesn't change much.

"We have one single room left," she says, after consulting her computer. "But I'm sorry, we don't accept dogs. You could leave him in your car and pop out to check on him?"

I recoil in horror at the very thought. Larry trusts me, and easy-going as he is, there's no way I'd even consider leaving him on his own in a car park for a night. I mean, he might get dog-napped.

"No. Thanks anyway, but we'll leave it..." I reply, walking forlornly away, back out into the night.

I take Larry for a stroll around the bushes to do his business, and go back to the car. I could, of course, just sleep here – I've done it before, and it's no big deal, not really. There's enough room, and it would only be for one night, hopefully.

I am turning the issue over in my mind when my phone pings. Out here in the big bad world, phone signals are not an issue.

I open the message and smile when I see it's from Priya.

"Sorry I wasn't around when you got in touch," the note says, "but just wanted to say hi, see how you're doing, and say we're back from our hols and at home again. We went to France, but I was a lot better behaved with kids in tow than when we went! Hope your trip around the country is going well, that you're seeing some amazing places, and living your very best life. Or whatever – gosh that sounds corny doesn't it? Anyway. Lots of love from your petite chou-merde xxx!"

It makes me laugh, the way she signs off. Maybe, underneath the kids and the jobs and the life experience, we're all still a little bit crazy after all.

I try to reply, but I don't really know what to say. I have seen some amazing places, but am currently in a parked car at the edge of a motorway, surrounded by lorries, smokers and drunk German teenagers. I'm not sure that counts as anybody's best life.

I look at some of the pictures I took down at the beach this morning, find one of Larry rolling in the sand, legs akimbo, the sun and the sea behind him. I send it to Priya, along with the message: "I seem to have been adopted by a stray dog called Larry the Lamb."

She replies immediately with a bunch of emojis and the words: "That is AWESOME! Where is that place??? How long are you there for? I am well jell!"

I explain that I was only there for one night, and that I'm on the road again, to which she replies: "Yeah. That makes perfect sense. Find paradise and swap it for a motorway! Have you lost your mind, Ells-Bells?"

I can almost hear the sarcasm dripping from her words – she was always a master of mockery – and wonder if she's right. I see one of the teenagers vomiting next to an overflowing dustbin and decide that she is – this is insane. Why am I here? Why am I considering sleeping in my car when there is a perfectly gorgeous hotel room waiting for me in Starshine Cove? Why am I being so stupid?

"Probably have lost my mind," I reply. "Maybe I need to go and look for it."

"Don't forget to check down the side of the sofa," she says, then adds the words: "Gotta go. Feeding time at the zoo and the kids are still in holiday mode. Stay safe and stay in touch xxx".

I close down the chat, and turn around to look at Larry.

"Priya thinks we should probably go back," I explain to him. "And Priya is a psychiatrist, and knows about this shit. What do you reckon? Think there'll still be room at the inn?"

He wags his tail, farts, and looks shocked by the noise. I take that as a yes.

Chapter Eleven

I manage to arrive the traditional way this time, and it is almost ten by the time I pull up in the car park. I sit for a few moments, seeing the lights shining from the mullioned windows, imagining the warmth of the room, the crowded bar, the sounds of laughter and chatter. I grit my teeth, feeling as though I'm about to run some sort of gauntlet of forced sociability. It's strange how I have ended up like this, so removed from the rest of the world, so reluctant to engage with normal human interaction – I'm a doctor, for goodness' sake, my whole job is about dealing with people.

Except, I know, that this is completely different. Working in drop-in centres in London isn't exactly a social life. I see people as patients, I see them at strange and usually difficult times in their lives, and I see their symptoms, not the whole of their existence. I know they are wives, husbands, mums, dads, sisters, friends, not just patients – but for me to do my job properly, it actually helps to compartmentalise, to keep all of that separate. I'm not totally sure when it started leaking into the rest of my life, but it has.

I take a deep breath, let Larry out of the car, and go inside. I see that although it is busy, it is not crowded. There is music playing, Smokey Robinson telling me he has the tears of a clown.

A quick scan tells me none of the locals I've already met are there, but I do receive a few inquiring looks, which tells me they are probably from the area, and that they recognise either me or the weresheep. I plaster a non-committal smile on my face, aiming for polite-but-discouraging-contact, and head to the bar. I need to get the key, and get out, I think. Simple.

Jake is there, and tonight he is wearing a plain white cotton shirt, opened a few buttons at the collar, that somehow makes him look even more exotic. He looks up from the glass he is cleaning, and raises one eyebrow. Okay. Maybe not that simple after all.

"Hi," I say lamely, "I'm back!"

"I see that," he replies, his mouth quirking up at the corner.

"I'm sorry I didn't say goodbye."

"I'll let you off – just this once. Someone called about a booking, but I held off – had a feeling you might end up darkening my door again. The great escape plan didn't quite work out?"

"No," I say, frowning, "I think next time I might dig a tunnel... Anyway, is it okay if we stay another night?"

"I suppose so. I can even stretch to another Starshine Special; you look like you need it."

"Why is it," I ask, "that you always seem to be subtly insulting the way I look?"

He grins, and casts his eyes over me. "There is nothing wrong with the way you look, Ella, believe me. Go on, take a seat. Matt'll take over on the bar."

I have no idea who Matt is, but assume he is the same barman I saw the night before. I move away quickly, not wanting to meet another new person – he might start psycho-analysing my choice of trainers or something.

I am keen to lay my weary head down for the night, but I know that I owe at least one drink to Jake – he kept my room for me, after all – plus I get the feeling that he understands, that if I say 'Sorry, I need some emergency alone-time' at any stage during our conversation, he won't judge.

I manage to find a small table tucked away in the corner, near the jukebox, settle Larry down and go over to look at it. It's better than sitting there twitching. It's one of those olde-worlde affairs, with curved glass and neon lights. It looks a bit like a fairground ride, now I come to think of it. A quick glance at the music listed on little handwritten cards tells me there is a fair amount of olde-worlde going on with the contents as well – lots of Motown and soul, 60s classics, country, a few compilations from the 21st century scattered among them. There's even a collection of famous operatic arias. I'm rooting around in my purse for change when Jake appears beside me.

"It's free," he says, shrugging. "I had the coin mechanism disabled."

"And again," I reply, "it is impossible to see you as a wheeler-dealer. What do you fancy? Kylie? Venga Boys? Puccini?"

"I'm more of a soul boy, but also partial to a bit of Spice Girls."

I laugh, and press the buttons that bring 'Spice Up Your Life' into the room.

"Thank you," I say, as we sit down. "For the drink, and the room."

"What about the Spice Girls?"

"Yeah, well, I thank God for the Spice Girls every night in my prayers. But...seriously. Thanks. You might have suspected I'd be back, but I didn't."

"You're welcome. Where did you go?"

"Oh, so many places. Fossil hunting. Ice cream eating. Mainly driving. Possibly a tiny bit of thinking. It was an ill-formed plan at this time of year, I now realise, with a dog in tow. Nowhere else would take us. Plus, I was talking to a friend – well, not talking, messaging, I haven't actually seen her for years – and she seemed to think I was mad to have left at all. I was thinking about it afterwards, why I felt it was important I moved on – I don't actually have a schedule; I could stay for as long as I wanted to. I realised it was for all kinds of reasons, but at least one of them was that I was scared that thing was happening."

"The falling in love with the place thing?"

"Yes. And obviously, that's not exactly a fate worse than death, is it? But it's also not something I'm ready for right now. I've recently broken up with someone, and I think I'm on the run from my own life. I'm just not sure I'm ready to stop running yet. Does any of that make sense?"

I have no idea why I am telling him all of this, or asking his opinion. I barely know the man – but something about him seems to make me open up in ways that more inquisitive people don't. Sheer contrariness on my part, probably.

He is silent for a few moments, looking at me intently, and then replies: "Yeah, it does make sense. I get it. I've been on the run myself in times gone by. Not physically, maybe, but definitely from anything that mattered. Anything that felt too complicated."

He doesn't elaborate, and I don't push him. Instead, I say: "Exactly. Are you sure you weren't actually a therapist before you moved here? I feel like I should be paying you for your time!"

"Definitely not a therapist. In fact I wasn't a man who was especially interested in other people at all. It's not a time in my life I'm proud of."

"Well, you're not like that now, are you? Now you make

time for your guests, and sit listening to the woes of the various stray humans that end up in your pub..."

"Not all of them," he replies, seriously. "And I feel obliged to add that I'm not just talking to you because I'm a nice guy. I'm a work in progress, but I'm not quite there yet. I enjoy talking to you. It can get lonely here, despite appearances – I stay busy, and I love living here, but I'm not quite like the others. They have ties, history, shared experiences. I'm still on the outside looking in a bit, which is how I like it for the time being. Most people who stay at the inn are in couples or families, and they certainly don't want me hanging around them..."

"Ah," I announce, pointing at him, "are you in fact saying that I'm doing you a favour, not the other way around?"

He laughs, and answers: "Maybe it's a symbiotic relationship. And on that note, I actually have a proposition for you..."

"Already?" I say in fake shock, clutching my hands to my chest. "But I haven't even had one Starshine Special yet!"

"Ha ha. Don't worry, your virtue's safe. No, my proposition is this – why don't you just stay for the week the room was booked for? Why don't you just treat it as a holiday? A pleasant stay in a luxury hotel in a beautiful place, with an extremely charming – it has been said handsome – host, and the whole of the south-west coast on your doorstep? Be as much involved, or not, with the village as you like – you're not trapped here, you have wheels, you have Larry, you have time. Why not just give yourself a break from the running, just long enough to catch your breath?"

Just long enough to catch my breath... Even as I repeat the words in my mind, I feel something unclench inside me. I feel a sudden rush of relaxation, of calm, of rightness. The last month has been a blur of hectic tedium, and I realise that I while I am still running, I am running on empty. That this isn't just something I *could* do – it's something I *need* to do. The trick will be doing it and then moving on, before Connie snares me in her sugar-coated web.

"Jacob Hennessy," I say, echoing her tone to him the day before, "you just might be more than a pretty face."

He raises his glass, and I clink mine against his.

"Here's to holidays," he says, smiling his perfect smile. "And spicing up your life."

Chapter Twelve

It is now Thursday, and I have settled into a gentle routine. Larry and I eat breakfast at the inn, and then we usually head out to explore.

We have visited so many beautiful places, seen so many beautiful sights – and they have been so much more enjoyable with another living creature to share them with. Admittedly, he's not much of a conversationalist, but that suits me just fine. He is happy to simply be at my side, to accompany me, to share my crisps and to curl up on my lap wherever we are. I take literally hundreds of pictures of him, and am starting to understand all those people who fill their social media posts with photos of their pets.

He is now also looking very smart after a trip to a grooming salon, emerging smelling of lavender and trimmed into shape. He wasn't as keen, and immediately found some poo to roll around in to make himself feel better – but I suspect he is a lot cooler, and that he can also see a lot better now his fringe has been cut. I probably need to do the same myself, as my hair is by this stage nowhere near a bob. I had to maintain a certain level of smartness when I was working, but must admit I am enjoying the freedom now that isn't an issue.

I quite like the blonde streaks from all my days in the sun, the slight tangle that all the sea air has given my hair. More than that, I like the honest sense of exhaustion I have by the end of each day – days spent walking and climbing and clambering and swimming in the sea. It is a different type of tiredness to work-tiredness; it feels hard-earned, like it gives you as much energy as it takes. Plus, it makes the reward at the end of the day even sweeter.

Every evening, I have gone back to the inn after a day of adventure. Every evening, I have enjoyed a Starshine Special, and a quick chat with Jake as we listen to music on the jukebox. It's nothing deep and meaningful, nothing earth-shattering – we respect each other's boundaries, and I simply enjoy it. It feels like a way of easing myself back into the world. He is, in a small, quiet way, becoming a friend – someone I can talk to about my day, someone who has a sense of humour, someone who makes me smile, all the way to my eyes.

And after that, I make the trek up those rickety stairs, to my pretty room with a view, and allow myself to enjoy it. I enjoy my shower, and I enjoy seeing the star-studded bay stretching out beneath me, and I enjoy the way Larry seems so settled. Mainly, I enjoy that wonderful feeling when you finally lay down your tired body on a comfortable bed, stretching sore muscles, feeling fresh linen against sun-kissed skin, glorying in the space and the softness and the serenity of it all. I never thought that the simple act of going to bed at the end of the day could be so glorious.

I have continued messaging Priya, and reopened lines of proper communication with Katie and Lucy, and spoken briefly to Mark about the need to disentangle our finances. We still share a joint account, where my final wages were sent, and that is obviously not something that can continue. He raised the issue of the house again, and I suggested what I thought was fair – there is no way that I would ask for half of it, as I only contributed a fraction of that. I know a good lawyer would grind their teeth in horror, but I really don't want to be greedy, or take more than I need. I am more than capable of supporting myself, and the sum we have agreed upon will cushion the blow for a while if I am careful.

In short, I have been having adventures, drinking cocktails, and Sorting My Shit Out. Jake was more right than he could have imagined – staying still hasn't just allowed me to catch my breath, it's allowed me to regain control of my own life. At least some of it.

Nobody has come forward to claim Larry, which is another wonderful piece of news, because I cannot imagine my life without this smelly lump of fur playing a starring role in every scene.

Today, my companion and I have stayed closer to base camp. We have explored the caves in daylight, and found to my delight that they sparkle almost as much as they do at night. The deeper you go into the cavern, the more shady it is, and if you stop and wait until the sunshine hits it just right, you are rewarded with a glorious shower of sparkle and shimmer. I whirl around in it, dancing beneath a glitterball entirely created by nature.

I see tiny chunks of the stuff on the floor, and realise that this is what Daisy the artist must use for her creations. I've been told she's in Australia for the summer, but I hope that one day, I can buy one of her pieces. A little bit of Starshine Cove to take away with me, a reminder of all that I found here.

We spend some time on the beach, and it is fuller than normal – by which I mean I see about 20 other people, all tourists from the look of it, all clearly enjoying their secret slice of heaven. It is a warm day, and the heat seems to float off the waves, rolling into a hazy horizon. I see a couple of boats bobbing around further out, and decide that I'd like to do that one day. Sail off into the sunset, and see how this place looks from the other side.

Eventually, we make our way along the beach and up the steps to the café. The flowers are in full bloom, and I spot a patch of swaying red and yellow gladioli that have blossomed as others have faded. Archie knows his stuff, and I suspect there is something to delight the eyes and senses all year round in Starshine Cove. I notice one of the little fairy creations peeking up at me from behind a thick green stalk, and bid her a good day as I walk along the path.

Inside, Connie is in full command mode, dashing around behind the counter, plating up sandwiches and pouring drinks and singing along to 'I Heard It Through The Grapevine' on the radio. I see Dan on waiter duty, and he looks thrilled about it, as well as a girl of about the same age who I assume is his sister, Sophie. Where Dan hides behind his rebellious appearance and fake-surly exterior, Sophie looks like the exact opposite – she has her mum's gorgeous golden curls, big blue eyes, and seems to enjoy chatting to the customers as she waltzes gracefully around the room delivering orders.

Connie spots me, and holds up a hand, waving me over to the counter. George is already there, Lottie in her traditional almost-comatose pose at his feet.

"The wanderer returns!" George announces, gesturing for me to sit next to him. "How goes it, traveller?"

"It goes...well, thank you. We've been having a nice time."

Connie places the orders on the counter, bashing her hand against an old-fashioned brass bell that presumably tells her waiting staff, or children as some might call them, that they are ready. Even from across the room, I can see Dan grimace in that way that only teenagers can.

"So," she says, propping her elbows up on the surface and

resting her face in her palms, "how are you finding life with Starshine Cove's most eligible bachelor?"

"Connie, I'm hurt!" George announces, passing a corner of toast down to Larry. "I thought that was me!"

"Maybe 60 years ago, babe," she replies, winking at me.

"Well, Connie," I reply slowly, "as landlords go, he's not bad. He has good taste in music and makes a mean cocktail, but I hate to disappoint you – no romance is brewing."

"Are you sure?" she says, pleadingly. "Because it seems such a waste of two gorgeous young people in the prime of their lives..."

"And by that, you mean that if we don't jump into bed with each other, we're being wasted?"

"Well, when you put it like that...yes! Anyway. There's time yet. I haven't given up hope."

I roll my eyes at her, and order a coffee. I am keen to get away from this subject, because I suspect it might make me blush. And if I blush, she will assume I am embarrassed, and if I am embarrassed, she will assume it is because I am hiding something. Like wild sex in the snug.

Jake is, without a shadow of a doubt, drop-dead gorgeous – but I am not in the market for a new man, even if he was interested in me, which I'd never be arrogant enough to think. There have been moments – accidental touches, brief encounters, a high-five that lasted slightly longer than it should have lasted – but nothing more than that. Nothing that would, in fact, make me blush.

The blushing part comes from something else entirely. The blushing part comes from the dreams. I seem to have replaced my usual rollercoaster REM of anxiety for something far more enjoyable. Jake has appeared in my nocturnal wanderings several times now, in a variety of circumstances – next to me in my car; in the sparkling cave; at Baker Street Tube station. Even, on one especially strange occasion, at the back of the crowd at an Alanis Morissette gig – dreams are weird. The one thing they all had in common, though, was that they ended with a kiss – a long, lingering, knee-buckling kiss that left me breathless and out of control and desperate for more. This dream-kiss is so vivid that I can smell his aftershave, feel my fingers curled into his hair, still remember the strength of his arms wrapped around me and his chest pressed against mine.

Each time, I have woken up hot, bothered, and mortified – to the point that I even spent half an hour on the slow wi-fi looking at dodgy websites about dream analysis, desperate to find some meaning other than the obvious one. Eventually I found an article that claimed sexy dreams aren't about sex at all, which is why you can sometimes have them about random people you don't even fancy – it's actually your dream state telling you that you're intrigued by that person, and want to get to know them better. Phew, I thought. Thank God for that.

I hide all of this from Connie of course, because she'd enjoy it just a bit too much. Instead, I glance around the café, seeing that most of the blonde-wood tables are full, that everyone seems content, that even the toddlers are sitting quietly with colouring books and crayons, babies are asleep in pushchairs, dogs are snoozing, people are reading and chatting. It is entirely possible that the village council have funded some kind of social experiment where they pump happy drugs into the water supply. Or maybe it's as simple as there not being wi-fi, and nobody getting enraged about the news on their phones, or seeing pictures of other people's holidays that look even better than theirs.

As I take my visual survey, Connie and George bantering in the background, I see one man, though, who doesn't look quite right. He appears to be in his 50s, and is sitting at a table for four with a woman I presume is his wife, and a boy of about 12. The wife and the boy have empty plates in front of them; the man has clearly just pushed his ice-cream sundae around in its

tall glass, and it's now a puddle of pink liquid and halved straw-
berries and bobbing chocolate curls.

There's something in his posture, something about the way
he is holding himself, that tells me he is in pain. It's the kind of
thing you see in waiting rooms – people trying to be brave,
trying to hide their hurts around others, trying not to show how
worried they are. His skin carries a sheen of sweat, which
nobody else in the air-conditioned room has, and his eyes are
staring into the distance.

His wife says something to him, and he doesn't reply until
she waves her hands in front of his face. I can almost imagine
what she says – something jokey about him being on another
planet or away with the fairies. I see him try to smile, and then
his right hand goes to his chest. He pats it firmly, like he's trying
to burp a baby, and I see him sucking in air way too rapidly.

He starts to flex his left hand into a fist, opening and closing
it and staring at it as though it belongs to someone else, and
without even knowing I plan to do it, I am off my stool and
walking briskly towards the table. I have seen these signs before,
and it often does not end well – and if I am wrong, then all that
happens is that I cause a bit of a scene and apologise to them
and feel a bit embarrassed. I can live with that.

I'm aware of Connie saying my name as I leave the counter,
and of Larry jumping up and following me. I ignore them both
and head quickly in his direction, weaving between tables and
prams and excuse-me-ing my way through. I keep an eye on the
man, who by this time has started to lean alarmingly to one side,
his face contorted in pain. Just as I reach him, he slumps,
crashes to the floor, his flailing arms sweeping the sundae glass
down with him.

His wife and son jump up in shock, scraping their chairs
back with a squeal, the woman shouting: "Geoff! Geoff! What's
wrong?" as she falls to her knees at his side. The boy backs up,
wide-eyed and scared, the hand-held video game he was playing

dropping to the floor, where it lands in a slick of melted strawberry ice cream.

The whole room goes initially silent, that peculiarly English thing happening where nobody quite wants to cause a scene, or intrude on something private. That only lasts for a few moments, before people dash over to try and help.

I push my way through, asking the crowd that has gathered to stand back, telling them to move the chairs and clear some space. I must do it with some authority, because everyone does exactly as they're told, as I crouch down and examine the man.

"Geoff!" I say loudly, taking him by the shoulders and shaking him. "Are you all right, Geoff?"

There is no answer, and it is very obvious that he is not all right – but this is what we were always told to do. This looks like a heart attack, but that's not always the case – people faint, pass out, have strange unexpected blackouts. It's not always the bad thing.

This time, though, it is the bad thing – I can't find a pulse, and he isn't breathing, isn't moving, isn't responding to the frantic cries of his wife and child.

Connie has run over to see what she can do, and I tell her to phone an ambulance immediately and tell them it's a category 1 condition, heart attack or cardiac arrest. She dashes away, and I shout after her: "Connie, do you have a defibrillator here?"

She shakes her head, curls flying, and yells: "Not here – in the hall!"

"Send Dan to fetch it, and make that phone call – now!"

I turn back to the man in front of me, knowing that I need to act quickly, but that I also need to stay calm, and keep everyone else around me calm. The first part isn't too bad – I, after all, have done this before. But for this man's family, this is terrifying.

"Does Geoff have any long-term illnesses?" I ask. "Any medical history?"

"No, nothing," the wife mutters, throwing an arm around her son's shoulders. "I mean, his own dad had a heart condition, and died when he was little, but...that's not going to happen, is it? There've been no signs of anything wrong at all! He's been a bit tired, but..."

I see her panic building, and see her son's face freeze at her mention of death. I don't have time to comfort them, so I just say: "Okay. That's helpful. I'm going to do CPR – it might look scary, but it's not hurting him, all right?"

They nod, and I check his airway before I place my hand on his chest, place the other on top, straighten my arms and start pumping. There was an advert a few years ago that told people to do CPR at the same beat as the song 'Stayin' Alive', and that was a clever trick – but not one that I really need. I have done this too many times, and it is second nature.

It is hard work, keeping up CPR, maintaining that pace, keeping the vital blood and oxygen flowing around a human body. I count silently as I go, pausing to give him rescue breaths, remembering the times we weren't allowed to do that during the pandemic. I've had Covid three times so far, and I'm willing to take the risk again.

I am working on him as Connie updates me, shouting instructions at me from the phone, telling me to do the things I'm already doing. Eventually she is quiet, obviously having told the operator what's happening. It feels like forever, but is probably only two minutes, when Dan runs full pelt towards me clutching the defibrillator case. I carry on with the compressions while he calmly opens it up and pulls out the device, unravelling the wires and the pads.

I pause the compressions, check for breath, and pull up his T-shirt. As ever, I'm struck by the lack of dignity – this poor man started his day like any other, enjoying a holiday with his family, and now he is lying here covered in ice cream, his clothing shoved aside, surrounded by strangers. An audience for the worst day of his life.

As soon as the device is turned on, a recorded voice starts to give me instructions I don't need, and I quickly attach the pads to Geoff's chest. The voice tells us all that it is checking the heart rhythm, and there is a tense wait until we are told that a shock is needed. Both the defib woman and I tell people to stand clear, and I lean back on my knees as it does its business.

There is no change in Geoff's condition, so I take up CPR again, continuing until finally, miraculously, I see signs of independent breathing. He is still not conscious, still hasn't opened his eyes, but he is breathing. I am checking his airway again and monitoring his breath sounds when the paramedics arrive and take over, gently pushing me to one side so they can carry on. I tell them what his symptoms seemed to have been in the minutes before, and update them on what I've found and done since then, and I leave them to it, telling them I will be around if they need me.

They soon have him removed to the ambulance, his wife and son going with him, and I find myself standing alone by the counter of the café, blinking rapidly. There is always this insane moment after an emergency procedure like that when you feel like you might be about to have a heart attack yourself. The adrenaline is still surging through your system, and everything in your mind and body is on high alert.

I see Sophie start to pick the chairs back up, and begin to clear up the mess on the floor – discarded sticky pads, a shattered sundae glass, the bright yellow video console. I see it, but I'm still trying to regulate my own breathing. Connie approaches me with a towel, and starts to wipe it over my body – I realise that I am wet, from ice cream and spilled coffee. I nod, and take it from her.

"I'm fine," I say, reassuringly. "Don't worry. Dan was a star, tell him thank you."

She gives me a cautious once-over, then replies: "Ironically, I suspect he's nipped outside for a vape. But I will. You stay here for a minute, madam – don't be dashing off."

I see her make eye contact with George, who immediately takes hold of my shoulders and steers me towards one of the stools. I sit down gratefully, suddenly exhausted, and smile as he lifts up Larry and places him in my arms. The dog licks my face frantically, obviously confused by everything that's been happening, and I murmur calm words that work for both of us, comforting myself as well as him.

The level of chatter in the café has suddenly shot up as everyone seems to talk to each other at once. I see Connie making her way through the room, offering refills on drinks, passing out trays of brownies, making sure that everybody is all right. This will be an interesting anecdote for everyone else here, maybe a frightening memory for some, perhaps even a wake-up call for others – but for poor Geoff and his family, it's going to be life changing. Even if he survives, there'll be a long, hard road to recovery.

Once she's finished her rounds, Connie takes up her customary place behind the counter. She gets me a Diet Coke from the fridge, and passes it over, hands shaking.

"That," she says seriously, "was amazing."

"Not really," I reply, managing to open the can without a visible tremble in my own fingers. "It's really good you had the defibrillator, and that the ambulance got here so quickly."

"There's an ambulance station about three miles away, which in rural terms is pretty much next door – but yes. It was lucky. Might have been a different story if it was at night, or at a weekend, or even a month later – it's only in use during tourist season, when there are more people here. Luck all round, I suppose – mainly having you here, Ella. You saved that man's life. Don't play it down – you didn't just save him, you saved that whole family from a lifetime of loss."

She seems even more affected than me, and I am I uncomfortable with the attention.

"Maybe, who knows? The hospital will do the real work."

She is drumming her fingertips on the surface, and her blue eyes have narrowed.

"How could you do all of that?" she asks eventually. "Is that your job, are you a doctor?"

I gulp down some of the Coke, and then reply: "Hummm... I went on a course."

"A course?" she says, smiling. "And how long was that course?"

Realising I've been well and truly rumbled, I answer: "Oh, about six years or so..."

She lets out a delighted laugh, and George pats me on the back.

"Well done, love," he says, sounding like a proud dad at prize evening. "Connie's right, that was amazing. No need to hide your talents under a bushel – it's hardly a shameful secret is it, being a doctor?"

"No," I answer, "not shameful – but you do learn to be cautious. I mean, one minute you'll be at a party, chatting to someone over a vol-au-vent, and the next minute they find out what you do for a living, and before you know it you're locked in the bathroom with a complete stranger, in your best frock and make-up, examining someone's swollen testicle or fungal nail infection. You wouldn't believe how many rashes I've been asked to look at over the years!"

Connie guffaws with laughter, and George gives me the kind of cagey look that I know means he was considering asking me about something himself. Hopefully not a swollen testicle.

"Well, you were a blessing today, Ella," he says, patting me on the shoulder. "It would all have been very different without you. I wouldn't have known what to do, and Connie here would probably have just wafted a croissant under his nose and hoped it brought him round. You have a gift, and it was a privilege to see you use it."

Huh, I think, as I nod and drink my Coke. A gift, a blessing...these words have not seemed relevant to my job for a long time, but maybe he is right. Geoff is still alive, and that means he has a chance. He might get to see his son grow up, and grow old with his wife, and one day view this all as a terrible thing that happened, but could have been much worse.

I made a difference – and I have to admit, it feels good.

Chapter Thirteen

It starts the very next day. I have had a lie-in, and wandered downstairs for a late breakfast. Miranda is on duty, as Jake has gone away for a few nights to visit his father in Warwickshire.

She ambles over at her understandably slow pace, and deposits a tray carrying my granola, along with a bowl of fresh berries and a little jug of honey. There is, as usual, also a sausage for Larry.

Normally, I'd thank her, and she'd give me a no-worries smile, and amble all the way back to the kitchen again – but today, she lurks at the side of the table, obviously feeling awkward. I see her open her mouth and close it again several times, and eventually decide I have to put her out of her misery.

"I love your T-shirts," I say, gesturing to today's version – a hot pink 'not-fat-I'm-pregnant' top.

"Oh, yeah, they're fun aren't they? I'm thinking of getting some more for after I've had the baby, but this time they'll say 'I'm not pregnant, I'm just fat'."

"Ha! That would be even funnier. How far along are you, if you don't mind me asking?"

I am always very aware of asking questions that haven't been invited. People are entitled to their privacy, to their secrets, and outside of a consultation, I work on the principle that if anyone wants to share, they will. Women in particular seem to be expected to divulge every detail of their reproductive health to complete strangers – everything from 'Have you got kids?' through to 'When will you be starting a family?', as though that isn't a deeply personal issue, and one that for some people can be a cause of a lot of pain. Harmless questions that can inflict a lot of harm.

I lost count of the amount of times people asked me and Mark those questions. We were the right age, we were a solid couple, we had established careers – yet friends and acquaintances and random people we'd met in the bar on holiday still seemed to think it was perfectly fine to say 'So, when will you two be hearing the patter of tiny feet, then?'

I found it intrusive even before Lizzie, but afterwards, every single time it felt like a punch to the gut. I often wondered how they'd react if I told them – if I responded to what they saw as a totally innocent query with the truth. That I had been pregnant, that I had lost my baby, that I had been consumed with grief and loss and guilt ever since.

Miranda, though, does not seem offended at my question – in fact she looks relieved.

"Five months," she says, placing a hand on her bump.

"Oh – maybe you'll get a Christmas baby then!"

"Who knows? Always thought that'd be rubbish, having your birthday the same day as Christmas. Bet people only get you one present for both... He's moving around a lot now. Do you...want to feel?"

I smile, and place my hand where she indicates. Sure enough, there is that joyous motion as the tiny human inside her kicks and cartwheels and says hello to the world. I never made it far along enough to experience this, and for a long time after I lost Lizzie, I found it difficult to be around pregnant women. I found it hard to listen to their happy complaints, or share their excitement and fears, or listen to the names they were choosing. I deliberately chose not to do any pre-natal work, and would quite literally cross the street to avoid a pregnant woman.

I was in too much pain of my own, and always felt a sting of unreasonable jealousy that didn't make me like myself very much at all – much as I tried to quash it, there was always a little voice in my head, asking why they got to keep their baby and I didn't. What made them better than me? Like I say, unreasonable – and luckily not too long-lived. It's not feasible in my profession to completely sidestep pregnancy issues, and, bit by bit, the feeling faded. It became something I recognised and managed and eventually it simply lost its hold over me.

Now, as I feel Miranda's baby kick, all I experience is a sense of wonder – even after all this time, even after years of being a doctor, I am still amazed at this process. At the thought of that tiny life in there, who will eventually become a baby, then a child, then a person with their own hopes and dreams and challenges.

I move my hand, and grin at her: "Definitely nice and active!" I say. "How are you feeling?"

"Oh, mainly okay, you know. Get tired easily. Jake's been great though, he lets me work what hours I can, and he's even put me a recliner chair in the back so I can put my feet up. But, well, I heard you were a doctor, and I wondered if I could ask you something?"

Ah, I think – here we are.

"Of course you can," I reply, patting the chair next to me so she can sit down. "But bear in mind I'm not a specialist, and even though I'm a doctor, I'm not your doctor."

She nods, and wrinkles her nose, and is obviously struggling to find the words. She looks so distressed that I am starting to worry there is something really wrong here.

"It's okay," I say reassuringly. "You can tell me."

Her face creases in embarrassment, and the words come tumbling out: "I've got piles, and they're really uncomfortable, and I just don't know what to do – this has never happened to me before and it's the worst thing ever!"

I bite back the laughter that is rising in my throat, because this is clearly not funny for Miranda. I assure her that it is very common, and talk about it in a matter-of-fact way that seems to console her. I give her some advice on diet and possible medication, and tell her to talk to her midwife about it.

"Okay," she says, staring at me intently. "That's good. But I won't be like this all the time, will I?"

She looks heartbroken, and I realise again how young she is. There has been no mention of her parents, or the baby's father, and suspect she has nobody around to support her through all of this.

"No, you won't. I promise."

"And another thing – someone told me I might poo myself during the birth! Is that true?"

I smile, and answer calmly: "I've noticed that people are always really keen to tell you horror stories when you're pregnant. My advice is to not listen – everybody's pregnancy and labour is different. Yes, that can happen, but it's not inevitable – and even if it does happen, much as you think it would be the most embarrassing thing in the world, it's not. Midwives and doctors will have seen far worse, and once you have that baby in your arms, you really won't care any more. All that matters is the outcome, not how you get there."

She considers this, and eventually nods firmly as she gets back up.

"Yeah. That's a good way of looking at it. Anyway, sorry to bother you – and I feel a lot better now. Thank you."

I wait until she is out of sight before allowing myself a quick laugh.

"Well," I say to Larry as I chop his sausage in half and pass a piece down, "what a way to start the day, eh? Piles and poo! At least it wasn't a swollen testicle…"

We eat our breakfast, and as I leave, I see Miranda cleaning the surface of one of the big tables. She is singing out loud, and smiling at something only she sees, and I feel a little thrill of satisfaction. She is happier now, and that is a pleasure to see.

I had been planning on a drive to Poole today, but instead I make a last-minute decision to stay local. I leave the inn, and wander around the green until I reach the village shop.

The shop – or Emporium as it is grandly titled – is run by Trevor the Druid, and is one of those places that stocks a little bit of literally everything. Tinned food, a small counter selling fresh meat and fish, pies and cakes from the Betties' Bakery, drinks and sandwiches. There are souvenirs and postcards, household items, toiletries, toys, books, fishing gear, a whole rack of weird but useful items like shoelaces and sewing kits and plug fuses. There's even one corner of it that is filled with videos for hire – the old-fashioned VHS ones in their chunky plastic cases. Basically, it's a one stop shop for everything from a multi-pack of Wotsits to an inflatable dinosaur.

Trevor himself greets me cordially as I pay for the chocolate éclairs I have in my basket, then solemnly announces from behind his wizard beard: "I can cure warts with nothing more than the power of my mind and flowers from the hedgerows, you know."

"Well," I reply, somehow not at all surprised, "that's great. I have a lot of time for herbal medicines."

"The ingredients are important, but so is the *power of the mind*."

He stares at me intently, as though trying to communicate something of great importance telepathically, and I nod again.

"Yep," I say, taking my change. "I can't argue with that."

He seems placated, and I leave, stifling yet another laugh – that seems to be my go-to mode this morning. He's right, though, to some extent – the power of the mind is one of the most important forces in the world, for good and for bad. Not so sure it can get rid of warts, but it definitely plays a vital role in how well we live our lives.

The power of my mind allows me to remember where George's cottage is, and also instructs my hand to magically lift up and knock on the door. For my next trick, I will attempt to levitate Larry into the air and make him do the Charleston.

I stand back, and look up at the house. It's one of the older buildings, large and sprawling, with a thatched roof and a bright red front door. There is a small courtyard garden in the front, and a flag flying at full mast. I glance up at the fluttering fabric and see that it is a picture of some kind of winged creature, with the word 'Pixieland' painted beneath it in bright pink letters.

George opens the door, and I am ushered in. Larry immediately dashes through to find Lottie, who is lying in a heap of golden fur by the fireplace. She thumps her tail once, and endures Larry's adoration stoically.

"I come bearing cakes," I announce, glancing around the room. It is a beautiful room, filled with light and air, the ceiling criss-crossed with dark wooden beams. The walls are decorated with paintings of the cove, and numerous framed family photos.

"You must be a mind reader," he replies. "I was just sitting here pondering a trip to the café. I'll get us some tea, shall I?"

As he leaves, I browse the pictures, smiling at one of the two little girls – Lilly and Meg – in a paddling pool with Lottie sitting between them. There are several of George and a red-headed woman who I assume was his wife, who I know passed away a few years ago, and plenty of people I don't even recognise, including Connie with a smiling man with golden hair and bright blue eyes. I see a wedding photo, a woman in a white dress with the same red tresses, grinning as she gazes up at a man I eventually recognise as Archie. He looks very different now, with his long hair and his beard, but underneath it all he was a bit of a babe.

I start to realise how little I know about these people – I have been welcomed, a little too thoroughly on some occasions, but I still don't quite know how all their lives interconnect. I have perhaps been guilty of seeing this place as some kind of wacky art installation, between the Druids and the Mystery Cricket and the general sense of wellbeing, but I know they are people like anyone else, with complicated lives and histories. Their bonhomie is, in some cases, maybe just what lies on the surface – a different kind of protective shell. If someone seems relentlessly happy, you don't tend to question them too much.

"Ah," says George, passing me a mug of tea that looks strong enough to floor a builder, "that's a nice one, isn't it? A very happy day. My daughter, Sandy, that is, and her Archie before the girls came along."

He points at the man with Connie, and tells me that is Simon, and then takes me to another framed photo, this one showing a young woman with darker auburn hair and a smile so mysterious she makes the Mona Lisa look like a blabbermouth.

"And this is Suzie, my middle one. I was a later starter, me, only met my wife when I was in my late 30s. Thought it would never happen for me. Thought love was a bit of a myth to be honest, until she turned up – rolled into the village in one of those Volkswagen camper vans, she did, and from the moment I met her I suddenly understood what all the fuss was about. She was younger than me, didn't think I had a chance..."

I laugh, and reply: "George, I think you'd have a chance with anyone."

"Thank you kindly, love, but those days are over. I was lucky once, and you can't expect more than one miracle in a lifetime, can you? Anyway. What brings you here? Not that I'm complaining."

I hear a touch of melancholy in his voice, and understand that showing me these pictures has made him sad. Perhaps they have been there for so long that he has become accustomed to their presence, their power, the fact that they are maybe ticking time-bombs of emotion. Now I've come along, and he's seen them all anew.

"Well, apart from the pleasure of your company, of course, I just wanted to pop in for a chat. That was a weird thing that happened yesterday, and I thought I'd check you were okay. Plus Larry asked me to bring him for a visit with Lottie."

"Ah," he says wisely, nodding, "you have a talking dog as well, do you? Chatty buggers once they get going, aren't they? Well, that was very nice of you. At my age – 87, in case you were wondering, and yes, I know, I don't look a day over 70 – at my age, you do get a bit more used to the ups and downs of life. But when it's a young one, like that man in the café, well...it doesn't seem fair, does it?"

As he speaks, his eyes roam across the wall of photographs, of memories, of his own life and the lives of those he loves.

"It doesn't, no," I reply quietly. "I called the hospital last night, by the way, and he's doing as well as can be expected."

"That's good... So, what kind of a doctor are you, anyway, in the real world?"

"The real world?" I echo, widening my eyes. "Are you telling me Starshine Cove isn't actually the real world? Because, you know, I've been having my suspicions it's all a bit too good to be true..."

He laughs so loud that Lottie lifts her head and stares at him, before flopping down again.

"No, it's real enough, my love. We just try very hard to see the bright side of life – which isn't too hard when you live here. We have each other, and we have this beautiful place, and we have a lot of love and laughter and fun. That's the key isn't it? Whatever life throws at you, you have to try and find the fun in it."

I can't help but smile along with him, charmed as ever by those sparkling blue eyes.

"Maybe it is," I reply, "and that's definitely something I need to work on. But in answer to your question, I've mainly worked in community health – GP surgeries, health centres, that kind of thing. I go around different places when they need an extra pair of hands."

I don't go into detail about my other experiences – because that really doesn't qualify as finding the fun.

"Oh!" he says, sounding impressed. "So you're one of those hokum doctors are you? Is that the right word? Or is it poke-'em doctors? Although after what you said yesterday, maybe you're more of a scrotum doctor..."

"You know perfectly well what the word is, you old fraud."

"I do," he replies, shaking his head. "But it's a long time since I've been able to see one. The nearest surgery to us is miles away, and getting an appointment is about as easy as putting a man on the moon. They do this thing where you have to call in the morning, and then you can't get through, and then even if you do, all the appointments are gone!"

It is a familiar story, and a complaint that I know has relevance all across the UK, not just here. It's one of the reasons I could always get work in the drop-in centres.

"That must be frustrating," I say, seeing that there is more to it. That as I suspected yesterday, there is something on his mind. "Especially if you're not feeling well."

"Oh, I feel fine, Ella – healthy as a horse, me, feel like I could do one of those Iron Man contests most days! It's just... well, I have this mole, you see, and I have to be honest, I've been a bit worried about it..."

I nod, and try to look surprised, and obviously completely

fail. He points one finger at me and grins as he says: "You knew there was something, didn't you? You could tell somehow. That's why you're here!"

"Yes," I answer, grinning back. "It's a little-known secret power they teach us in medical school. Anyway, if you want to, you can show me the mole. I do like a good mole."

He considers it for a few moments, and then replies: "All right, can't see as it'd hurt. But I warn you, I'm going to roll my trouser leg up now, so prepare yourself – you're only flesh and blood!"

"I'll do my best not to swoon," I say, as I pull some disposable gloves out of my bag. He raises an eyebrow, and I say: "Never leave home without them. Now come on, don't be shy."

He leans down and shows me the offending mole. I take a look at it, and ask a few questions about when it first appeared, and if it's changed at all. I can tell by the way he answers that it is genuinely concerning him, much as he tries to hide it. I also suspect from its size and shape and colour, plus what George is telling me, that he may be right.

"Well," I tell him once we're done, "the good news is I don't think you're about to drop dead any time soon, George. The not-so-good news is that I do think you need to get it checked out. I genuinely think it'll be easy to deal with at this stage, but you can't ignore it. If you're struggling to get an appointment with your GP, maybe there's a drop-in nearby? Or a lot of surgeries these days do a thing called an e-consult – we could fill out the form, send them some pictures, maybe get a referral quicker that way?"

Of course, given the wi-fi reception around here, we might end up having to do it on the fire escape of the Starshine Inn surrounded by teenagers.

"Would you help me with that, Ella?" he says once he's gathered himself. "I'm not bad on the tech stuff considering I was born before electricity was invented, but I'm not a natural. I could ask one of the grandkids or Archie or Connie, but...well, I don't want to worry them without cause, do I?"

"I could definitely help you with that, as long as you do it before I leave – I'm only booked in until Sunday."

He looks marginally surprised, and says: "You know what, I'd forgotten about that. Suppose I'd got used to you being around brightening the place up."

Ha, I think – that's a first, me brightening a place up. I already like George, but now I think I might be just a bit in love with him.

"Tell you what, why don't me and you go on a sneaky coffee date?" I ask. "I could do with a few supplies from the outside world. We can do it tomorrow if you like. I'll even drive."

I see his eyes light up, and realise just how much this has been playing on his mind – how hard it must have been for him, shouldering the worry, not wanting to burden his loved ones. Seeing him so relieved fills me with a warm feeling deep inside, and as we say our goodbyes and I walk across to the café, I am smiling happily to myself. I've felt so useless for so long and not even recognised that fact. I'm sure Priya would have a term for it, but I'm just accepting it for what it is – a win.

As soon as I think of her, I stop and send her some photos of the cave, even though they hardly do the place justice. She replies: "Wow! Every pic you send me of that place is amazing. Can I come and visit? Or maybe just bring my girls down there and, you know, leave them with you while I go shopping in Paris?"

"Tough day?" I respond.

"Tough morning. Tired out and pissed off. No apologies for language, it makes me feel better. How's you?"

"Did CPR in the café (all good). Talked about piles over breakfast. Just been shown a mole."

She sends me crying-laughing emojis and adds: "I've been cleaning up projectile vomit from two sick little people all night.

I have chunks of it in my hair, and the shower is broken. At least you're being useful. Enjoy the feeling."

I am, I decide – at least for now.

By the time I walk into the café, it is almost 11am, and the place seems to be in something of a lull, a quiet spell between breakfast and lunch. Only a few tables are occupied, and I spot Connie sitting on a tall stool at the counter, chewing a pen and doing a crossword. Adele is on the radio, saying hello.

Connie stands up as soon as she sees me, clearly preparing to go and find something delicious from her display of delights.

"No, I'm fine, honest!" I say, as I take a seat next to her. "I couldn't eat another single thing, and I've had so much tea I might wee myself."

"Right. Well, we've all been there, I shan't judge. Evelyn called in earlier."

"That's nice," I reply quickly. "Who the heck is Evelyn?"

"She's Geoff's wife, from yesterday?"

"Oh! Gosh...how is he? How is she?"

Connie points to a spot further down the counter, where I see a box of Quality Street and a cuddly teddy with a balloon tied to its paw. They scream 'hospital gift shop'.

"He's doing okay. Regained consciousness during the night, and apparently doesn't remember much about it at all. She's been warned it won't be easy, but they're hopeful he'll recover. The docs there told her that without the immediate CPR and the defibrillator, he wouldn't have made it. They were impressed apparently, at the level of first aid training the Cove Café has provided its waitresses! Anyway, she was hoping to see you, but she had to dash. She left those for you as a thank you, along with a card."

I retrieve the card, which is addressed to 'The waitress with blonde hair', and peel it open. I am met with a picture of two sausage dogs, and the words 'thank you for being a friend'. The writing inside it is scrawled, which is perfectly understandable, but I manage to decipher it and read out loud: "Thank you for everything you did yesterday. You saved Geoff's life, and we will always remember you – you're a hero. With love from Geoff, Evelyn and Lucas."

Lucas has written his own name, and added a little drawing of a smiley face. It is unbearably sweet, and I tuck it away in my bag.

"So," Connie says, her eyes mischievous, "you look very pleased with yourself this morning. Anything I need to know about?"

I could tell her about Miranda's piles, or George's mole, I suppose – but that would be rude. Instead, I decide George is right – you have to find the fun in life.

I glance around as though I am making sure nobody can hear us, lean across the counter, and whisper into her ear: "Jake and I made wild passionate love to each other on the beach last night!"

Her eyes pop open, and her mouth forms an astonished circle. She claps her hands in glee, launches herself off the stool, and jumps up and down on the spot, much to Larry's confusion.

"Oh my God! I knew it, I knew it! What was it like, tell me everything...I want all the details!"

I am doing a countdown in my head, wondering how long it will take, and by the time I reach six she stops her happy dance, and frowns.

"Hang on a minute," she says, looking at me suspiciously, "Jake's away isn't he? Not back until tomorrow?"

I wink at her as she finally realises she's been had, and laugh at the expression of combined disappointment and delight on her face.

"You're not a hero," she says, throwing a tea-towel at me, "you're evil! How could you mess with my mind like that? I was looking forward to getting some really first-rate gossip then as well! What a bloody let-down! Never mind, I suppose there's always tonight..."

"What's tonight?" I ask, not sure I want to know.

"It's Friday isn't it? Naked karaoke at the village hall, of course."

Chapter Fourteen

After that, Larry and I set off on one of our adventures, heading to a nearby beach called Eype. For some reason the name makes me laugh, and every time I say it in a high-pitched tone, Larry looks up at me like I've announced something of great importance. Maybe it's his real name, who knows?

I do actually find a fossil today – hidden in some sand and tangled branches by the base of a baby-sized cliff, revealed when I poke it with my highly technical gadget: a big stick. It is broken in half, but I am delighted as I brush off the crusted sand and see perfectly curled circles in the stone. A consultation with Google tells me it is an ammonite, and once upon a time it was an ocean-dwelling mollusc.

I pocket my treasure, and head back to Starshine full of wonder, planning a whole new career for myself as a fossil-hunter. I could be just like Lara Croft, but without the cartoon boobs.

I plan to go out for dinner, thus avoiding the village hall, and any possible hint of naked karaoke – just in case. You can never be too sure with this lot.

As I park up, I see that Jake's car is back in its usual spot, and hope everything is okay. Inside, I am greeted by Matt on the bar, and a new server I have never seen before but who seems to know who I am. I suppose my fame as a fossil-hunter has already spread.

"Everything all right?" I ask, lurking by the doorway that leads to the stairs. "I saw Jake's car outside."

"Oh, yeah, he's fine," Matt replies, as he pulls a pint of IPA, "he's on the roof terrace. Go on up. He won't mind, you're a friend."

"I'm more of a paying guest," I point out.

"Nah. We have lots of paying guests, and Jake doesn't spend anywhere near as much time with them as he does you. You're a friend, whether you like it or not. In fact, can you do me a favour and take your friend some water? He walkied down for some earlier, said to bring it up when we were quiet. Except it's never been quiet."

I nod, and Matt pulls a bottle out of the fridge and passes it to me. He pauses, and gets another.

"For you and Larry," he explains. "It's just down the back, can't miss it."

I head down the corridor, bypassing my stairs, and reaching another doorway. I had no clue there was a roof terrace, or how to find it, but I follow the hallway to more steps, and at the top of them I reach a green door. I know we're in the more modern extension at the side of the building, but beyond that I am completely lost.

I'm not sure if it's a roof terrace for customers, or if it's just Jake's, or if this will be like walking into someone's home. Unsure of the etiquette, I tap the door with my knuckles, and open it.

The terrace isn't large, but it is breathtaking. Perched so high, the views of the cove and the sea stretch into infinity, the late afternoon sunlight reflecting on the turquoise waves, the distant shape of red cliffs curving around the coast in a blaze of colour. It is so beautiful it makes me sigh.

I tear my eyes away from the sea, and am confronted with something else that makes me sigh. Jake is lying on a mat on the terrace, wearing nothing but a pair of olive-green cargo shorts, eyes closed and headphones on. He clearly doesn't know we are here, and I allow myself a guilty moment of sheer pleasure as I look at him.

The gorgeous face is matched by an equally gorgeous body, lean and tanned and muscled, long legs stretching out, a perfectly contoured chest with a plume of dark hair feathering down to his waist. His arms are crossed beneath his head, biceps fairly shining in the sun, and his deep brown waves are wild and tousled. Jesus, I think, it's like he was created in a lab – it doesn't seem fair that one man should have so much going for him.

I feel a tiny curl of desire creeping across my stomach, a physical yearning that I haven't experienced for a very long time. Maybe not since I first met Mark. We weren't exactly setting the world alight in the bedroom department by the end, and it has been over six months since I last touched a man in a way that wasn't either professional or simply affectionate. What I feel when I look at Jake in that moment isn't either of those things – it is much more basic than that.

I can feel the flush crawling over my cheeks, and am suddenly way more hot than I should be. I turn around, deciding that I will just leave the water here, and run away. It seems like the only safe solution to my predicament. I don't enjoy feeling like a peeping tom pervert, and there is a cold shower most definitely calling my name.

Larry, though, has other ideas, and I look on in horror as he runs straight over to Jake, and starts giving his face a thorough tongue bath. Give a dog a sausage and you've got a stalker for life.

Jake sits up in surprise, looking understandably bewildered

but soon recovering. He pulls off his headphones, and scratches Larry behind the ears, looking around and spotting me. I freeze for a moment, and tell myself to get a grip. I have seen male bodies before, and I will see them again – plus Jake isn't a mind-reader, thank God, so he has no idea what kind of reaction seeing him like this has provoked in me.

"Hi!" I say brightly, walking towards him. "Matt asked me to drop off some water for you...sorry to intrude. My dog has no concept of boundaries."

Larry is, by this stage, nestled on his lap and licking his chest, which in all honesty sounds like a really great place to be.

"No problem," he says, "good to see you. Pull up a chair."

He moves Larry, and stands up, stretching his arms over his head and yawning. Look away, look away, look away, I tell myself, fumbling as I pick up one of the fold-out wooden chairs. Jake grabs his discarded T-shirt and puts it on, which goes some way towards defusing the situation.

I make myself busy getting Larry's little portable bowl from my bag, pouring him some water, and swishing my hair in front of my face while my blush fades down to something that can't actually be spotted from space by a passing satellite.

Jake places the other chair next to me, and takes a long pull from the water. Somehow, he even manages to make the act of drinking look sexy.

"I thought you were away until tomorrow?" I say, glancing around at the terrace. It is a lush little place, much of the surface covered in terracotta pots filled with dazzling flowers, a small herb garden off on one side rich with the smell of rosemary and mint, troughs spilling over with lavender and bright-pink zinnias with petals that look like they're made of velvet. I reach out and touch one, finding that they feel like velvet too.

"Yeah, well, that was the plan," he says, looking troubled and running his hands over his face. "It was dad's birthday, and me and my brother both went home for it. Thing is, with my dad... Well, he's a bit of a dick, to be frank."

I laugh at his honesty, and am rewarded with a grin.

"Right," I reply, sipping some of the water left in the bottle. "Well, families can be complicated. Mine live abroad."

"That's the stuff of dreams for us. Don't get me wrong, I love him – he's my dad. But he's also pig-headed, rude, arrogant and just plain hard to be around. Every time I go back, I promise myself I won't be baited, won't rise to it. And every time, he manages to get under my skin."

"I get it. You love him, but you don't like him?"

"Exactly! They're two very different things, aren't they? Anyway. I did a runner, and came back here..."

"To your happy place."

He ponders this for a moment, then nods. "Yes. To my happy place. I have cover in the bar and the kitchens for another night, so I thought I'd just head up here, away from everybody, and try to calm down."

I gesture at the terrace, and say: "It's really lovely up here. And I'm sorry if I disturbed your zen moment."

He waves it off, and quickly replies: "Nah, that's okay. I'm not very good at zen, to be honest. I was trying really hard, but I was already getting bored."

"I was always the same at meditation classes. Just totally sucked at it."

"Well, nobody's perfect. Sorry if I unloaded there – not everybody is fascinated by my dysfunctional family, I realise."

"What about Connie? She's fascinated by everything."

He looks at me, and shakes his head. "You're the first person here I've talked to about my family. Guess you're just lucky!"

"Or maybe you just recognise another emotional hermit when you see one, and reckon I'll keep your secrets safe. Which, by the way, I will."

"You may be right," he answers. "Anyway, I hear you've been busy."

"Ah. Word has spread, has it? It was a pretty intense situation, have to admit. I think I'm a bit better at intense than meditating."

"And how are you feeling now? Did it..."

He trails off, frowning, and I take a guess at what he was about to say: "You want to say 'trigger me' don't you?"

"I do! But I'm worried that makes me sound like I'm 15 and making a TikTok video. I might start talking about journeys and feelings next and then I'd hate myself for all eternity."

I laugh, and shake my head. "No, it didn't, actually. I mean, I wish it hadn't happened, for that poor man's sake. But I'm glad I was there, and I'm glad I was able to help. It actually made me feel...useful."

"Well, you've definitely become a legend round here. Booking into Starshine Cove for a week, casually winning hearts and saving lives – Connie will live off that for years! They're probably at the meeting right now, planning to commission some kind of statue in your honour..."

"Meeting?" I say, confused. "I thought it was naked karaoke tonight?"

"Maybe later. But every other Friday, the village elders get together to discuss important matters, like which film to show at the next screening, and whether the yoga mats need replacing, and who gets to bat in Mystery Cricket."

"Why aren't you there, then?" I ask. "You run the Starshine Inn; that must qualify you as an elder!"

"I'm 42, thank you very much. And I am invited. I just...don't go."

"Why? Are you worried your inner boss man will come out, and you'll start acting like one of those monsters who deliberately spoils other people's sets in Monopoly?"

"I am like that when I play Monopoly, and no, that's not the reason. Maybe it's because I'm not quite fully assimilated yet. Maybe it's because I'm usually busy here. Maybe it's as simple as me being scared they'll make me play Mystery Cricket."

I nod, and decide I can see the logic in that. I wouldn't fancy a faceful of jelly either.

We both sit in a comfortable silence for a while, watching Larry investigate the plant pots, looking on as the sun starts to slide slowly into the sea. I am struck by how easy this feels – how easy it is to be around this man. How easy it is to like him, to talk to him, to be myself around him. Once I've wrestled my libido under control, anyway.

I have spent a long time living with a man who felt like a stranger, and a month on the road talking to nobody but baristas and shop assistants. It has taken some time for me to warm up, to dare to peer into the world of others again – and Jake has been a big part of it.

"So, you have the night off?" I ask, as Larry curls up in the shade of a trellis that is covered with tumbles of sweet-smelling pink jasmine.

Jake nods, and I say: "I have a proposition for you."

He grins, clutches his hands to his chest, and replies: "Already? But I haven't even had one Starshine Special yet!"

"Ha! Very funny. I was wondering if I could take you out for dinner. Somewhere nice. I'm leaving in a couple of days, and I'd like to say thank you. And don't worry, your virtue is safe."

He looks into my eyes, and gives me such a heart-melting smile that I fear I may fall off my chair. Maybe he can read my mind after all.

"Virtue, much like normal, is over-rated," he replies. "But yes. It's a date."

Chapter Fifteen

We drive to the nearest big town, and enjoy a very civilised meal together in a small Italian restaurant tucked away on a cobbled side street.

Jake tells me more about his mum, and the summers he spent in Rome as a child, and I show him photos of my parents' place in Portugal. I tell him stories from medical school, and he recounts his first steps in the business world. We talk about films and music and friends and travel. We talk about everything, and yet nothing, all at the same time. We seem to have come to an unspoken agreement to keep the mood entirely light.

Larry is back at the inn, where his blankets have been set up for him behind the bar and where he is perfectly happy receiving lots of fuss and treats. I feel like a mum having a night off from her kids, even if my kid is furry and has four legs and isn't that demanding. Even more excitingly, I am wearing a dress.

This might not sound like very thrilling news, but it is nice to feel fancy for a change. Between the travelling and adventuring and the sun and the long hours of driving, I haven't exactly been living like a princess recently.

That doesn't bother me, but I'd be lying if I said it didn't feel good to have a long bath in fancy bubbles, to blow dry my hair in a style rather than just to stop it being wet, to put on some make-up and a spritz of perfume. I don't have high-heels with me, because they weren't top of my priority list when I was leaving London, but I do have some nice strappy sandals. I have even painted my toenails coral pink, with varnish I found on the shelves on Trevor's Emporium. It matches the little rosebuds on my new dress, and I feel fit for a royal wedding.

Jake has made a similar low-key effort, in a black short-sleeved shirt and a pair of smart jeans and cologne that smells of wood and spice and exotic places. I suppose, to the staff in the restaurant, we actually do look like we're on a date.

By the time we finish up our tiramisu, I have had two glasses of red wine, and am feeling exceedingly mellow.

"This was nice," I say, leaning back in my chair and smiling at him. "Though I'm so full you might have to carry me back to the car."

"Damn," he replies, "I was just about to ask you to do the same for me...but yes. It has been nice. Ready to head back, or do you want to go somewhere else for a drink?"

I think it over, and shake my head. He is driving, so it'd just be me drinking, and that's never a good look. I might end up asking for a kebab on the way home, or forget that this isn't a date at all and behave inappropriately.

"No, I don't think so," I reply firmly. "It's getting late."

"It's half past nine," he says, grinning.

"It might only be half past nine, but on countryside time, that's practically midnight, and I might turn into a pumpkin if I don't get back before the chimes strike twelve."

"I think you might have that story mixed up, Cinders...but okay, come on, then. We can walk along the river back to the car and try and shift some of this pudding."

He pats his utterly flat stomach, and we pay the bill. There is a small scuffle over it, which I win, and after a short and picturesque stroll along a bank-side path, we are safely tucked away in Jake's Audi.

He puts music on – something soulful and warm that I don't recognise – and we drive home in that comfortable silence that I have started to treasure. Connie has asked me a million questions since I arrived here and Jake has asked very few, yet he still knows me better than anyone else in Starshine Cove. Strange but true.

By the time we arrive back at the inn, I am in a kind of trance – the comfort of the car, the companionship of the man, possibly the wine. I don't even want to get out.

He switches the engine off, but neither of us moves. We turn to look at each other, and we both smile, and a moment of pure magic passes between us. He reaches out, and takes my hand in his, and kisses my fingers gently before letting go. The briefest of touches, but enough to make me my heart beat faster.

"So," he says, quietly, "you're leaving on Sunday."

"I am," I reply, my voice sounding a lot steadier than I feel. "Yes."

"I don't usually say this to hotel guests, but I think I'll miss you."

"I don't usually say this to people who run hotels, but I think I'll miss you, too..."

"So maybe," he continues, tucking a strand of hair behind my ear, "we should make the most of the time we have left together. Maybe you'd like that last drink up on the roof terrace?"

I look into his eyes, and know that the answer should be no. That I am not ready. That I am just out of one relationship, that I am still a mess, that I need a friend more than I need a lover. That for me, there is no such thing as no-strings-attached – if I spend the night with this man, it will complicate things. It will make everything so much harder. It will result in nothing but emotional chaos that I am ill-prepared to handle right now. It would simply be wrong, and I definitely shouldn't do it.

But, as a wise man recently told me, the key to life is always trying to find the fun in it – and I'm sick of being sensible.

"Yes," I finally reply. "I think I'd like that very much."

Chapter Sixteen

It is almost dark, the light hazy and warm, hovering between the end of a hot summer's day and the start of a balmy summer night as though it can't quite make up its mind which one to choose. Jake takes my hand as we get out of the car, walking slowly towards the inn, every step seeming to heighten the sense of excitement. I am about to do something reckless, something crazy, something purely spontaneous, and every fibre of my being is utterly thrilled about it.

I am not this person. I am not usually reckless. I do not have holiday romances with handsome strangers; I am not the kind of woman who allows herself to be swept away in the moment.

Except, I know, as soon as I left London and my career and my life behind, I started to change. And now, here, in this tiny place at the end of the world, I am changing even more. I am evolving, and everything from the touch of Jake's skin against mine, the sensation of his fingertips tracing my palm, the promise in his gaze, tells me that it is a change I shouldn't fight. It is a change I don't want to fight.

We pause before we reach the door, standing beneath both the light of the sun as it lingers, and the moon as it rises. I look up, touch his face, smiling as my fingertips run lightly across skin, his stubble, the shape of his jaw. He skims his hands down the bare flesh of my arms, pulls me close, holding me tight as our bodies press together. It is delicious, and divine, and it has only just begun.

"Are you sure?" he asks, his eyes shining.

"No," I reply, letting my fingers briefly tangle into his hair, "but I'm definitely having fun."

He laughs, and says: "Fair enough. Game face on before we go in, unless you want Connie to hear about this and pop round with her spy glasses."

I reluctantly disentangle myself from his arms, consoled only by the thought that I will soon be back there, and we walk through the door and into the inn.

It is just after 10pm, and it is usually fairly quiet by this stage – but tonight, there seems to be some kind of party going on. The place is absolutely rammed, every seat taken, every corner filled, every nook and cranny overflowing. I spot Trevor, and the Betties, and so many other people. It's as though every single inhabitant of the village has come to the pub at once.

As we enter, Connie emerges from the centre of the hubbub, and shouts: "She's here, everyone! Strip off your clothes and start singing!"

My eyes widen, but luckily nobody starts to disrobe. Instead, I am horrified as they all join voices in a ragged chorus of 'For she's a jolly good fellow', following it up by swamping me in a blur of faces and smiles and greetings and hearty pats on the back.

I glance back at Jake, who to be fair looks as surprised as I am, and mouth: "Help!"

He shrugs, and I know he is clearly as much in the dark as me. We are dragged apart by the flow of the crowd, and I have no choice but to go with it. Slowly, after I have been passed from person to person and been congratulated by strangers and fended off many offers of drinks, the crush lessens. I am left standing, in shock, with Connie and George.

"Excuse my language," I mutter, still trying to process it all, "but what the fuck was that?"

"That," replies Connie, poking me in the chest with a finger, "was just a little celebration. To thank you for what you did yesterday, and for what I've since found out you've been doing for George, the secretive old goat."

I glare at him through narrowed eyes, and he throws up his hands.

"Sorry, love," he adds, "she got the thumb screws out, and I felt so much better for having talked to you. Just try and enjoy yourself, eh?"

I was enjoying myself, I think. I was enjoying myself very, very much – and was, in fact, fully prepared to be enjoying myself a whole lot more, possibly several times over, for the rest of the night. I look around, and see that Jake has disappeared behind the bar. He meets my eyes and laughs, giving me a 'what can I do?' face.

This, I think, as Connie and George usher me over to a table, is not how I'd expected this night to end. I am somewhat mollified when we reach our seats, and I see Larry curled up with Lottie. He jumps up when he notices me, and we are gloriously reunited.

Jake joins us, presenting me with a Starshine Special even though I hadn't asked for one, whispering: "It's a double, thought you might need it…" before he pulls up a stool next to me. I can feel his thigh hard against mine, and despite the fact that we are in a crowded room surrounded by lunatics, it still feels good.

Someone has been at the jukebox, and I hear 'Dancing Queen' by Abba kick in. A few people begin boogying along, and I soon start to recognise more faces – people who have wished me good morning; men and women I've passed on the green; some I've seen in the café. Even, totally bizarrely, Dr Wong, who is busting out some unexpectedly good moves on the impromptu dance floor.

"We had our meeting," George explains, sipping a pint of what looks like Guinness, "and we decided we wanted to do something to show our appreciation."

"You could have sent flowers!" I say quickly, still blinking with the surprise of it all. I'm not great with surprises, especially as the last one I got was finding my partner enjoying a lap-dance from his mistress.

"And where would be the fun in that?" he asks, patting my hand. "Flowers are nice, but nothing says thank you like an impromptu party! I'm afraid we're all possibly a bit drunk, because we've been here since eight waiting for you to get back..."

"About that," says Connie, her eyes flickering beneath the table, clearly spotting my hand resting on Jake's knee, "where have you been? Matt just said you'd both left, all dolled up!"

"Masquerade ball at James Bond's holiday home," I say quickly, hoping to close down that particular line of inquiry.

"Oooh, nice. Hope you drank plenty of Vespers. Anyway... we didn't just have a meeting and decide to come to the pub, although that would be par for the course. It wasn't a normal meeting where you just happened to come up in conversation. No, the whole meeting was actually all about you."

"What do you mean, all about me?" I ask suspiciously, gulping down my Starshine Special so fast I almost choke.

"She means, love," George continues, "that we have a proposition for you."

I feel Jake shake with laughter next to me, and nudge him. Sadly, it seems that my virtue is in fact perfectly safe at the moment, much as I'd been hoping it wouldn't be.

"What kind of proposition?" I ask, not sure if I want to know.

"We want to offer you a job," he continues. "In all serious-ness, and party aside, we want to offer you a job. We can pay you a part-time salary, provide you with accommodation, and the Betties have promised all the free cake you can eat. I know it's not London, not the glamorous big city lights, but there's a place for you here, Ella, and people who need you. Will you at least consider it?"

I stare at him for a moment, completely dumbstruck. I expect Connie to chime in, but she is uncharacteristically quiet, looking as serious as I've ever seen her. Bloody hell. They actu-ally mean it.

"Look, that's really kind of you," I say, gazing from one expectant face to another, "but it's not that simple. There's paperwork, and regulations, and insurance, and inspections, and I'd need a surgery, and..."

I run out of reasons at that point, and Connie makes the most of the pause to add: "I know it's a lot to ask, and a lot to think about. And yes, I'm sure we'd have to jump through some hoops – but there is a surgery already. Our last doctor left about 15 years ago, so it might need some updating, but there's still a room in the village hall that he used. I'm sure we could sort it. Look, we're not asking you to answer us right now – I know this is a lot, and I know we hijacked you when you probably had other things on your mind, but do say you'll think about it."

The way her eyes pass across me and Jake tells me she knows exactly what other things I had on my mind, but at least she doesn't start joking about it.

"Would it really be so terrible?" she says, smiling gently. "To stay here a little while longer? With as many cakes as you could eat?"

"Ha," I reply, shaking my head. "You have no idea how much cake I can get through..."

I wonder if she has a point, though. I think about the way I have felt since I found this place. I think about Larry, and the beach, and the magical cave. I think about Miranda and George and how good it felt to help them. I think about the way I have rediscovered some sense of purpose, remembered how to smile, been lifted up by the beauty of these surroundings and the kindness of these people. I think about the man sitting next to me, and how this might complicate things. I think about all of it, silently, as I watch Dr Wong climb onto a table and start twerking to Beyoncé's 'Crazy In Love'.

"Would I get my own walkie talkie?" I finally ask, because for some reason that seems important.

"A gold-plated one," Connie replies, winking at me. "Studded with diamonds."

I nod, and glance at Jake. His handsome face is completely neutral, and I have no idea whether he's thinking this is a great idea, or getting worried that his one-night fling might be about to turn into something significantly more demanding. Still, I decide, this is a decision I have to make for myself, a decision that needs to be about my future, not one that is based on sex, no matter how potentially fantastic it might have been.

"I'm not saying yes," I tell them. "It's too big a deal, and I have a lot of things to consider. But I'll think about it, okay?"

Chapter Seventeen

Jake has made it clear that the party needs to end at 12, as he has paying guests to consider. I see at least some of those paying guests – my nodding-acquaintance breakfast companions – getting on down to Queen B on the dancefloor, laughing their heads off.

Now that I've promised I'll consider their offer, George and Connie seem intent on making the most of the rest of the night. They ply me with drinks, and share gossip, and tell me about the annual snowman contest in winter, and Connie shows me photos of her oldest son, Michael, who I haven't yet met.

She hasn't, at any stage, mentioned a husband or partner, and I do wonder about that – but tonight is most definitely not the night to inquire. Tonight, it is all about finding the fun. I see Jake moving through the crowds, laughing and chatting, and feel a tug of regret that it's not the kind of fun I'd been anticipating. Every now and then he sees me watching, and gives me the kind of smile that tells me he knows exactly what I'm thinking.

Ah well, I tell myself – maybe it's for the best. Maybe I was about to make a mistake. Or maybe I was about to have the best sex of my entire life, who knows?

I see Dan – easily identifiable with his bright green barnet – sidle towards the jukebox, and steel myself in case we're about to be subjected to a blast of Slipknot. Instead, he has read the room, and the Beastie Boys come on, telling us we have to fight for our right to party.

"Ooh, I love this one!" declares Connie, earning a surprised look.

"What?" she says, laughing, "just because I look like Dolly doesn't mean I only listen to Dolly! Come on, let's dance…"

I decide that if I can't beat them I might as well join them, and allow her to drag me to the centre of the room. A quick glance around assures me that I don't need to worry about how I perform – this is an entire village full of people who all dance like nobody's watching.

Jake joins us, and the surprises continue when he breaks out into a deeply unexpected hip hop routine, complete with jumps and spins and criss-crosses. We form a little circle around him, clapping our hands, Connie screeching with laughter as he starts body-popping.

"Pub Daddy!" she exclaims, waving her hands in the air. "You got some moves on you!"

He gives her a small bow, and we all pause as the song ends – that weird netherworld at a do when you're not sure if you're going to like the next one or not. Nothing worse, is there, than when you're on a high from 'I Will Survive' and for some reason the DJ chooses that moment to bring everyone down with 'Everybody Hurts' by REM?

I needn't have worried, as the next one up is 'Jump Around' by House of Pain, and within moments the entire room is doing as they're told – and jumping around. I see George bobbing on his seat, and Connie is going full pogo, and the Betties are doing a gentle synchronised hop. I see Dan and Sophie screaming the lyrics at each other as they make giant leaps, and even Larry is joining in. The whole room seems to be shaking in time to the beat.

I see Matt behind the bar doing his own version even as he pulls pints, and Dr Wong still on a table, protecting her knees and keeping it small, and I see all of the people I have met tonight come together in one gloriously silly moment. I see Jake opposite me, grinning with complete abandon as he jumps, and the whole thing is so joyful that I can't help feeling the same. I throw myself into it, knowing I'll ache in the morning but just not caring – I am alive. I am among friends. I am, in all kinds of ways, jumping around.

Jake reaches out and takes hold of my hands, and we jump together, higher and wilder with each bounce, shouting along to the few words we know, collapsing against each other as it all finally comes to an end.

We twirl and spin and laugh, and I hear Connie mutter: "Crikey, that song lasts forever..." as she walks gingerly back to the table, rubbing her lower back as she goes.

"She's not wrong," I say to Jake, wiping sweat-stuck hair away from his forehead and smiling up at him. "Good cardio workout, that."

"The best kind."

"Almost," I reply, winking at him. It's infectious, I decide – stay here long enough and you have to wink at someone at least once a day.

I tell him I need a drink, and start to make my way to the bar. By this time the pace has slowed, a few people gamely left dancing to Johnny Cash and his 'Ring of Fire'.

I sing along as I walk, still laughing inside, deciding that I have definitely found the fun today.

All of that changes when I look up, and see a solitary figure standing by the bar. He is still in his work suit, tie pulled down, hair uncharacteristically messy, a look of absolute shock on his face. I stop dead in my tracks, the song lyrics dying on my lips, the riot of noise around me fading to a static buzz. I stare at him, blinking rapidly to clear the sweat from my eyes, wondering if I am imagining it all.

"Hey," he says, giving me a lopsided grin, the one that used to drive me crazy. I am most definitely not imagining it.

"Mark," I say, forcing myself to stand next to him. "What are you doing here?"

His answer is lost to me, as Johnny chooses that moment to hit the chorus, and the whole pub joins in. I shake my head, and glance back. At the small ruck on the dancefloor, at Larry chasing me across the room. At Jake, who is walking towards us.

I feel trapped, and helpless, and confused. My lives have just collided, and I am caught in the crossfire. I want to run back to Jake, to explain, but I have no idea what I would say. Instead I meet his eyes, put as much reassurance into my expression as I can.

"Everything okay?" he asks, looking from me to Mark. He is not a fool, and he soon figures it out, I can tell.

I nod, and struggle to speak, tripping over my words as I try to form them. Jake smiles at us both, the very picture of a professionally convivial host, and says: "Right. Well, I'll leave you to it."

Mark is trying to shout over the din, but it's no use – I can't make out a word of it, and I'm distracted by watching Jake anyway.

In the end I simply grab Mark's hand, and pull him away behind me.

Chapter Eighteen

He follows me up the stairs, Larry at our heels, and as I shut the door behind us the music from downstairs fades to a more distant hum. I clamp my eyes shut and shake my head, trying to clear my mind.

I turn around and see Mark staring at Larry in confusion. Larry in turn is sniffing his smart shoes, obviously trying to discern if he is friend or foe, or if he comes bearing sausages or crisps.

Mark dumps his travel bag, hesitantly reaches down and pats his head. He is not one of life's natural dog people, and looks a bit relieved when he isn't immediately savaged.

"Why is there a dog in the room?" he asks, frowning.

"Because he's my dog, and he belongs here," I reply simply. "More to the point, why are you in the room?"

He shrugs, and I see him consider and reject a whole variety of replies. He is obviously tired, though, and just answers: "I wanted to see you. I finished work, went home. It was empty. It always feels empty now. So...I decided to come and find you."

He sounds so forlorn as he says this, looks so bewildered, that I bite back the snarky reply that I feel forming in my mind. There are things I could say at this point – about the house not being empty last time I was there, about Kim, about whether she ever managed to disentangle her lacy black bra from the light fitting in our guest bedroom. I say none of these things, because Mark does not look like he could handle them.

I find that I run through angry and bitter very quickly, and land eventually at simply confused. I have not seen him for over a month, and truth be told, I haven't thought about him that much either. I switched off from him and our shattered lives together as soon as I left, and I haven't wasted a lot of emotional energy on wondering what his world his looked like since that day. I don't think that makes me a bad person – he made his choices – but it does make me a bewildered person. One minute I am jumping around, and the next I am falling over, landing in the murk of my past.

He tugs his tie even lower, rubs his eyes, and yawns. He looks around the room, takes in the pastels and the prints and the bookshelves and the sunflowers, and says: "Nice. Very country kitsch."

"It's not kitsch," I reply, kicking off my sandals and checking Larry has fresh water, "just country. You look terrible, by the way."

"Thank you," he says, managing a small grin. "I'd say the same, but actually, you look...amazing. Can we talk? And can I sit down? No, actually, can I lie down?"

He looks longingly at my bed, and I shake my head firmly.

"Help yourself to the spare," I say, pointing towards it.

I still have the bottle of wine, and Mark looks like he needs it. I open it up, pour him a glass, and pass it to him. It's a sign of how exhausted he is that he doesn't do that pretentious little wine-connoisseur tasting thing first. He just drinks it, and makes no comment about its provenance of what kind of grapes it's made from. I pass him a shortbread biscuit, and take myself off to the en-suite. Larry stays with Mark, on guard duty in case he drops a crumb.

I stare at myself in the mirror, and almost don't recognise my own reflection. I am less groomed than I was at the start of the evening, but in a good way – my hair is wild, my cheeks are flushed, my make-up is very slightly smudged. But there is, undeniably, a different light in my eyes, a different energy to the way I feel.

I get my purse out of my bag, and pull free the folded picture of Lizzie. I have always hidden this ritual from Mark, which perhaps has been half of the problem – I have hoarded my pain, closed in on myself instead of reaching out. I give her a quick kiss, put her safely away, and take a few deep breaths before I go back out.

Mark has completely discarded his tie and jacket, and is stretched out on the small single, staring at the ceiling. He looks slightly restored by the wine, and I perch opposite him on my own bed. It is not the bed I expected to end up in tonight, and he is not the man I expected to be sharing a room with.

"How did you even find me?" I ask. "This place is a bit of a secret."

"Damn right it is," he replies, turning to face me. "I got lost about 15 times, ended up asking for directions at a McDonald's. As for how I found you...well, top class detective work I suppose. I got an email about the car being repaired here, and you've been using the joint account card at some place called Trevor's Emporium."

"Right. Fair enough. I've not exactly been living off the grid, have I? Anyway. That still doesn't explain why you're here."

"Like I said, I wanted to see you. It just...well, it didn't feel right, the way we left things. And, you know, I missed you."

"What about Kim?" I ask, keeping my tone neutral. I don't have the energy for a fight, but it seems like a fair question to ask.

"Oh God, Kim," he says, hiding his face in his hands. "That's over. It was so stupid. It meant nothing. You know that, don't you?"

I look at his face, see the genuine regret in his eyes. I don't hate him, I find. That would maybe be easier.

"It didn't mean nothing, Mark – it meant we were done. Once I'd recovered from the shock of seeing Kim's boobs jiggling around, do you know what I felt about it?"

He shakes his head, and I continue: "I felt nothing. I wasn't even that bothered. I don't want to be cruel, but it was actually a bit of a relief – you set me free."

"Wow," he says, clamping his eyes shut as though he is trying not to cry, "if that was you trying not to be cruel, I'd hate to be around you when you're making an effort..."

"I'm sorry," I say gently, reaching out to place a hand on his arm. "I didn't mean to hurt you. But it's over, and you know it as well as I do. It's nobody's fault, it just..."

"It was after we lost the baby," he says quietly, "I know. Nothing prepares you for something like that, does it? I didn't know how to behave around you. You seemed so...together. After that initial few weeks, the procedure, you seemed...like you forgot about it. I know you didn't, Ella – I know that. But I didn't feel it. You just pulled yourself up and went back to work and stayed calm while the whole bloody world was exploding around us. Our loss felt like it was...sucked up into everyone else's. We never got the chance to deal with it."

I close my own eyes, for exactly the same reason, feeling the sudden sharp sting of tears. He is right. That is exactly what happened – there were ongoing lockdowns, and a media frenzy, and so much conflict. So much fear and hate. And in the middle of all that, we were just two people, trying to cope with a new reality we didn't understand. At a time when we should have come together, we stood apart. I wasn't calm – I was comatose.

"I know," I say finally. "And I wish it had been different. I wish I'd been different."

"Maybe it still can be," he replies, looking into my eyes. "Maybe it's not too late. I don't think it is, Ella. I've been thinking about you all the time, hating myself for what I did to us. I can be better. We can be better – come home and give us a chance. I still love you. I don't think it's over yet – if it was, I wouldn't be here. I wouldn't have spent so long missing you."

I look at this man, this man who I once loved enough to build a life with, start a family with, and all I feel is sadness. All I feel is an empty place where that love used to live. I have spent years in the ghost of a relationship, and I don't want to be haunted by it any longer. I want to be free.

"It is, Mark," I answer. "And I think you understand that, too. It might seem like the solution right now, for us to try again, but it's not. It's just putting off the inevitable, and at some point, further down the line, we'll have to face up to that. I don't want us to be enemies, and I'm truly sorry for everything that's happened – but it's too late. I think it was too late a long time ago. We're different people than we were back then, and we need to lead different lives."

"That's just not true!" he says fervently, sitting up and spilling his wine. "It was just a glitch. It was a mistake. We can fix it, Ella – we were together for a very long time, and I'm not ready to throw that away."

He sounds determined, and I know that in this moment, he means every word he is saying. I let myself play with the idea for a moment – imagine going back to London with him. Imagine a simpler world with less choices and less complications. I realise that world comes with less of everything, including happiness.

"You can bring the dog!" he adds, obviously unsettled by my silence.

"No, Mark," I say simply. "I...don't want to."

Mark is not a person who takes well to being told no. He has always been the same; it is part of the package – part of what makes him him.

"You don't want to?" he repeats, frowning. I see emotion flicker over his face, and he clenches his fists.

"What about what I want, what I need?" he asks, his tone quiet but bordering on angry. "I know I'm the one who had the affair, Ella. I know that, and I am willing to own that mistake. But it wasn't just me, was it? You backed away years before Kim. We lived together but we were apart. I was hurting too, and every time I tried to reach out, you shut me down, pretended everything was fine, that we were fine, that the whole fucking world was fine..."

The fact that he is swearing tells me how upset he is. That this is real, not just him attempting to manipulate me and get his own way. That he has suffered too, that he still is.

"I know, Mark," I say soothingly. "It wasn't just you. I wish I'd handled it all better. I wish I'd been less selfish, more able to cope with it all. But that time has gone, and nothing we say or do now can change it."

"You make that sound very easy," he replies, staring past me at the wall. "Like you've just flicked a switch and I'm gone..."

"No," I answer, reaching out to touch his hand. "It wasn't easy. It isn't easy. But it is right – we only get one life, Mark, and I don't want to spend it regretting the past. I need to move forward, and so do you."

He opens his mouth as though he is going to disagree, then seems to change his mind. A dejected smile plays on his lips, and instead he says: "But I miss you so much, Ella. I really think you should come home – at least see what that looks like. Give us a chance. Give me a chance."

"Mark, I can't. I won't. I have to give *myself* a chance... I don't know how things will work out for me, I don't know where life is going to lead me, but I do know that going back to what we had isn't it. I'm sorry, but the answer is no."

He nods, and says: "Right. Just like that? You don't want to talk about it? To know about why I had the affair, about how I felt the last few years, about my life without you?"

"Maybe," I reply, "one day. Maybe one day I will want to know all of that. Maybe one day, we will sit down with a bottle of wine, and share all of that. But right now, I can't – and I'm not going to drive myself crazy, take a step back, just because you want me to, Mark. That might make me sound ruthless, but I think I need to be alone – I need to sort myself out, and I won't do that if we just slide back into our old lives. I don't think that would be good for either of us. It's not really what you need either."

He rubs his eyes and shakes his head and lets out a frustrated growl that makes Larry's ears pop up.

"You don't get to make that decision for me!" he says, angrily.

"No, I don't. But I do get to make it for myself. Nothing you say is going to change my mind, Mark – so either leave, or accept that."

He stares at me as though he can't believe what he's hearing, as though he is preparing his counter-argument. Something in the set of my face must tell him that it would be wasted.

He sighs, and flops back down onto the bed. He is quiet, still, as though someone has taken his batteries out.

"Okay," he says eventually. "Fine. I convinced myself that I'd talk you into it. I wish I had. But you've changed, Ella, and... God, maybe that's a good thing. For you at least. But I had to see you. Had to find out for sure. On the drive, I was sure I'd get you back – then I walked in here, looking for you, and there you were – looking the happiest I've seen you for years. I'm glad, really I am. Even if you did steal my car."

I recognise this for what it is – an attempt to back down, to lighten the mood, to outrun the cloud of intensity that is hovering around us. I recognise it, and I grab hold of it.

"I didn't steal your car," I reply quickly. "I just borrowed it, on a permanent basis. I assume from the fact that you drove here that you have a new one anyway."

"Yeah. Bright red Porsche. I might as well have 'mid-life crisis' tattooed on my bloody forehead."

He stifles a yawn, kicks off his shoes, and flops back down. He suddenly looks deflated, as though he might crash out at any second. He's had a long drive, and a tough conversation, and none of this has gone the way he probably imagined it might. It's like all the energy has fizzled out of him.

"Do you mind if I stay here?" he asks, gesturing at the child's bed his feet are hanging out of. "I don't think I have it in me to go anywhere else right now. Then tomorrow, maybe we can talk some more – sort stuff out properly."

I can still hear the sound of music from downstairs, and know that the party is still going on. That Connie will be dancing, the beer will be flowing, Dr Wong and Dan might have formed a mosh pit. I know that the party will have to continue without its guest of honour. I will find Jake in the morning, and explain and apologise, but I can't do it now.

I look back at Mark, and see that his eyes are already half-closed. His expensive clothes are rumpled, and his face bears lines I have never noticed before. He is older than I recall, and carries his own scars. I don't have the heart to kick him out, especially as his new car is probably too small to sleep in.

"Okay, Mark," I say quietly, standing up and pulling the duvet over him. He is already asleep. I draw the blanket over him, and draw a line beneath our time together.

Chapter Nineteen

I wake up the next morning feeling rough. A combination of slightly too much alcohol, way too much jumping, and a restless night of unpleasant dreams. Having Mark walk back into my life has chased away the blush-inducing variety, and brought with it the unwelcome return of the worry-inducing ones instead. I spent the whole of my sleep running away from zombies, forgetting my PIN number, and trying and repeatedly failing to find the right key to unlock the car door when Larry was trapped inside it.

Thank you, Mark, I think, as I get up and make my way into the bathroom to get dressed. Larry is at my heels, keen to go out, and the man himself is still comatose. I poke him on the shoulder, and he comes to in a shudder of groans and slobber. He blinks his eyes a few times, obviously disorientated, then stares up at me in surprise.

"Wakey wakey, Rip van Winkle," I say. "Time to get moving. I'm taking the dog out for a walk. How long do you need to get yourself sorted?"

Mark is the kind of man who usually takes a while with his ablutions, but he can tell from my tone that this isn't an option this morning. He sits up, pulls a face as he sniffs his own armpits, and replies: "Shower, shave, clean clothes...twenty minutes?"

I nod, and leave him to it. I feel nervous as I make my way down the stairs, uncertain as to what I will say to Jake. Uncertain what I will say to Connie and George about their job offer. Uncertain about everything.

I spot a few tables that are occupied, and quite a few people looking worse than usual. One poor woman actually has her head laid flat on the wooden surface, a packet of paracetamol nearby. As I am a medical professional, I instantly diagnose an epidemic of hangovers will be sweeping Starshine Cove this morning, and that the pace of life will probably be even slower than usual.

I don't see Jake at all, which is something of a relief. I need to clear my head, trawl through my thoughts, look at things in the cold light of day rather than the hot light of lust.

Larry runs ahead of me, down the steps to the beach, and we spend our twenty minutes chasing waves, peeing on suspicious-looking seashells, and picking up poo in small black bags. I only do the last one, honest.

I can't say that it helps me come to any lucid conclusions, but it does at least blow away the cobwebs, and the very slight hint of a headache that I'd felt the minute I opened my eyes this morning.

I perch on one of the big rocks, and message Priya. We have been in regular contact recently, which has been an unexpected bonus to my life imploding.

"Almost slept with Jake," I type. "Then got offered a job as Starshine Cove's doctor. Then Mark turned up and begged me to go back. Advice?"

I see the little symbol saying she's typing, and laugh when she answers: "Shit. Go for a long walk on the beach?"

"Already done that," I answer, adding some smiley face emojis. "No clearer."

"Make a list," she suggests. "Pros and cons of all scenarios. Don't forget to include multiple orgasms on the plus side."

Ha, I think, putting my phone away. She has always been a fan of a good list, Priya – and it might not be a bad idea.

I give it an extra ten minutes, because Mark always takes longer than he says he will, and by the time we head back into the inn, he has just emerged. His hair is still damp, and he's wearing his weekend uniform of jeans and a Scotland rugby shirt.

I point at a table that is halfway between us, and meet him there. Larry immediately goes into sit, because he knows this is the place where the sausage magic happens. Mark stares at him and grins.

"That is one weird-looking dog," he announces.

"Yeah, well, what he lacks in looks he makes up for in personality. You okay?"

"Will be, as soon as I get some coffee inside me..."

As he says it, Jake emerges from behind the bar. I see him pause, and wonder what this must look like from his perspective. I'm not so full of myself that I imagine him heartbroken, but I also know that from the outside looking in, it appears that I have just spent the night with my ex when all the signs were pointing to me spending the night with him. I am awash with embarrassment, and can't wait until we have a moment to ourselves and I can explain.

He approaches our table, looking as though he is immune to the hangover epidemic, maintaining an air of calm friendliness that I am in complete awe of. How he pulls that off is a total mystery – unless, it occurs to me, it's because he just doesn't give a damn. Here's me, flapping away, worrying at it all, and here's Jake, Mr Congeniality, without a care in the world.

"Good morning," he says politely, "what can I get you both? I assume Larry's order will be the same as usual."

He is so professional, so brisk yet well-mannered, that I am starting to wonder if it's Jake at all, or if he's been kidnapped by space aliens, and they've beamed down a body double.

As he heads away, I stare after him, confused. I shake my head, and realise that Mark is talking.

"What?" I say, turning back to face him. "Sorry, what did you say?"

"I said," he replies, patiently, "are you and him, you know...together?"

"Me and Jake? Together?"

"Yes. Like, together in a way that involves nudity."

"No!" I exclaim, horrified at the course this conversation is taking.

"Well, I can't say that I'd blame you. I don't think I've ever seen a man that good-looking in real life. How come you moved to the arse-end of the country and ended up finding a male supermodel?"

"I don't know," I snap back, "maybe it was just karma."

He holds up his hands placatingly, and replies: "Sorry. I didn't mean it to come out like that. I just, well... I don't know quite how to behave, to be honest. This is kind of like the morning after the end, and I'm a bit freaked out, and when I got here last night, I'd convinced myself I'd be able to talk you into coming home. Instead I walked in and saw you dancing with a bloke who looks like he's just stepped off a film set. I'm...wobbly, all right?"

I see the sincerity in his eyes, and nod. "All right. And maybe there was a bit of a spark there. Last night, with him, there was a moment...I don't know what would have happened. I don't know what any of it means. I have no idea what I'm doing with my life, and I was probably about to mess everything up anyway..."

"Ah," he announces, as Miranda delivers our coffee, taking in the scene and quickly shuffling away again, "then maybe it's a good job I came along when I did. Maybe I saved you."

"Yep," I reply, "that's exactly it. Saved by the bellend."

He snorts out a laugh, and I am surprised to find that I am capable of joining in. He reaches into his bag, and produces a sheaf of A4 papers.

"I had all these with me," he says, waving them around. "All the legal stuff about the house. I had this plan, you see – I thought I'd take you out for dinner, and tell you I wanted you back, and then rip them all up in front of you in a grand gesture."

"Well, I'm glad you didn't do that, Mark. Then you'd have needed to print them all out again. Leave them with me, and I'll get everything signed. Are you going back to London after breakfast? I actually do have a date this morning."

"Oh, right – hot one?"

"If you find 87-year-old grandads hot, yes. But I do need to get moving."

He smiles at me, and nods, and tells me not to worry, he'll be out of my hair before long. There is still an air of sadness to him – maybe there always was, but I was too wrapped in my own to even notice. I realise that despite the complications, despite everything, I am glad that he did this. Glad that we got to see each other again.

"Thank you," I say, laying one of my hands on his. "For trying. Just because we're not together, that doesn't mean we can't be friends."

"Perhaps," he says, after a moment of hesitation. "I'm not sure I'll be much good at that, but I'll give it a go. Hey, maybe Jake's got an equally good-looking sister you can introduce me to, and we could be one of those weird modern families…"

"He has a brother. Happy to hook you up if you like."

"Nah, I'll swerve that one, thanks. What's your plan, anyway? Where's next on your grand tour?"

Ah, I think, now there's a question. I have a lot of thinking to do. A lot of considering. A lot of soul-searching. Possibly, a lot of miles to put between me and Starshine Cove if I decide to chicken out. I could do that – I could be packed up and gone in minutes, hit the road with Larry and never look back. It would certainly be a lot easier than having to do all that thinking.

"They've offered me a job," I murmur, leaning down to ruffle Larry's mane.

"Who has? The Illuminati?"

"Kind of. The villagers. They want me to stay here, and be their GP."

Mark turns this over, and I find myself keen to hear his views. He is, after all, someone I have shared my life with for a very long time.

"And how do you feel about it?" he asks.

"Confused. I mean, look at this place – it's gorgeous. And they do need a doctor. But...well, I haven't worked in the same place for ages now, and it makes me feel nervous. I'm worried about getting too involved, staying too long..."

"Caring too much?" he suggests, raising one eyebrow at me. Damn him, I think, he's right.

"Yeah. But now I say it out loud, that sounds awful doesn't it? I mean, I'm a doctor. It's part of my job description to care."

He puts down his coffee, and runs his hands through his hair, and looks at me seriously.

"Ella, you're a human being as well as a doctor. And what you went through...the way it was with work, with the baby, with us... I think you can forgive yourself for switching off, you know? But for what it's worth, I think you should give it a shot."

"You do?" I say, frowning. "Why?"

"Because you're happy. Because you're enjoying your life.

Because something seems to have switched back on inside you. Because you deserve it."

I stare at the table, and feel a rush of emotion I have nowhere to put. I sip my coffee, and bite my lip, and force myself to meet his eyes.

"Maybe you're right," I say. "And thank you. But I'm still keeping the car, you know that, right?"

"I wouldn't have it any other way. Now, come on and wave me off – I think I'll skip the food. All this fresh air and wholesome honesty is making me feel a bit sick. I need to get myself to the land of smog and shallow relationships."

Chapter Twenty

I am standing at the bottom of a very steep, very pretty cobbled street. The incline feels almost vertical, and is lined on one side with old houses and cottages that seem to tumble in a ramshackle rush towards us. I find myself wondering if the homes inside all have sloping floors, as it seems impossible to imagine them any other way. The other side is bordered by ancient-looking walls, which George has told me surround an abbey built by Alfred the Great. I don't know much about history, but I'm guessing that was a long time ago.

"Recognise it yet?" says George, gesturing upwards. "From that Hovis bread advert in the 70s?"

"I was born in 1984," I reply, much to his disgust.

"Bah," he replies eloquently, "you're practically a baby! Anyway, this is Gold Hill, and it was very famous back in the day. Been in all kinds of TV shows and films. On calendars, and chocolate boxes, all that good stuff."

I glance around at the picturesque location, a place that feels like it could have been transported from a different era, and I can see why. If cobbles could talk, these would have a few tales to tell. It looks as though it's barely changed in centuries.

"It's beautiful," I say, looking on as an especially brave child comes running down it at full pelt, arms windmilling, screaming in delight as his mum yells at him to slow down. "Are we...you know, going to climb it?"

"That's the plan. I come here two or three times a year to do exactly that, Ella – it's my version of an MOT. I used to run up and down it as a lad, and I can't say I'm capable of that any more – but as long as I can still get to the top of this hill, I reckon there's life in the old dog yet."

"Well," I say, as we start the long trek up, "I'm not sure it'd work as an NHS test, they tend to involve these new-fangled concepts like blood pressure and cholesterol levels, but I see where you're coming from. What's at the top?"

As I ask, I'm already feeling the burn in my calves, and am hoping that the answer might be an oxygen mask and a saline drip. I am a relatively fit person, but the sharpness of the slope is something my legs are not accustomed to. I have Larry on his lead, pulling slightly ahead of me, but he's not exactly a sleigh dog and doesn't help much.

George tells me that once we're at the peak, we will be rewarded with the best view in the entire world, and also cake. Could be worse, I suppose. We make occasional small talk as we climb, but mainly we are quiet, concentrating on achieving the summit. By the time we do, I feel like we should be able to plant a flag and claim it in our name.

He pauses at the top, and takes a few moments to recover, his thick white hair damp with sweat, his blue eyes sparkling with pleasure.

"Looks like I'll live to see another day," he announces, then gestures at the view. I turn around, and discover that he really wasn't kidding.

The panorama stretches out for miles below us: a glorious patchwork of green fields and rolling hills and woods and hedgerows as far as the eye can see. The sun is painting the landscape a vibrant shade of gold, and it is hard to imagine a more beautiful place to pause and catch your breath.

"I never intended to come here, you know," I say as we gaze at the vista laid out before us, "to Dorset. Thought I was just going to drive on through. I had no idea that it was so beautiful; to be honest I didn't even really know where it was."

He nods, and tells me I'm not the only one, and leads me towards a bustling town square. We find a cosy corner table in a tea room, and George orders us a full cream tea for two. I am about to object and say I only want coffee until I see another table getting theirs delivered, and decide I'll force myself. Freshly baked scones, jam, cream, tiny little sandwiches and miniature slices of Victoria sponge...who am I to argue with such splendour?

I get out my phone, and together George and I fill in an e-consult form on his surgery's website. It takes a little while, and I make sure George is telling me as much as he can, and we upload some pictures I took earlier. Much as this stuff has made life easier for a lot of people, I can totally see why someone of George's age – often exactly the demographic who most needs to use the health service – might find it confusing.

By the time we finish, our little stand of delights has arrived, along with a pot of old-fashioned loose-leaf tea and delicate china cups decorated with roses. They look so dainty I'm scared I might break them.

"So," George says, nodding at my phone, "what happens next? When do the little men inside that device tell me what's going on?"

"They should get back to you within 48 hours," I explain, "and although I can't say for sure, I'd guess they'll refer you for some tests."

"Right," he replies, looking pensive. "And do you think I'll be all right, love?"

I am not an expert in this field, and I am not going to start throwing the 'C' word around over scones, but I suspect he has an early stage skin cancer that should, hopefully, be well within the scope of modern medicine to treat. I explain this in terms that I hope reassure him, and he seems to accept it.

"Thanks, Ella. It's a weight off my mind knowing I'm not just ignoring it any more."

"Yeah," I reply, passing Larry a tiny wedge of ham from one of the sandwiches, "just ignoring it probably wasn't the way to go – but now the wheels are in motion, try not to worry too much about it. I'm sure you're going to outlive us all, George."

He seems to think this is true, and who am I to argue?

"So," he says eventually, as I knew he would, "have you given any thought to our offer?"

"Not as much as I'd like," I reply. "Things got...busy, last night. I haven't had time to really consider it. Like I said, I wasn't even planning on coming here, never mind settling down!"

"Well, you can't argue with fate, my love. You might not have planned it, but here you are. I've lived in Starshine the whole of my life, and can't think of anywhere better. But maybe for someone as young as you it isn't as exciting as the big wide world."

I am silent, remembering my last day in London. The noise, the traffic, the disabled pigeons. I'm not sure any of that qualifies as exciting, but it was definitely different. Even if I don't stay here, I'm not convinced I'm even remotely ready to go back to the city. I decide that I don't want to think about it now, that it would spoil my scones.

"Tell me about your family, George," I say, changing the subject. "If that's not being nosy..."

"Nosy?" he says, looking surprised. "You think that qualifies as nosy, when I've known Connie Llewellyn for years? That barely qualifies as a question!"

"She does have a way about her," I reply. "Less nosiness, and more just that she's genuinely interested in people?"

"That's about the size of it, love, yes. Diplomatically put. So, if you really want to know, I'll give you the potted version. It's not the happiest of stories though, I have to warn you."

George always seems to be the very picture of positive energy, but I had suspected there was more to his history than meets the eye. The sadness that crossed his face when he showed me his family photos, the way he seems so determined to not let life defeat him. I smile and nod encouragingly, and he continues: "Well, first of all, Connie's actually my daughter-in-law – I'm not sure if you knew that?"

"No! I didn't...so Sophie and Dan and Michael are your grandchildren?"

"For my sins, yes. As well as Lilly and Meg, bless them. So, Connie arrived in Starshine a long time ago. She was a bit like you – from the city. All glitz and glamour, she was. Designer this and designer that – proper little diva."

He smiles at the memory, and I try to reconcile my view of present-day Connie – sassy for sure, but usually found in jeans and trainers – with this younger version of her. I find it impossible.

"So, she ran her car into a ditch, and was spitting feathers by the time we got her out. Some choice language about country bumpkins and the like. That's until she saw Simon, my eldest. He was a bit younger than her, and if I say so myself, a very good-looking man."

"Chip off the old block then?" I say gently, winking at him. Damn, I think – that's it. My wink for the day. I'm going to have to start rationing them.

"If you say so, dear. Anyway. Love at first sight for those two, it was, and cut a long story short, she stayed, they got married, started a family. And Sandy, my youngest – well, she was a bit of a thespian. One of those little girls who was forever putting on puppet shows, and holding recitals in the living room. She never took it that seriously, but every year she'd be in some kind of am dram production in town; she loved it. One Christmas, she was playing Cinderella in a panto, and Archie was in the audience. He was smitten, she felt the same, and again, a happy marriage and two gorgeous little girls."

He pauses, messes with a sandwich he shows no sign of eating, and I sense that this isn't easy for him.

"And Suzie?" I ask, remembering the third photo he showed me.

"Suzie was cut from different cloth. More like her mum, who was a bit of a wanderer until she arrived in Starshine. Suzie...well, to be honest, love, I'm not entirely sure where she is right now. It was never enough for her, this place, not like it was for the others. She went off to university in Newcastle, and she never really came home again. I get a postcard every now and then, telling me she's all right, and I've built up quite the collection over the years – the last one was from Barbados, would you believe! *Barbados!*"

He repeats the word in utter amazement, as though there could be no more exotic location on the whole of the earth. I suppose for a man who seems so content with his own little corner of the world, it must seem unreal.

"It's beautiful there," I reply. "I visited on holiday a few years ago."

"Isn't that strange?" he says, gazing out of the window. "Maybe you met her. Maybe you had a drink with her at the bar, or passed her in the street, or sat next to her on a bus."

"Maybe I did," I answer, finding it unlikely but not wanting to burst his bubble. Stranger things have happened, and perhaps if I show him my holiday snaps one day, he'll spot a familiar face in the background.

"Anyway," he says, leaning back, pushing his plate away. "This is the sad bit, so get your napkin ready. It was in Decem-

ber, back in 2019, when it happened. Sandy was pregnant with
Meg, and she started to have contractions. She was a couple of
weeks off her due date, and got a bit worried, and...well, in the
end, Simon said he'd drive her to the hospital just to get
checked. Thought it might be those – I forget the name, those
practice ones..."

"Braxton Hicks?"

"That's the thing. Archie was in town anyway, doing some
Christmas shopping, and Simon managed to get hold of him,
and he was going to meet them at the hospital. I stayed at home
with Lilly, who was all excited about getting to meet her little
brother or sister. She wanted to call her Tinkerbell if it was a
girl, and, well, Tinkerbell even if it was a boy – obsessed with
fairies, that one. She loved the story of Peter Pan, Thumbelina,
anything like that. Her mum used to read her the tales from
picture books, and she had all the films on DVD. Eventually she
got everybody in on it."

"I've noticed," I reply, recalling the woodland trail, the little
hand-made fairies that seem to pop up all over the village, the
Pixieland flag in George's front garden. If ever there was a place
willing to embrace a little girl's fancy, it would be Starshine
Cove.

George rubs his eyes, and shakes his head. I see a slight
tremor in his normally steady hands as he picks up his teacup
and takes a sip.

"Well, the weather wasn't great that winter. There'd been
some snow, and then some ice, and when they reached the big
roundabout near the hospital, a lorry that had been delivering
supplies spun out of control and hit Simon's car. Archie was
already there, no clue what had happened, waiting for them in
the maternity unit. Even now I can't get that image out of my
head – the thought of that poor man, pacing around the corri-
dors, wondering if that was the day. If that was the day he got to
meet his new baby..."

For the first time since I've met him, George looks truly vulnerable. Despite his age, despite the fact that we have been talking about him getting tested for a potentially serious condition, he has never seemed anything less than robust and full of vitality. Now, as I look across the table, he carries every one of his years and more. I reach out, take hold of his hand, give his fingers a gentle squeeze.

"You don't have to talk about this," I say quietly, "some things are just too hard, I know. I understand."

He keeps hold of my hand, and replies: "I suspected you might, sweetheart. But that's okay. I'm okay. Well, I'm not, but I never will be when it comes to this. That's only right and proper. Life moves on, and you have to move with it – but that doesn't mean you have to forget them, does it? The people you lose along the way. It's easier to talk about now, but it'll never be easy. For a long time afterwards, I wanted to blame someone – wanted it to make some sense, you know? But it was nobody's fault. It was just an accident. Just one of those sad things you see on the evening news, or read about in the local paper – except this time, it was happening to us."

The random nature of life is something that never ceases to amaze me. Working in medicine, you see such extreme examples of it – how resilient the human body can be, surviving the most horrific of ordeals, or the opposite, where a simple decision to cross a road or climb a step can end someone's story without warning. We tell people to eat well, to exercise, to avoid smoking or drinking too much – and all of that is important. All of that helps, but it's not a forcefield that protects you from all of life's threats. Nothing does that.

"In the end," George continues, "Archie did get to meet his baby that day – he did get to meet Meg. They managed to save her, but not Sandy, and not Simon. We all lost so much – for me, two of my children; for Archie, the love of his life; for those two little girls, their mum – Meg never even got to meet her.

Connie, the kids...well, you can imagine. It was brutal. I wasn't
sure how any of us were going to survive it."

I had by that point started to suspect that this story wasn't
going to have a happy ending, and I have been trying to prepare
myself for it. To not crumble. To not start crying, because I have
no right.

He sees the look on my face, and pushes one of the napkins
towards me. I obediently pick it up and dab the tears from my
eyes. I have failed, and am embarrassed that George is now
consoling me.

"How did you survive it?" I eventually ask. I think about
Connie, and the easy way she laughs, her infectious winks, her
mischievous sense of humour. I think about those little girls, and
their secret fairy forests, and I think about Dan, hiding his
sadness with his hair dye and his vaping. I think about George, a
man who has lost his wife and two of his children, and doesn't
even seem sure where the third one is. About Archie, creating
gardens full of beauty and life while he raises two children on
his own. How did they survive all of this? Not only survive, but
seem to thrive, to go on living so fully and so thankfully?

"Ah...well, it wasn't easy. It helped that we had the children
to think about. A newborn is a newborn, whatever the circumstances, and they take a lot of looking after. Lilly was only three,
and she just didn't understand. She'd lie in bed at night, asking
when Mummy was going to come and read her stories to her –
she did that for months, convinced that eventually, she'd just
walk through the door and they'd carry on with the Lost Boys
and Peter Pan and Wendy... Connie's kids were all in their
teens, and that's not the easiest of times anyway, is it?"

"It's really not," I reply, remembering how awkward and
miserable I'd been at that age, even with a loving family
around me.

"To be honest, love, it's all a bit of a blur – the shock, the
funeral, all of that stuff. We focused on the kids, and we focused

on each other, and the whole village seemed to come together. In a small place like this, it was a loss that hit everyone. It affected the whole community – the pain, the anger, the hole they left in our lives. But that also meant that the recovery was communal – there was always help with the baby. There was always food freshly cooked for us, logs chopped, dogs walked, lifts to school for the kids, someone on hand to open the café... I suppose we just looked after each other, Ella, as best as we could.

"That makes it sound simple, and it wasn't. It was hard and slow and painful, and we were all at different stages at different times. We still are, truth be told. It's not the kind of thing that ever leaves you, that you ever get over – you just learn to manage it. To be positive for other people's sake, and, eventually, for your own. Life is short, and you never know what's around the corner, and if there's one truth all of this taught me, it's what I told you yesterday..."

"I remember," I reply, "you told me that whatever life throws at you, you have to try and find the fun in it."

"You were paying attention after all! Whatever you decide to do, Ella, I hope you remember that, at least."

"I will, I promise. And to be honest, life is a lot more fun when you're around, George."

Chapter Twenty One

By the time we get back to the village, it is late afternoon. George heads home, and I decide that I need to see Connie.

I find her just closing up the café, her hair scooped up in a wild bun that seems to be exploding over her head, a smile of welcome on her face. Looking at this woman, it is nigh on impossible to imagine the pain she has endured, the courage it has taken to continue to greet life head on.

Before she gets a chance to speak, I wrap her up in a huge hug, squeezing her so tight she lets out a small squeal.

"What was that for?" she asks, looking surprised but pleased.

"Just because."

"Right. Well, that explains everything. Can I tempt you to a cuppa, or a bucket of wine?"

"The former sounds good," I reply, joining her as we stroll to her house. I've not been inside before, and am unsure what to expect. She lives with her children in one of the newer homes – by which I mean perhaps 19th century – set back from the green. The pink Fiat 500 is parked outside, and I see that Archie has been at work on the garden. A collection of fairies is arranged in an old chimney pot, surrounded by pale purple Michaelmas daisies and trailing lobelia in shades of blue.

She opens the door – unlocked, obviously – and I follow her through into a hallway that is cluttered with boots and coats and the detritus of family life. I spot a snorkel mask hanging from a hook, an old skateboard, a couple of abandoned backpacks that suggest an infestation of teenagers.

"Sorry about the mess," she says, looking back at me over her shoulder, "I'd make an excuse, but it's always like this."

I join her in the kitchen, and enjoy browsing its quirks as she makes a brew. It is a large room, taking up the whole of the back of the house, and it is clearly both well-used and well-loved. There is an old-fashioned Aga, and a Belfast sink, and copper pots and pans hanging from the ceiling like exotic jungle vines. The island in the centre of the room is adorned with knives in blocks, with bottles of oil and jars of home-made jam, with flour-smudged papers covered in hand-scribbled recipes.

The huge fridge door is entirely coated in magnets and notes and pictures; bright daubs of rainbows and fairies that I can tell have been created by the girls; postcards, receipts, train tickets, letters, appointment cards and scrawled lists. Not a single inch of the actual fridge is visible.

"That's my external hard-drive," she says, presenting me with a mug. "It might look like chaos to you, but it makes perfect sense to me."

"Fair enough," I respond, walking around the room and spotting a photo of Dan and Sophie when they were maybe six or seven years old. Dan is adorable: wide-eyed, big grin, messy hair; both of them have identical missing front teeth.

"I keep that there to annoy him," she says, "and by the way, he seems to have been inspired by your heroics in the café the other day. Started talking about medical school!"

She sounds vaguely scandalised by this, and I raise an inquisitive eyebrow as I ask: "And that's a bad thing?"

"No, of course not, it would be a lovely thing – but only if it's what he really wants. And it's not easy, is it? All those years of training, and then the long hours, and then all those rashes and strange men's balls…"

"It's not easy, no. But who knows? He might love it. He might be brilliant at it. He certainly stayed calm enough the other day."

She nods, and seems to consider this, and replies: "He did, didn't he? I just…well, I want whatever he wants. All that matters to me is that he's happy."

This is a very Connie thing to say, but now of course I have a much better grasp of why – how precious her children are; how she has had to be both mum and dad for years now; how the weight of that love defines her. How she, more than anyone, values the importance of making the most of every day.

We settle at a large pine dining table, after she pushes aside a scattering of magazines and school textbooks and a box full of tangled hair bobbles. Larry disappears off to sniff at the bin, obviously hopeful for scraps. I realise that he is hungry, that I have not quite got the hang of this dog mama thing, and that I have no food with me.

I explain to Connie, and she immediately goes to the fridge, emerging with a cooked chicken breast that she shreds to ribbons within seconds, plating it up for a grateful Larry to devour.

When she sits down, she looks at me over the steam of her mug, and narrows her eyes.

"He told you, didn't he? That's what the hug was all about?" she asks eventually. She names no names, but it is clear who and what she is talking about.

"He did," I reply gently. "And I'm so sorry. I hope you don't mind me knowing."

"Lord, no! It's not a secret – but it's also not the kind of thing you dump on random visitors as soon as they arrive, if you know what I mean? I miss Simon every single day, and my heart breaks for my kids, not having him around, and that will probably never go away either. But despite all of it, I don't have any regrets about coming here, and I'm still happier than I was in my previous life."

"I hear you were a designer diva who looked a bit like Angry Barbie..."

"Ha! Not far wrong. I was living the dream in London – big job, glowing reviews, write-ups in all the papers. I'd just been offered a spot as a judge on a new reality TV show about cooking, and I had an agent, and I'd signed a contract with a publisher for a recipe book...but I was bloody miserable, love. Looking back, I wasn't just miserable, I was depressed – my whole life was my work. I only had colleagues, not friends; I only had sex, not relationships. I'd even stopped enjoying my work – I just hated everything about myself. I took off in the middle of the night, and did a runner. You're familiar with the concept?"

I nod, and confirm that I am indeed.

"So, when I ended up in that ditch, I was at an all-time low. I didn't do it on purpose, but...well, I was being careless. I was literally all out of care. Then I looked up into the bright blue eyes of the man who became my toy-boy, my lover, my friend, the father of my children, and all that changed. I had almost 20 years with him, built this life with him, found a family that was the size of a whole village. So yes, it's all very sad, and will never stop being sad – but it wasn't the end. I don't always feel like that, but I try very hard to be grateful for what I've still got."

I think about this home, with its clutter and mess and unapologetic air of chaos, and am filled with admiration for Connie, for George, for all of them. Admiration for them, and a slight sense of shame at my own less-than-firm grip on life. We have all suffered, we have all faced challenges – no life escapes them.

"You're very brave," I say simply, wondering if will ever find my own courage.

"Indeed. I deserve a medal just for putting up with Dan's death metal playlists. Look, I don't want to put pressure on you – you have to find your own way through whatever you're facing, and staying here might not be the right choice for you. We do tend to get a little over-enthusiastic, but I'm aware that this place isn't magic for everyone – plenty of people have left, have wanted something different, moved on. But can I at least show you what's on offer, so you can make a more educated decision about it all?"

I agree, and as soon as we have finished our tea, we head to the village hall. This is another building I've not been inside before, but it was clearly a school at some point in its history. Now the central hall that might once have been used for assemblies is, Connie tells me, where they hold their cinema nights, classes, and meetings. There are offices set up in the former classrooms, and I get a peek at a different side of Starshine Cove – the side that involves running successful businesses. I glance through the doors, and can guess which one is Connie's – the one with the desk you can barely see beneath a mountain of books and pads and files.

At the back of the stage area she ushers me into the room that was once the surgery. It is dated but clean, with a consulting area and a curtained-off zone that I know will contain an examination couch. A full-sized anatomical skeleton model stands in one corner wearing a top hat and wonky sunglasses, which makes me laugh – clearly the last GP must have had a sense of humour.

The equipment that is left is basic – shelving units, an unopened box of latex gloves, a set of scales. I know the essential tools – the stethoscope, the blood pressure monitor, the pulse oximeter, the diabetes tests – will probably have been packed away in the doctor's bag and taken on to the next place.

Most of us are very protective about our own equipment, a habit you soon pick up after years of losing stuff. Mine is in the boot of the car, which is where I'd expected it to stay.

"Dr Randolph retired," she explains, going over to adjust the skeleton's shades, "moved to the Lake District to be near his family. I know this isn't much, but whatever you needed, we'd be able to get for you..."

I nod, and stay silent as I prowl around the room. I can already imagine using it, picture the changes I'd make, the layout I'd choose. The people I could help. Even picturing it is frightening, feeling like a mental commitment I'm not sure I am ready to make. The timing is off – maybe if I'd found this place in a year's time, I'd have been thrilled. At the moment, I'm simply not sure.

"Right," says Connie, looking at my expression. "Come on, I'll show you the place we thought you might live in...if you wanted to, obviously."

Our next stop is the bakery run by the Betties. She knocks on the door of the little building next to it, and Little Betty emerges. It is not late, but she is wearing a dressing gown and pink fluffy slippers. Her face lights up when she sees us on the doorstep, and we are invited into a cosy room that is dominated by a big sofa and an enormous flatscreen TV. Big Betty is snuggled up on the couch, and pauses what looks like an action flick, a man in army fatigues frozen in place as he brandishes a machine gun.

"*SEAL Team*," Big Betty says, grinning. "Our current favourite. Have you come to look at the attic?"

"Yes, if that's okay? Don't want to interrupt the massacre..." Connie says, gesturing at the TV.

"No worries. Give me a minute."

She discards her slippers and replaces them with slip-on Skechers, then leans down to kiss Big Betty on the lips. I hope I hide my surprise, and tell myself off for making too many assumptions about people, spotting their matching wedding rings and realising that they are much more than friends.

We follow her outside again, and to the back of the bakery, where we find a parking space and a set of external stairs.

"Now, the thing to remember," announces Betty as she opens the door, "is to duck."

She does exactly that, avoiding a sloping ceiling in a way that speaks of bitterly learned lessons. It's not a problem for Connie, who is vertically challenged, and it's actually okay for me, as I come in at the perfectly average end of things when it comes to height.

I find myself in a spacious room that must run across the whole length of the bakery. There is a small kitchen area, a sofa that I expect turns into a bed, and a door at the back that will, I'm sure, lead to a bathroom. It is basic but cosy, clean and tidy and decorated in rich cream tones, and the whole place is filled with the smells of sugar and spice and all things nice. One of the advantages of living above a bakery, I suppose.

There are skylights in the roof, and at the far end of the room is a window in the shape of a porthole, which I find myself immediately drawn towards. I push back the pale yellow curtain, and see exactly what I expected to – a perfect view of the beach, framed in a circle of glass. I stand and stare while the other two chat, not really hearing a word of it. I am gazing out at the sea, lost in the gentle roll of the waves, the shimmer of the sun, the sight of a man standing at the edge of it all, throwing pebbles into the water.

I turn around, see both of them looking at me expectantly.

"I know it's not much," says Betty, gesturing at the room, "but I always think it's nice. A bit like a hobbit hole."

She's absolutely right, I think – it is a tiny retreat built for one. A place where you could feel cosy, and warm, and safe. As with the surgery, it is all too easy to imagine myself here, curled up with a book and glass of wine and Larry.

The dog seems to agree, as he has already jumped up onto the sofa and twined himself into a tiny ball of fur. He gives me a look from beneath his shaggy eyebrows, and it's one that seems to say 'What are you waiting for? We're home!'

"What do you think?" Connie asks, frowning slightly. "Don't you like it?"

I do like it, I think. I like it a bit too much.

Chapter Twenty Two

I find Jake where I'd spotted him from the hobbit hole, right at the edge of the retreating shoreline. He is sitting on the sand, obviously having given up on filling the sea with pebbles, now just staring out at it, looking serious.

Larry spies him and runs over to deliver the traditional greeting, and I lower myself down next to him.

"Hi," I say simply, resisting the urge to reach out and touch him. "Are you thinking deep thoughts? Composing poetry?"

He looks at me and smiles, replying: "Nah. Just clearing my mind before the dinner shift. I've been for a run."

I take in his trainers, the damp T-shirt that is clinging to his chest.

"I see that. Good way of clearing your head. Look, Jake...can we talk?"

"We are talking."

"I mean, really talk. I'm sorry about last night. That didn't quite go to plan, did it?"

He doesn't meet my eyes, and I can tell that he is trying to figure out what to say next. I have spent the whole day with Connie and George, people who are open and sharing and wear their hearts not only on their sleeves, but on every item of clothing they own. Jake, like me, is a different kind of creature. We hide our hearts under as many layers as we can.

"It's okay," he says eventually, stroking Larry's ears. "It was probably for the best. I don't think either of us was thinking straight."

I recall the touch of his fingers against my palm, the scent of his cologne as I nuzzled his neck. The strands of his thick hair falling through my hands. No, I decide, we weren't thinking at all – we were just feeling. While it lasted, it was dazzling, blinding – but now we need to see clearly.

"Probably," I agree, "but...well. I'm sorry it all ended like it did. Obviously, I didn't know Mark was coming. And nothing happened, Jake – he stayed in the spare bed. It wasn't some big romantic reconciliation."

"Honestly, Ella, that's none of my business, is it? It was just...a moment. It happens. It's not a big deal, it's not important. We barely know each other, really."

He isn't being rude, and he doesn't sound angry, but there is a sense of distance in his tone that I find I don't like. Whether I stay or whether I go, Jake has been a big part of this weird stage of my life, and I don't want things to end badly between us. His friendship matters to me in a way that I never expected.

"I was pregnant," I say quickly, before I can change my mind. "A few years ago. I lost the baby, and I was working in a hospital, and it changed everything. It's a long story but not a complicated one – I closed down after it happened. To Mark, to my family, to my friends. To everyone. I didn't even tell my parents. Coming here, meeting you, meeting the people who live here... Well, it's been the first time I've genuinely felt connected to the world for a very long time. You can sit there and pretend we barely know each other, and maybe you'd be right – but I don't think so. Sometimes, you can know people for years and still not understand them. Sometimes, the opposite is true."

I feel his arm go around my shoulders, and he pulls me close next to him. I lean my head on his shoulder, and say: "I didn't tell you that so you'd feel sorry for me, Jake. I told you that so you'd know that you matter. Even if I go tomorrow, I'll always think of you as a friend."

He drops a light kiss on top of my hair, and holds me even closer.

"I'm so sorry, Ella – that's a terrible thing to have happened to you. And you're right, of course you are – we do know each other, in the ways that count. You've...well, you've somehow snuck under my skin, and I suppose I didn't know how to react to that..."

"I could suggest a course of anti-fungals," I reply, "maybe some hydrocortisone cream?"

"Ha!" he says, laughing. "I'm not entirely sure I want to get rid of you, truth be told. Last night it all seemed simple. This morning...not so much. What are you planning to do?"

Stay here, I think, in your arms, on this beach. Forever.

"I don't know," I reply. "Part of me wants to run, if I'm honest. I don't feel ready for this, for any of it. For being part of a community. For having patients I actually see more than once. For staying still."

"For me, and whatever this is?"

It is a fair question, but it is not an easy one to answer. I don't want to hurt him, but he deserves the truth.

"Yes, maybe," I say quietly. "I'm a bit of a disaster zone, Jake. I have no idea how I'm going to feel from minute to minute, never mind longer term. I could wake up in the morning, and check out of the inn, and check out of this place, and never come back. Or I could decide to stay, to give it all a chance. But if I do...well, it can't be based on the fact that I fancy you rotten, can it?"

"I don't know," he replies, laughing. "Decisions have been based on less. But...okay. I get it. I understand. I'd be lying if I said I didn't have any concerns either. Last night was..."

"Last night," I complete for him, "and it was amazing. But we were both working on the basis that I'd be leaving, weren't we? Neither of us had any idea what was about to happen, that they were going to ask me to stay. It was exciting and thrilling and definitely a ten on the anticipation scale – but now it's a lot more complicated. Now, it would matter. It wouldn't just be something fun, something we could both walk away from – it would be something entirely different."

"Something that maybe neither of us is ready for," he replies, nodding. "I know. I've not exactly got the best of track records myself when it comes to romance. My marriage was... well, in the spirit of sharing, it was awful. Had been from the beginning, and it finished when she sent me a text saying she was moving out. I was with my mum in Italy at the time, when she was near the end."

"God," I say, shocked. "She sounds like a monster..."

"No. She wasn't. And if she was, I helped make her one."

"She didn't find you in bed with your PA, did she?"

"No," he says firmly, "in part because my PA was a 52-year-old man called Claude. But I was always working, and she was always second best, and that took its toll. She wasn't the kind of woman who was used to being second best, and whatever love we had for each other seemed to turn to contempt as time went by. She wanted a lot more than I could give her. Still, the way she did it was...not good. That left its mark. I've been a bit traumatised by text messages ever since – maybe that's why I like this place so much: I don't get many.

"Since I've been here, there've been a few flings, but nothing serious – and that's suited me, to be honest."

I feel a flicker of jealousy as he says this, and am amazed at my mind's ability to trip itself up – how can I feel jealous of a man I am effectively telling myself I should walk away from? But whether it makes sense or not, I still feel it. Bloody stupid mind.

"Maybe that's why we get on so well," he says, grinning down at me. "Because we're both complete screw-ups. Though to be fair, you've at least formed a meaningful relationship with a weresheep."

I glance down, see that Larry is currently eating sand, chewing it up, and then coughing it out again. I'm not sure he's the best judge of character.

"Yep, and maybe that's about all I can cope with right now," I say, filled with regret but knowing it's true.

He nods, and we are both silent for a few moments, lost in our thoughts, a world apart even though we are physically close.

"It feels like we're both trying to make some sort of decision," he says, standing up so suddenly I almost slip down into the sand. "When we don't have to. We're both trying to control something when maybe the best thing to do is let it go."

"What do you mean?" I ask, taking hold of his offered hand and hauling myself to my feet.

"I mean, perhaps we should just...wait and see. I don't think that comes naturally to either of us, but it's actually the only sensible response. You might stay here. You might go. We might end up together. We might just stay as friends. We might not be able to stand the sight of each other before long. The point is, we don't have to decide any of it in advance – we can just let if unfold. See what happens."

I brush sand off my bottom, and frown up at him. Just let it unfold...I'm really not sure I like the sound of that, but perhaps that means I'm just scared. I'm scared of wanting too much, of rejecting too much, of feeling too much – and just letting it unfold sounds risky. Like the kind of thing you should get vaccinated against.

"Well, after tonight, I'm officially homeless," I say, as we walk back towards the steps. "So I've got to make some decisions at least."

"Impossible to be homeless in Starshine Cove," he replies, grinning. "Too many people would invite you to stay. Plenty of spare rooms and caravans and beach huts, and failing all of that, Trevor the Druid would set you up in a tent inside his replica Stonehenge."

"Does he actually have a replica Stonehenge?"

"No – but he does have a replica of a local stone circle in his garden. Has parties there on the solstices, where everybody drinks his home-brewed wine. It's terrifying. The point is, stop worrying so much – stop setting yourself deadlines and targets and trying to colour inside the lines all the time. If you go, I'll be sad to see you leave, but I'll survive – as will you, as will Starshine Cove. If you stay, take every day as it comes, and don't freak out about us – I won't be trying to seduce you over candlelit dinners in the snug, or tempting you out for a secret rendezvous in the caves. We both need our breathing space, don't we?"

The image of Jake seducing me anywhere at all is actually a very enticing one, but I understand what he is saying. He is backing off, in the nicest way possible. He is giving me a way out of the maze. He is allowing me the distance I need to decide which way is up.

I nod, and follow him up the wooden steps, Larry at my heels. Breathing space. Maybe that is exactly what I need – exactly what I was looking for when I threw my bags in the back of Mark's car and ran.

"Hey," I say, as we pause outside the inn, "if I did stay, does that mean you'd be my patient?"

He stares at me and laughs out loud.

"Not a chance in hell," he replies, firmly. "I'd rather go and see Dr Wong."

Chapter Twenty Three

I wake up the next morning to be greeted by the first bad weather I've seen in Starshine Cove. I pull open the curtains in my room, and gaze out at a slate-grey sky and slashes of rain hammering down onto the bay. A few dog walkers are out there, raincoats on and hoods up, determined to battle their way through the elements.

"Maybe this is a sign," I say to Larry, who is chasing a loose sock around the floor. "Maybe this is nature's way of telling me to leg it."

Except, I realise, as I stare out to sea, it is still just as beautiful. In some ways, even more so, the clouds and the gloom and the tiny stripes of fugitive sun giving the view a certain romantic broodiness. It has gone from being a picture-postcard perfect vision to being the kind of place where Lord Byron or Wordsworth might stride forth, creating works of poetic genius. I can imagine this view in snow, and sleet, and storm – and I think I'd probably still think it was gorgeous.

I drag myself away, get dressed, feed Larry, and realise that whatever I decide, my time in this room has come to an end. I pack my belongings, tidy up the bed, look around with a sense of melancholy. I remember being little, and my parents having this ritual whenever we stayed anywhere – we'd walk around, saying goodbye to everything, on the morning we left.

It feels fitting to resurrect it, and I wander my domain, announcing 'Goodbye, bath!', and 'Farewell, wardrobe!', and 'So long, candy-stripe duvet cover!'

Larry looks at me like I've lost the plot, and I pause in the doorway, feeling a simmering sense of sadness. I close the door behind me, wondering if another will open.

We head down the steep and twisting steps, my suitcase bouncing and jarring as we go, and I stop to catch my breath at the bottom. I look out at the inn, the tables laid for breakfast, the other guests with their wheelie bags and coats and the resigned looks of people whose holiday has come to an end.

They will be loading cars, filling petrol tanks, setting routes on their satnavs. They will be heading home to whatever the week ahead has in store for them – work, kids, family. They will be saying goodbye to Starshine Cove, and telling their friends about it, trying and failing to point it out on maps. Perhaps they will take souvenirs: pebbles from the beach or knick-knacks from the Emporium or cakes from the bakery – perhaps they will already be planning a return trip next year.

I know nothing about these people, and probably never will – we are ships passing in summer, bumping hulls on our way to somewhere else.

I see Jake behind the bar, and our eyes meet. He smiles, and nods at me, but stays where he is. He is giving me my breathing space, and I am grateful. Being near him is confusing; it clouds my mind, makes my senses whirl like a compass spinning when a magnet is too close.

I nod back, and drag the case outside. Larry is keen to go, seeing me head to the car and expecting a full day of superlative adventuring, new things to pee on, novel dogs to sniff, fresh treats to steal. I open up the boot, stash the case next to my medical bag, and close it firmly. I am packed. I am ready.

The rain has calmed to a steady drizzle, and I pull my hoodie up around my hair as I walk firmly away. Larry yaps once at my change of direction, then follows.

Together, we walk past Trevor's Emporium, the usual racks of postcards and almanacs and copies of his history booklet safely moved inside. We pass the bakery, both of us involuntarily sniffing at the aroma of freshly baked bread. I glance upwards, notice the tiny porthole window, its yellow curtains closed.

We move on in front of George's cottage, where Larry stares down the path towards the door, ears raised and shaggy head turned on one angle as he listens out for Lottie.

We make our way across the little side street that is home to Connie and her children, and I hear a blast of angry guitar music wafting from a window that must be Dan's.

We cross the green, where not so long ago I first witnessed the joys of Mystery Cricket as I ate raspberry cheesecake and drank lemonade and wondered if I'd slipped into an alternative reality. I'm still not sure I haven't.

The patio is empty today, the umbrellas dripping rain onto soaked stone, the windows of the café steamed up from so many customers sitting inside. Larry stays close by my side, nervous at the presence of so many people he doesn't know, and I spot Connie dropping off an order to a table full of men in walking gear. She nimbly jumps over their walking poles and heads back to the counter, spotting me as she approaches.

She looks up at me, and her face is a picture of restraint – I know how hard it is for Connie to stay quiet for more than a few seconds, and suspect she might explode if she tries to do it for too long. She raises her eyebrows at me as I sit on one of the tall stools by the counter.

"Okay," I say finally, putting us both out of our misery. "I'm in."

She laughs and claps her hands and does a little dance, and I grin along with her. I don't think even I'd known what I was going to say until the words came out of my mouth.

"I have conditions, though," I add seriously.

She nods so hard her curls waggle, and replies: "Anything!"

"I need some kind of rear entrance to the surgery, so people can come and go in private – I know you probably all have a hive mind, but let's at least try for some confidentiality. I'll need some new equipment. And, most importantly of all, no more winding me up about pretend naked karaoke."

"Oh," she says, frowning, "does that mean we'll have to start doing it for real?"

Part Three

Happy Place

Chapter Twenty-Four

Five weeks later

Connie insists on an opening ceremony for the surgery, which is no great surprise. Lilly and Meg are given the honour of cutting the ribbon, under close supervision, and with a cheer from the small gathered crowd, I am up and running. There is a doctor in the house, and that doctor is me.

My first patients of the day are a mum and baby, looking for help with nasty nappy rash. My second is an elderly man who wants to talk about his severe flatulence. My third is a lady with constipation. It seems to be a lower-half kind of day, which isn't at all unusual. I'll never understand why people get so embarrassed about these things – I mean, come on, we all have bottoms, don't we? And they all behave in pretty much the same way. Despite this, there's pretty much nothing guaranteed to make a patient squirm in their seats as much as talking about poo.

I also carry out a couple of blood pressure checks, and prescribe some antacid medication, and check out a toddler's ear infection. And...that's it, the rush is over, and my first session is finished. I sit back in my chair, and smile to myself. I've probably seen less patients in an entire day here than I would in a couple of hours in London. Nobody was desperately sick, nobody swore at me, and nobody tried to steal my prescription pad. All things considered, it was a win.

I finish up some paperwork, and look around at my new empire. As requested, I now have a separate back door, and a small waiting room that isn't in the main hall, so patients don't feel like they're putting on a show when they want to talk about their health. I have some shiny new equipment, a computer with my very own dongle, and the skeleton has had a brush up – in addition to his top hat and shades he now has a bright pink feather boa, courtesy of the girls' dressing up box. They've also provided a potted spider plant, complete with fairy.

In the end, Connie had the bright idea of contacting the existing surgery, which is in the nearest town. We came to an agreement that I would set up as a satellite, on a trial basis for 12 weeks, at the end of which everyone will sit down and see what might happen next.

It's taken a while to sort out the formalities, and I used some of that time visiting my mum and dad in Portugal, and going to see Lucy in Ireland. I've finalised the legal stuff with Mark, and moved into the attic room above the bakery, which is now looking a lot more like home. Larry stayed with George while I was away, and is also with him during surgeries – dog friendly is one thing, but nobody wants an inquisitive hound sticking their nose into their personal business. And I mean that quite literally.

I have been back for five nights now, and on each of those nights, I have as usual finished my day with a drink at the inn, accompanied by Jake. Now I'm not on holiday, though, I've swapped out the daily cocktails for cranberry juice – I'll save the hard stuff for weekends.

Things with Jake have been...nice. That's a bland word, but it's the right one. We have enjoyed our chats, and put the world to rights, and shared more of ourselves, but we have done it in a purely platonic way. At least, mainly platonic – I'd be lying if I said there wasn't always that hint of something more just beneath the surface: the momentary thrill when our hands accidentally touch, a lingering look as I make my farewells and head home. It could be so much more than it is, but I can only take so many changes at once.

I am logging out of my computer system when Connie arrives. She puts a small white paper bag on my desk, which I know will contain something deeply sugar-based, and plonks herself down opposite me.

"Do you have an appointment?" I ask in mock-formality, trying to ignore the bag. How everybody in this village isn't a diabetic is beyond me.

"No, but I hoped you'd fit me in... I don't just come bearing a croissant. I've brought you something exciting as well."

"Is it contagious?"

"Well, it does pass from person to person..."

She rummages around in her huge bag, which seems to be as organised as everything else in Connie's orbit, and eventually emerges with a walkie-talkie. I am stupidly excited to get my own, even if it's not gold-plated.

She makes a triumphant 'Ta-da!' sound as she lays it on the desk, and gives me a brief run-through of the instructions. As the instructions basically amount to switching it on, going to a channel and pressing a button, I don't feel overwhelmed.

"Now," she says seriously, as I experiment with it, "we've been talking about your call sign, and we have some ideas. I've left a notepad out at the café for the last week, and people have written their suggestions down."

"Oh," I reply, as her head disappears into her bag again. "Is there anything wrong with, you know...my name?"

She finally finds the notepad, and gives me a sympathetic look.

"Oh Ella, haven't you been here long enough to know that just won't work for us?"

"Yeah, okay. What have we got then?"

She starts to read the list out loud, making me laugh as she gives a commentary on who suggested what. The ideas include Dr Who, Dr Dre, Dr Spock, Dr Phil, Dr Doolittle, Dr Beat, Dr Sleep, Dr Strange and, alarmingly, Dr Frankenstein. There is also Dr Jones, which we both immediately rule out as it's impossible to say it without following up by singing the chorus of the Aqua song – totally inappropriate in a medical emergency.

"I'm not feeling any of those," I say, shaking my head, wracking my brains and coming up blank. "Leave it with me."

"Maybe you could ask Jake what he thinks..."

"Maybe I could," I reply, narrowing my eyes at her. "Are you building up to an interrogation? Because I warn you, I have a wide selection of syringes, and I'm not afraid to use them."

"Oh, you are no fun at all!" she exclaims, petulantly.

"Don't pout, Connie, you're too old to carry it off."

"How very dare you! I'm 53, and I'll be pouting until the day I die! But seriously....not an interrogation, just a question, from one friend to another, woman to woman – have you shagged him yet?"

She laughs at the outraged look on my face, and pats my arm.

"Sorry. Just did that for effect," she says. "And because I'm nosy. I just...well, you two seem good together. I thought it might even develop into a Three L situation."

I know I'm going to regret it, but I can't quite stop myself from asking: "Three L situation?"

"Yep," she answers, counting them off on her fingers as she speaks: "The Three Ls – Love, Lust and Like. Though not necessarily in that order."

It's actually a pretty accurate shorthand for what, it seems to my less than expert eyes, you need to make a relationship work. I think I had all of them with Mark, in years gone by. And with Jake...well, two out of three ain't bad. I like him, for sure. I lust after him, especially when I'm asleep and can't stop myself. But love? That doesn't feel like an option that's available to me right now.

Connie is looking at me thoughtfully, and I end this line of conversation as effectively as I know how – by suggesting it's about time she rolled up her sleeves and submitted to a blood pressure check. She bleats and argues, but eventually gives in.

I tell her all is well, and we spend the next few minutes discussing a plan to introduce wellness appointments for the over 50s in the village.

It is enough to distract her – but not quite enough to distract me.

Chapter Twenty Five

Life continues in a similar vein for the next few weeks. I get to know my patients, none of whom are overly demanding, and also begin to make some house calls to the residents who have trouble getting out and about.

I meet dozens of people, most of whom simply want to introduce themselves rather than look for medical help, and also visit a lovely couple called Ed and Viola. They're in their 90s, but still live independently in the highest house on the hill that tumbles down to meet Starshine Cove. While I'm there, I spend more time listening to their life stories than I do on any physical exam.

In fact, that's one of the biggest adjustments I have to make all round – not rushing, not pushing, not trying to get to the heart of a diagnosis within my allotted few minutes. In a busy health centre, it's a numbers game – out here, the only number that seems to matter is how many cups of tea I can drink before my bladder explodes.

I have been to visit Miranda at home, and found that she lives alone in a spotless but cramped flat out near the retail park. I have to admit I am a little concerned about her, especially as she seems to be so isolated from any normal support network. When I very gently raise the issue of the father or her family, she shuts down straight away and I back off. She reminds me a bit of Larry when I first met him – prickly and scared, though admittedly she smells a lot better. I hope that I might be able to tempt her a little closer, bit by bit.

George has had his appointment with his GP while I've been away, and is now waiting on a referral to have his mole investigated – he seems cheery enough about it, and has taken to calling it Adrian if it comes up in conversation.

I have meetings with the main branch of the GP partnership, which I value – it's a chance to make contacts, to gain a better understanding of the services in the area, and, vitally, remind myself that there is a world outside of Starshine Cove. I am happy here in many ways, but I'm also reluctant to fall completely under its spell just yet. The trial period goes both ways.

I take Dan with me to some of the meetings, as he seems to be taking this medical school thing a lot more seriously than I'd expected. He's done some shadowing of the routine health checks, and I mentor him on the basics, and on my advice he's applied for a job in a care home. I worked in one myself when I was a teenager, and I probably learned more about actual patient care and the realities of aging during those two years than I did in the first few years of medical school.

He knows he has to work his backside off to make his grades, and jump through the many hoops that medical school demands, and he seems fine with all of that – but he was decidedly unhappy when I told him the green hair probably wouldn't fly.

"Why not?" he asked, outraged. "Does it make any difference what colour someone's hair is, or what they look like, as long as they're a good doctor?"

"Absolutely not," I replied, patiently, "and once you're qualified you can get a full-face tattoo of Spider-Man's mask if you like – but medical school is competitive, and the people interviewing can be conservative. They might not be, but it could be a risk. Up to you, pal."

Like most teenagers, he didn't love being told what to do by the Man, and I added: "Look, I know you, and I think you'd make a great doctor. People on an interview panel don't know you, and they don't have long to make a decision about you. All I'm saying is that you should think about it."

He seemed mollified by the fact that I thought he'd be a great doctor, and I've left it alone since – I can mentor him, but I can't manage him. That's his job.

On the non-work front, I went to a sing-along screening of *Grease* in the village hall, where Connie and Sophie dressed up as Pink Ladies and George and Dan were T-Birds; I've done a Zumba class, and Matt the barman persuaded me to come along to his Real Ale Club, which proved to me what I'd always suspected – that real ale would be Satan's drink of choice.

Today, it is Friday, and it is my day off. It is also my birthday, and I am woken up by Larry yapping his head off. He had the snip last week and has only just forgiven me.

The melodious sound of a disturbed dog is not the best of ways to be woken up, and he's certainly not doing it to the tune of 'Happy Birthday'. I make my way groggily towards the door, but when I open it, there is nobody there. Instead, I find a small white box left on the step. Larry is extremely interested in it, which leads me to believe it is either edible, or a decomposing fish, both of which he finds irresistible.

I bring the box inside, and cautiously cut the pale blue ribbon it's tied up with. I am greeted by a small but perfectly formed cake, the words 'Happy Birthday Dr Zhivago' piped onto the white icing. Dr Zhivago was eventually my agreed-upon call name on the walkies, not that I've had to use them yet.

I have been very careful not to tell anybody about my birthday, because I fear the worst – huge surprise party, brass marching band, strippers, Connie jumping out of a cake wearing a cheerleader outfit. Clearly, though, someone has rumbled me.

I quickly pull on some clothes, and take Larry downstairs, glancing through into the bakery and seeing the Betties hard at work. As ever, the smell is enough to make me swoon.

"Morning!" I say, poking my head around the corner. "Are you responsible for the mystery birthday cake?"

"Ooooh," replies Big Betty, her face smeared with flour and a mischievous grin on her face, "how did you guess?"

"I don't know. Just call me Miss Marple, I suppose. And thank you, that was very sweet of you. I'm just a bit confused about how you knew."

"Maybe we broke into your place and stole your passport," she replies, "from your go-bag."

"I don't have a go-bag," I say, "I've told you several times now, I'm not a Navy SEAL or an undercover CIA operative."

"That's what they all say," she answers, tapping her nose, "your secret's safe with us."

Little Betty, elbow deep in dough, adds: "Ignore her, love, she watches too many films. We know because you filled in a form for the rental agreement."

My rent is £1 a month, but I still have a contract. That, I think, explains it – but does also raise other questions.

"Right. Did you...tell anyone else?"

"We didn't, my darling," replies Little Betty reassuringly. "Thought that if you wanted a party, you'd plan one yourself. But you're part of the village now, and everyone who lives in the village gets a birthday cake on their big day."

"What? Everyone?"

"Oh yes," she says, kneading away with vigour, "everyone. We keep all the dates in a notebook. Just a little gesture."

It might be a little gesture, but it is a lovely one, and

somehow not at all surprising. I thank them again, and leave them to their very important work. I have nowhere to be, and a cake to eat.

"What shall we do today, boy?" I ask Larry, as we do a slow circuit of the green. I am now totally accustomed to saying good morning to people, to returning waves, to chatting about the weather. It feels almost normal, and I'm fast approaching the stage where I might even stroll around at night without keeping my door keys clenched in my hand as a make-shift weapon.

"We could go on an adventure," I say, "maybe head inland for a bit? Go to Somerset maybe, we've not done that before, have we?"

It is mid-September and we are being treated to what will probably be the last few glorious days of summery weather. The intense heat of August has been washed away by a week of rain, and now the skies have been left clear and blue, the air calm. It is still absolutely tip-top adventuring weather – but I am feeling the call of the familiar today.

"Or, call me crazy," I continue, "we could just go home, watch TV, and stay in bed all day...what do you reckon?"

Larry is distracted by chasing a magpie across the green, so I decide for both of us. Netflix and chill it is, except not Netflix, because I don't have it here. I will have a deliciously lazy day, possibly a Buck's Fizz or two, and I will maybe head over to the inn for a sneaky Starshine Special before the night is over.

We stock up on a few essential supplies at the Emporium – dog food, crumpets, orange juice, a bottle of Prosecco – before browsing the entertainments section. My little hobbit hole comes complete with a VHS machine and a DVD player, and I spend a fun few minutes choosing before I decide on *Dirty Dancing*, *Step Up* and *Titanic*. That should keep me busy. This is shaping up to be the perfect day, in fact.

I chat to Trevor as he rings my basket up, and he nods at the films.

"Busy day planned?" he asks.

"Busy doing nothing," I reply, gleefully. He looks at me intently, and I half expect him to deduce, using the Power of the Mind, that it is my birthday. I am a tiny bit disappointed when he doesn't – they just don't make Druids like they used to.

By the time I get home, the postman has delivered a few cards, which is lovely. Mark has sent me one that has a picture of a Labrador on it, and the words 'Shit happens – dogs help'; all three of my university gal pals have bothered; and my mum and dad have even remembered. That sounds weird, but sometimes they forget – love them to bits, but they can get so carried away with their sun-soaked retirement that little things like their daughter turning 39 can slip their minds. I give them a quick call, and am blessed by the gods of phone reception – it seems to be better now I'm higher up.

Duty done and cards displayed, I prepare myself a feast of freshly buttered crumpets and birthday cake and Buck's Fizz. I lay everything out on the little dining table, and sing 'Happy Birthday' to myself with gusto. This, I decide, is self-care at its very finest.

I get the video of *Dirty Dancing*, and it slides into the old machine with a satisfying clunk that reminds me of being much younger. I snuggle beneath the sofa, Larry at my side, glass in hand, crumpets on a plate on my lap, and sigh as Baby starts to talk about the summer of '63 as she drives towards the family holiday that will change her life. There is something so very comforting about watching a film you've already seen 100 times, isn't there?

I pass the rest of my birthday like this, and wouldn't have it any other way. The year before, Mark had taken me to a fancy restaurant in Mayfair, where I'd felt uncomfortable for the whole evening. If someone had told me then, amid all that conspicuous wealth and women dripping with diamonds, that I'd spend the next celebration alone apart from a dog, in an attic above a bakery in deepest darkest Dorset, I wouldn't have been able to imagine how my life would get from point A to point B. I'm still not sure how it's all happened, but I have to simply accept that it has, and that I am most definitely happier today than I was this time last year.

I watch *Step Up* next, still a guilty pleasure, and save *Titanic* for last. I push aside my usual reservations – assessments of how much room there actually was on that floating door, and what a waste it is when Rose throws her priceless Heart of the Ocean necklace into the sea instead of, I don't know, donating it to charity – and simply go with the flow.

I have had quite a few glasses of Buck's Fizz by this point, and my breaks to take Larry out for a wee have been getting quite exciting as I traverse the steps to my room. By the time I reach the end sequence, and Rose glides up the staircase in Titanic Heaven to be reunited with Jack, I am ruined – crying so much that I might need a lifeboat myself. It is a good cry, though, a cathartic cry – a letting-go cry that is making me feel better, not worse.

Larry doesn't quite understand this, and is snuffling at my face, squirming on my lap as he tries to console me.

"It's okay, boy," I tell him, stroking his floppy ears, "all is well…"

We are both surprised when the walkie-talkie suddenly flares into life, and I stare at him in confusion as a voice says: "Pub Daddy calling Dr Zhivago, over…"

Larry jumps off my lap and goes to bark at it, which is a completely understandable reaction. I retrieve it from the bookcase, and really hope there isn't some kind of medical emergency going on somewhere in Starshine Cove – I am not drunk as such, but I definitely wouldn't drive a car.

I fiddle with the still unfamiliar controls, and reply: "Dr Zhivago to Pub Daddy…um…over?"

"Dr Zhivago, your presence is required at the cave ASAP, over."

"Oh God," I reply, as much to myself as him, "nobody's dying, are they?"

"Not as far as I know," he replies, sounding amused. "And don't forget to say over, over."

"Okay. See you there. Over."

Larry is jumping up my calves, obviously confused – he can hear the familiar voice, one he associates with sausages and affection, but not see the human it's attached to.

I clear away my dishes, run a brush through my hair, and get changed into fresh clothes. I fear I smell a little like a gerbil after my day of hibernating, and apply a quick spray of perfume while I'm at it. I can tell myself Jake is just a friend as much as I like, but I still don't want to remind him of a rodent.

I check the bottle of Prosecco and see that there is still some left, which reassures me that I can't be too inebriated, then make my way out from the attic, leaving my safe space for the big wide world.

Chapter Twenty-Six

It is going dark outside, and the village is quiet – apart from the gunshots coming from the Betties' living room. I smile at the thought of them snuggled on the sofa together, watching some villain get their ass kicked. I see lights on in all the homes that are scattered across the hillside, tiny twinkles of welcome against the landscape, and listen to the birds singing their last rousing chorus of the day. I wave to Trevor the Druid, who is lying flat on the green staring up at the emerging stars. I'd have found that off-putting not so long ago, but now it seems like an entirely normal thing.

I skirt the back of the inn, and make my way with Larry down to the beach. I feel a flicker of excitement at the thought of seeing Jake, but also still have some concerns about Connie jumping out of a cake.

"Are you alone?" I shout, as I make my way towards the mouth of the cave.

"Yes!" comes the amused reply, and I smile as I clamber over loose rock and head towards him.

As I approach, I am greeted with the most magical sight – myriad lights tumbling across the cave walls and roof, casting glowing stripes that illuminate the shine and shimmer. A sparkling rainbow dance of shine and iridescence is flowing all around me.

I stare, lost for words, as the glimmering beams move from place to place, as reds and golds and greens glitter all around me. It's as though I am inside a disco created entirely by nature.

I see Jake, standing up to greet me. At his feet he's laid out thick blankets, a picnic basket, a cocktail shaker. There is a small glowing glass orb, a snowman inside it, casting the strobing lights around the cave.

"Happy birthday, Ella!" he says as I walk towards him, Larry galloping ahead to check for predators and spare food.

"How did you know?" I ask, still looking around in wonder at the constant twinkle, the ever-moving light picking out different colours and shapes with each turn. "Did you break into my flat and steal my passport from my go-bag?"

"Um...no. I took a copy of your driver's licence when you checked in. Which now sounds really boring in comparison."

I do a slow twirl, following the light, marvelling at each jewelled crevice and curve, eventually coming to a stop in front of Jake. I reach out and hold his hands in mine, and say: "This is so beautiful. Thank you."

He nods, and gestures to the blankets. I settle myself down, and am soon presented with my very own Starshine Special. He opens the basket, and I see a selection of treats – olives, cheeses, crackers, tiny pots of chocolate-coated nuts, sugar-dusted cookies, tiny fruit tarts.

"Oh!" I exclaim, realising that I am hungry. "This is... divine. And the light – where did that come from?"

"Ah," he replies, nodding, "that was from Trevor's Christmas stash. I thought it was a bit nicer than shining a torch around."

As he speaks, the strobe passes across his face, then moves on to a rich sheen of silver stone on the roof.

"It's like I've fallen into a fairy tale," I reply, "the cave, the echo of the waves outside, the view, the revolving snowman…"

"Don't forget the Kettle chips. A vital ingredient of every fairy tale." He stares at my face, and asks with a note of concern: "Are you all right? You look like you've been crying."

I swipe at my eyes, and decide to confess.

"I have. I've been at home all day watching films, and it was great, but then I finished off with Titanic…"

"Ah. Well, that explains it. Even I cry at Titanic."

I laugh, amused at the thought of this man, this reformed alpha male, silently weeping at the tale of Jack and Rose.

"Always thought she could have scooted over on that door, though…" he says, passing me a small box of truffles.

"I know, right? But still…it's up there in the top ten for me."

This leads us on to a conversation about our favourite movies ever, then the TV shows we watched as kids, then to our first gigs, and our first holidays without parents, and a heated debate about whether Ross and Rachel were really on a break in *Friends*. As ever, we never seem to run out of things to say to each other – the chatter flowing naturally from one subject to another, punctuated by frequent laughter and comfortable pauses where we eat and drink, then pick up the thread again as though we've never stopped.

He's just finished telling me an anecdote about his brother, Josh, and the night he got locked in the local pub and had to be rescued by police through the cellar hatch, and I am crying again – this time in amusement. Larry has settled in a small ball in the middle of the blankets, and I have finished my latest Starshine Special. The snowman is still going great guns, beams of beauty swirling around us. I look at Jake, and am struck by how much I have missed this – these simple pleasures, the straightforward sharing of time and self with another human being. It has been, quite literally, years since I felt this way.

"Thank you," I say again, feeling suddenly serious.

"You're very welcome. It's your birthday."

"Not just for this," I say, gesturing around me at the picnic and the cave, "for everything. I know we usually avoid anything too deep and meaningful – henceforth known as D&M – but thank you. Ever since I arrived, you've been...amazing, and I am so grateful."

He smiles, and it is a killer smile – slow and steady and intense. The kind of smile that says more than words ever could.

"Again, you're welcome," he replies. "And I did get you a gift as well. I didn't know if it'd be too much, if—"

"I'd run screaming from the caves in terror?"

"Yeah. Too much D&M seems to have that effect on both of us. But...well, would you like to see it?"

"Duh," I reply, widening my eyes at him. "Of course I would!"

He nods, and pulls a small package from his jacket pocket. He passes it over, and I find myself holding a black velvet pouch. Mark has bought me jewellery before, and it's always come in fancy boxes and he usually 'accidentally' left the receipt in there just so I'd know how expensive it was – ironically, I didn't even think of packing any of it when I fled. As with so much I left behind that day, it just wasn't me any more, if it ever was.

This, though, somehow feels even more magical, more precious. I take my time, examining it in my hands, finally pulling open the drawstring at the top.

A necklace slides out into my palm, and I lift it up in the shadowy light. At first it looks like a pretty but ordinary item of jewellery, the kind you could see in a shop window in any town – a long silver chain, and dangling from it some kind of dark material fashioned into a pear-shaped drop pendant. It takes the snowman to show me just how special it is, and I gasp in delight as the illumination criss-crosses over the stone, and it bursts into life.

I hold it up, and as the light flickers across it, it is transformed from black into a ball of colour. Deep reds and purples, streaks of gold, all shining in my palm.

"It's one of Daisy's pieces," Jake says, looking from the necklace to my face as though he is trying to decide if I like it or not.

"Jake, I absolutely love it – it's the most wonderful present I've ever been given! It's even better than the Heart of the Ocean!"

I fumble around trying to put it on, and he comes closer, positioning himself behind me to help. His fingers brush my skin as he lifts my hair, and I feel the warmth of his breath against my neck as he fastens the clasp. It is an innocent but almost unbearably intimate act.

When he's done, he doesn't move away, and I lean back, nestling myself against his chest. I feel him take a surprised breath, and his arms wrap around me. We sit, entwined, surrounded by the shine of the caves, serenaded by the distant crash of the waves.

"This," I finally say, turning my eyes towards his, "has been an almost perfect day."

"Almost?" he whispers, holding me closer.

"Almost."

We don't speak, because the time for words has passed. He leans down, and kisses me. It is a glorious kiss, tender and passionate and full of the promise of so much more. It is a kiss that makes my dream encounters with this man seem tame in comparison, and I am trembling in his arms by the time it ends.

Now, I think, pulling him down for more, it is perfect.

Chapter Twenty-Seven

The next morning, I wake up in Jake's arms, in Jake's room, in Jake's world. I am momentarily disorientated, taking in the deep blue walls and the dark wood furniture and the detritus of another person's life.

I look at Jake, deeply asleep, his hair falling across his face, and sigh. Damn the man, he's even perfect when he's in a coma.

Larry is curled up at the bottom of the bed, and wags his tail when he sees me moving. I gently extricate myself from Jake, get dressed, and sneak away. It is stupid o'clock, just before 6am, and I can probably make it out without being spotted by any of Connie's drones.

I allow myself one more glance at Jake before I leave, relishing the sight of his tanned skin, the curves and straight lines of muscle. I find myself blushing at the memory of the night before: the complete abandon, the way any inhibitions I ever had were shredded away beneath his touch.

We didn't talk about things – there was no breath left for conversation – and I know we will need to. I know life will now become more complicated, that I have invited something mysterious and frightening into my world.

I know this, but I decide to simply not care for a little while longer. I am on a high, and reluctant to come down from the mountain top.

I close the door quietly, and make my way outside. It is still not fully light, and as I make my way down the steps to the beach, the first fingers of sunlight are struggling to break free. I walk with Larry, realising that as I stroll, I am smiling. I am reliving, and remembering, and it is making me glow with happiness.

No matter how complicated things might get, I tell myself, I should always try to remember this sensation – the welcome rush of life that is flowing through me. Physically, I am tired – but in every other way, I have more energy than I can ever recall having.

The sea is coming in towards us, a gentle boom and hiss as the waves hit the sand and retreat, and gulls are circling in the sky as it begins to lighten.

I sit down, cross-legged, and lay my palms on my knees. I am aware of a bundle of warmth at my back as Larry settles, and I stare out at the sea, and breathe.

I breathe deeply and slowly and I inhabit every single fraction of that breath. I ignore the nagging thoughts and concerns that are starting to crowd into my mind now it is fully awake, and I remind myself of what matters: here, now, this moment. The sound of the water and the touch of the beach on my bare feet and the simple joy of taking one slow breath after another.

I stay like this for a while, long enough that the lingering gloom is chased away by day, long enough that I start to recognise the patterns the waves weave into the sand, long enough that when I glance at my phone, I realise that I have been sitting here, still and silent, for almost half an hour.

I blink, clearing away my daze, and laugh. Larry comes to investigate, and I give him a cuddle before I stand up and stretch.

"Holy shit," I announce to the world, filled with joyous astonishment, "I think I just meditated!"

Chapter Twenty Eight

On the surface, life continues as normal. I see patients, I carry out checks, I make home visits where I am plied with tea and home-baked cake. I feel myself being sucked into the world of Starshine Cove, and have no urge to resist – I start to realise that not only is resistance futile, it's bloody stupid.

I've spent so long hiding, running, avoiding any entanglements – and none of it made me happy. None of it kept me safe. This, these simple routines and the gentle ebb and flow of village life, does make me happy. It is an almost unrecognisable sensation, and I am firmly instructing myself to simply enjoy it, to not over-think, to not try and peek around corners and spot the upcoming catastrophes.

This is, as we all know, harder than it sounds – but it is made a lot easier by the presence of Jake in my life.

Since our first night together, we have carved out many more. We have talked, and laughed, and had glorious amounts of life-affirming sex. We have explored the light and shade of our lives, the good, the bad and the ugly.

He tells me more about his marriage, about his mother, about how much he still misses her. I have told him about the way my work drained me of emotion, and I have even shown him my cherished picture of Lizzie.

While we get to know each other, though, we have decided to keep it secret from everyone else – because this is new, and fragile, and precious. Partly we are simply private people who don't want to face the Spanish Inquisition, but I am also aware that part of me is just afraid – afraid that if we drag this thing into the light of day, expose it to the corrosive raw materials of reality, that it will fade and fizzle. That I will lose it, and I will suffer. I am trying to quash this side of me, but I am a work in progress – I have spent too long expecting the worst for that to disappear overnight.

The Betties tend to go to bed early, so either I sneak out to see Jake, or he comes to mine once he's finished work for the night. Keeping it secret is, as he points out, also a lot of fun.

Today, I wake up alone, in my own bed, and find that I now automatically reach out to the other side of the pillows, expecting to find him there. I make a hmmph of disappointment as my brain catches up with my body – we both have busy days, and both needed our rest. Jake is going to see his business manager in London, and I have meetings with the extended integrated care team to discuss local provision and how to improve it.

That doesn't sound as much fun as a shag-fest with my handsome friend, but it is important, and I even find myself looking forward to these things now. I'd have run a mile this time last year, preferring only to parachute in at the start of the day and leave without a backward glance at the end.

I've arranged to meet Dan after his morning lessons and take him along with me, because it will all help with his applications to medical school or, alternatively, completely put him off applying.

I spend a lazy morning pottering around the flat, drop Larry off with George, and briefly chat to him about life, the universe and Adrian. He's had his mole removed and it is now being tested to see exactly what it was and if any further treatment is needed. George remains sanguine about the whole thing, and has an almost child-like belief that everything will be all right in the end. This is something I can only applaud him for.

I call into the café to get a takeaway coffee, and find Connie busily plunging the sink while she croons along to Shania Twain. She sees me arrive, points at the water that's almost at the overflow, and sings: "That don't impress me much!"

"Yikes," I say, peering over the counter, "that looks fun. Do you need help?"

I ask this genuinely, but also hoping that she says no – I am much better with human plumbing than mechanical plumbing.

"Nah," she replies, putting down her plunger and shaking her hair out of her eyes, "I'm an old hand. It's quite cathartic, a good old plunge..."

She winks as she says this, naturally enough, somehow managing to turn a basic domestic task into something smutty.

"Dan says he'll meet you in town later," she continues as she prepares my latte. "He's not going into college though. Just couldn't get out of bed this morning."

"Is he okay?"

"Yes. He's just a teenager. It comes with the territory. Talking of beds, and things you can do in them, how are you and Jake?"

I narrow my eyes at her, wondering if she's somehow figured it out, or if she's just fishing. I decide that a strategic retreat would probably be the best move, telling her there is no me and Jake, paying for my coffee and making a hasty exit, trying to hide the grin on my face.

There is a part of me that would love to tell her – it would be so nice to have someone to talk to, to giggle with, to turn to if I start to get the jitters. But we are not teenage girls, and I am way past the stage where I can sit with a pal and doodle love hearts on exercise books, practising my signature with my new love's name... I think I am, at least.

I drive into the nearest big town, Dorchester, which these days feels like a buzzing metropolis, and fill my time doing touristy things before my meeting. I walk through pretty civic gardens, browse shops, read up on the area's Thomas Hardy connections, and even treat myself to a visit to the Dinosaur Museum. I know how to live.

By the time I reach my meeting, there is no sign of Dan. I call Connie on the landline, and catch her just after the lunch rush has finished.

"Sorry!" she says, sounding harassed. "I meant to call you – he's sent you a message but it's probably not come through. He's full of cold, thought it best not to come. In fact he says to tell you he's diagnosed himself with bubonic plague."

"Right. Well, I hope not. Have you tested him for the usual?"

"Yep, and it was negative – he'll be fine, love, don't worry about it."

"Okay," I reply, as I walk towards my new colleagues, "well, you know where I am if you need me. I can pop in and check on him later if you're worried."

"Thank you, but I'm not, honest – kids get these lurgies all the time. Nothing a day in bed and a paracetamol won't deal with."

She is right, of course, and probably has far more experience with these things than I do, having raised three children of her own. I put it out of my mind, and spend the rest of the day in the meeting. I learn a lot, and contribute some ideas, and I come out of it feeling strangely invigorated. There are plans to roll out a mobile breast screening unit, and I find myself looking ahead already, mentally compiling notes of who should attend, those who will go without question and those who I know will take a bit more persuading.

By the time I have come home, walked Larry, and eaten dinner, I am ready for the next stage of my day – and the secret date that Jake and I have planned. Well, it's at the inn, so I don't suppose it's that much of a secret. Maybe I will go in disguise.

I call Connie before I leave, and she reassures me that Dan is still in bed, sweating it out but fine, and I make my way to the pub.

It is, as usual, fully booked, but as autumn kicks in a sense of quiet is settling around the whole village. The bar is busy but not packed, and the customers are clearly residents rather than passing tourists. I sit and read – *Far From the Madding Crowd*, which I'd picked up in a bookshop in town today – and find that I can picture the scenes so well, the countryside coming to life so vividly now that I live here.

Matt is on duty, and Jake arrives later than planned, walking into the room just after 10pm. He has come straight from London and is still wearing his business clothes, and I find that my heart does a little dance when I see him walking towards me. Something about the suit, the slightly loosened tie, nudges one of those Ls that Connie always talks about into overdrive.

"You look like someone from the cover of a Mills & Boon," I say, as he places our drinks down on the table top and sits next to me. "Like some ruthless businessman who has a steamy relationship with his secretary."

He raises his eyebrows, tugs the tie even lower, and replies: "Well, if that was something you'd be interested in pursuing, all you'd need is a pair of specs and your hair pinned up..."

I laugh, and blush, and decide that as we are in public, it would be inappropriate to offer to take some dictation there and then.

"How was your meeting?" I ask instead.

"Good. Productive."

"Did you buy Jupiter?"

"That would be silly. Maybe Mercury. Yours?"

"Excellent," I reply sincerely. "Lots of organisations with lots of letters in their titles, but yeah, it was great."

He smiles at me, and says: "You look excited. And not just about the secretary thing."

"I am," I answer, sighing and leaning back against the velvet-coated booth, "and it feels good. I wasn't sure, when I said I'd stay, if I really would. If I'd get to the end of the trial and just write it off as an interesting experience, and move on to the next thing. I wasn't sure I could handle it."

"Handle what?"

"All of these people – not just patients, but people. Being part of a community again. The pressure of actually...caring, if that makes sense?"

I feel his hand on my thigh as he replies: "It makes perfect sense. Letting yourself care about people is a risk, always. In business terms, you could fill a spreadsheet with it – the risk versus the reward, the profit offset against the potential loss. And now? What do you think now?"

The end of my trial will be here before I know it, and I've been trying to figure out what I will do next. I have also been trying to disentangle my feelings for Jake from that decision, which of course is impossible. Especially when his hand is on my thigh, and my thoughts are clouded by where else it might journey.

"I think," I reply slowly, meeting his eyes, "that I will probably stay. I think the profit outweighs the loss."

He nods, and sips his drink, and remains silent for a torturous few moments. This thing we have, me and Jake – it is lovely. It is sweet and it is fun and it is sexy as hell. But we have never put a label on it, never discussed the future, never had that grown-up conversation about what it might be long term.

As he sits there, quiet and serious and considering, I am momentarily floored by uncertainty: what if he doesn't want me to stay? What if this isn't his ideal outcome? What if he's compiled a spreadsheet about me as well, and I end up in the wrong column? What if he's about to tell me it's over?

It is an awful feeling, one that fills me with dread – and it is a feeling I recognise as my default setting before I arrived here. That toxic combination of anxiety and alarm, the mental tensing of muscles to prepare for the next blow.

I take a deep breath, remind myself that I am more than this now – I am stronger, I am more resilient. That I will be able to cope with whatever life throws at me.

Jake finishes his drink, and puts his arm casually around my shoulder in a daring move of public affection.

"That," he finally says, gently pulling me closer to him, "is what I hoped you say. I didn't want to put any pressure on you, but the thought of you leaving... Well, it didn't fill me with joy. I like having you here. I like what we have together. I like you being in my life. Now, unless you have any objections, I think we should retire to my chambers and celebrate."

Chapter Twenty-Nine

Jake's 'chambers', as he calls them, are actually a suite of self-contained rooms at the back of the inn. They don't have the best of views – out onto the car park – but once the curtains are closed it is gloriously private.

I am woken up in his bed, way before I want to move, by Larry yapping and licking my face. I calm him down, and yawn as I look at Jake beside me. He is fast asleep, and I feel a rush of tenderness as I take in the shadowed outline of his features: the cheekbones, the lips, the dusting of dark stubble on his jaw. I realise that I could stare at him for hours and not get bored of the view, and I fear I am coming perilously close to the third L. The scariest one of all.

Larry is still agitated, and I glance at my phone, wondering if it's later than it feels. No, I see, it is just after 4am, and still completely dark outside. I notice that I have two missed calls, both from Connie, and sit up, suddenly alert.

I quietly throw on my clothes, and follow Larry out of the bedroom and into the lounge. He runs to the coffee table, woofing and circling as we near it, and I am groggy and confused and not at all sure what has unsettled him so much.

I spot my abandoned bag, and am gripped with a sense of unease. The bag contains my walkie, and I left it in another room all night. I am not on call, there is no obligation for me to be available 24 hours a day, but still...what if I missed something? What if Connie needs me? What if Larry is squawking because someone was looking for Dr Zhivago?

I grab my bag, rummage around for the walkie – but unlike the phone, there is no way to know if I've missed anyone. Connie had called just after two, and again half an hour later. There is no message, but that could be because the signal dropped out. It could have been a pocket dial. She could have been drunk and looking for a partner in crime – but it could be something else.

I make a decision, shove my feet into my trainers, grab a fleece and leave the inn. Larry stays at my side as I jog across the green, calling at the attic to retrieve my medical bag, then heading straight for Connie's house. If the lights are off and all looks well, I will have lost nothing; I will simply go back to bed and sleep for a few more hours.

As I arrive outside her home, I see that the living room light is on, as well as one of the upstairs bedrooms. I knock on the door, and within seconds she answers. Her hair is wild, her cheeks are red, and she looks flustered.

"Oh! Ella! I'm so glad you're here," she says, ushering me inside. "I tried the phone, but it's crap, and I tried the walkie, and I sent Sophie round to get you, but..."

She is wittering, hands flapping in the air, looking small and bewildered in her pink flannelette pyjamas.

"I'm here now," I say, sounding a lot more calm than I feel. "What's wrong? Is it Dan?"

She nods, and her words spill out in a rush: "Yes! He was okay when I checked on him before I went to bed, just a bit hot and bothered, but enough himself to tell me to eff off and stop hovering...but, well, I'm his mum, and it's kind of my job to hover, isn't it? I tried going to sleep but I couldn't, I kept sneaking in to check on him. And the last time I did, he was even more hot, and he wasn't making much sense, just blabbering...and I'm probably totally over-reacting, but I'm worried this might not just be a cold!"

I ask her a few more questions, and she tells me he hasn't got out of bed other than to use the loo since the day before. She hasn't taken his temperature, but tells me he's feverish to the touch, and that when she switched the lights on, he hid his face under the duvet.

We always tell parents to trust their instincts about their children, and even though Dan is hardly an infant, he is still Connie's baby – and she is not the kind of person to be so easily rattled. I hide my own fears as we make our way upstairs. I notice Sophie's door is open, and she waves at me from her perch on the side of her bed, face pale and tired.

By the time I kneel by Dan's side, I know there is something very wrong. He is still, his skin is clammy, and when I take his temperature it is registering at 39.5. I try to talk to him, but he is delirious, pushing my hands away as I examine him, recoiling from every touch.

"Has he been vomiting?" I ask Connie. "Headache?"

"No to the first, yes to the second...is he okay, Ella? I shouldn't have waited should I?"

She sounds distraught, and I send her downstairs to get a glass of water just to give her something to do. While she is gone, I extract one of Dan's legs from beneath his tangled sheets, push up the jogging bottoms he is wearing. I use my phone torch to check over his skin, and blink away the panic when I see a small patch of red and purple blotches.

I hear Connie running up the stairs, and when she passes me the glass of water, I gulp it down – I don't need a drink, but I do need the glass. I press it against the rash on his calf, and the spots do not fade. I lean back on my knees, and take one long breath. I want to cry. I want to yell. I want to bang my head against the wall – but I don't have time for any of that.

"Connie," I say quietly, "we need to get Dan to hospital."

"I knew it!" she wails. "I shouldn't have waited! I just kept thinking he'd be all right in the morning…"

"You called me," I reply firmly, clamping down on my own guilt at not answering her, "and now we have to act. Would it be quicker to take him there ourselves, or call for an ambulance – you know better than I do."

I see her mind kick into action, and eventually she replies: "Quicker if we take him. But how? How will we get him there? I don't think he can walk down the stairs!"

She is right. He is too sick, and he is also too big for us to carry. I run through the possibilities – I don't want to ask George for help, because despite all of his claims to eternal youth, he is in his late 80s. Archie has the girls to look after, and as yet I don't know exactly what we're dealing with here – I don't want to expose him or them to anything contagious.

"Sophie," I shout along the hallway, "go and get Jake. He'll be asleep, but if you bang on the window, that'll wake him up. Tell him what's happening and tell him we need his help, and to bring his car."

Dan is way too tall to lie in Connie's Fiat 500, and Jake's is much bigger. I tell Connie to pack a bag, more to occupy her than for any real reason, and use her landline to call admissions at the local A&E. I describe his symptoms and outline my initial diagnosis, then go back upstairs to sit with him. He briefly comes to, his eyes lucid for a split second, and he mutters: "Bubonic plague?" before crashing out again.

I hear a car pull up outside, and meet them downstairs. Jake is in his workout gear, his hair ruffled on one side and flat on the other, his eyes shaded with deep concern as he looks at me.

He reaches out, takes my hand, starts to murmur reassuring words.

"I'm fine. Thank you," I say briskly, leading him upstairs. "Help us get Dan into your car. Sophie, will you be all right to stay here?"

I see her and Connie exchange looks, know that she wants to come with us, see that Connie is conflicted about leaving one child alone and in distress to care for another one.

"Can you drive?" I ask her, receiving a nod. We decide that Jake and I will take Dan, with Connie, in the Audi, and that Sophie will follow on. I spend a few moments talking to her first, checking that she is capable of driving, that she is not too upset, that she will be safe. I know this family's history, and I know how this will be even more traumatic for them than for most, and I need to know that I'm not putting anybody else at risk by allowing her to come with us.

Once I'm sure, Jake and I manage to half support, half carry Dan down the stairs, laying him as safely and gently as we can across the back seat. Connie cradles his head on her lap and talks to him softly. I see her fear, her desperation, and I clench my eyelids tight shut when I feel tears start to well up. I have been of little use to them tonight, but I'll be even less if I let myself break down now.

We start the car and drive away, and I see Larry's little head looking at us through the front window, where he is perched on an armchair and looking confused. Sorry, bud, I think – but this is one place I can't take you.

Jake seems to understand that I can't talk right now, and concentrates on driving as quickly as he can while being cautious of the winding roads and poorly lit lanes. I've never known a journey seem to last as long.

It is not a large hospital, not by London standards, but they greet us with efficiency, getting Dan onto a trolley as Jake drives away to park up and meet Sophie. We put on the masks we are given, and follow inside.

I introduce myself to the on-call emergency registrar, and

talk him through things while he makes his initial assessment. After that, Dan is wheeled away down the corridor, where I know he will be put into a gown and scheduled for tests.

"What will you be doing?" I ask the doctor, as Connie and I trail at his heels. I don't know this man, and he looks to be about 12 years old – I know that can't be true at his level, but I am reluctant to let go until I'm sure Dan is in safe hands.

He looks from me to Connie, clearly uncertain of our relationship and probably wondering why an out-of-hours GP seems quite so personally invested. Connie quickly improvises: "Ella is Dan's doctor, but also my sister."

It is a bare-faced lie, and one that I would normally immediately correct – but I know it will make my position here easier to deal with, so I decide that now is not a time for ethical quandaries.

The doctor nods and replies: "Well, I suspect you're correct, it looks like meningitis. So, we need to find out what kind, and to do that, we'll need some bloods, and a lumbar puncture to start with."

Connie's eyes fly wide open, and she stops dead in her tracks.

"Won't that hurt him? Aren't they awful?" she asks, desperately.

I place my hand on her shoulder, and explain: "Not as bad as you think, and he'll be well looked after. Plus, Connie, it's necessary – I'd tell you if I didn't agree, okay?"

She nods, and we follow the doctor. We walk through the departments that are still so horribly familiar to me, past what we used to call Minors, and Majors, and Resus, all the way to the Rapid Assessment Unit. A nurse in a mask is already drawing blood, and another doctor is filling in notes, and everyone is working under the constant glare of overhead fluorescent lighting.

The noise of the place is hitting my brain with all the

subtlety of a jackhammer: the beeps of the monitors, the hiss of a nebuliser, the chatter of the nurses, the squeak of trolley wheels on lino, the aggressive yells of an angry patient somewhere in the distance. The soundtrack to my old life.

Dan himself has opened his eyes, is looking around in confusion and fear. Connie is at his side straight away, suddenly casting aside her own panic, her own worry, to talk to him in calming tones, telling him everything is going to be okay, that he mustn't be scared.

There often isn't time, when you work in a busy hospital, to explain what you're doing – sometimes, you have to skip that part, and simply do it, no matter how distressing it can be for the patient and their families. Tonight, though, I am not working here – and I can at least help with that.

I stand on the other side of the bed, careful to keep out of the nurse's way as she takes Dan's arm and starts the process of setting up an IV. I see his eyes flare in fear, and put my hand on his forehead, stroking back his half-green, half-black hair.

"It's all right, Dan," I say calmly. "You know what this is, don't you? The nurse is just setting up an IV. That's just a fancy name for the tube, and the tube connects to a bag, and the bag will probably contain antibiotics."

I glance at the doctor for confirmation, and he nods. I'm relieved to be right – if this is bacterial, and if Dan has sepsis, then every minute could be important. Starting the drugs now rather than waiting for the test results is the right move – and it would have been so much better if he'd been here even earlier.

Dan's eyes are bleary and I'm not sure how much he is understanding, but I carry on talking, walking him through the steps, reassuring him, explaining how it all works as they also hook him up to fluids. When the time comes for the lumbar puncture, I do exactly the same. He is almost unconscious by this stage, which actually makes things easier – at least he's not squirming around.

I sit next to Connie, me holding her hand, Connie holding Dan's, and explain every stage of the procedure to both of them. I see a curious glance from the specialist nurse in charge, who is obviously wondering who I am and why I know so much about medicine, but it goes smoothly enough.

When it's over, I manage to corner the doctor again, and ask him if he's going to send Dan for a brain scan. There are all kinds of risks associated with meningitis, and swelling on the brain is one of them. He looks at me patiently, tells me firmly that if necessary, he will, and strides away. I can't say that I blame him – nobody likes being told how to do their job by a complete stranger, and nothing I have seen here leads me to believe that these people are anything less than professional.

After a while, Dan is moved to a small single room on a ward, and I leave Connie with him while I go and find the others.

They are in the waiting room, surrounded by the usual parade of sprained ankles and tummy aches and asthma attacks. A man in one corner is kicking the vending machine, and a woman is haranguing the triage nurse about how long they've been waiting, pointing out that they were here hours earlier and other people are 'skipping the queue'. The nurse explains the basics of triage to her with a practised tone, and I walk over to Jake and Sophie, trying to shut it all out.

"He's been admitted," I say to Sophie, who looks like she's about to cry. "They've done some tests, and we'll know more soon. Sophie, I'm so sorry I wasn't there when you came to look for me..."

She brushes it off, but I see Jake stiffen slightly. I wonder if he is feeling the same underlying guilt as I am.

I give Sophie directions to the ward, and am left with Jake, standing beneath those punishing lights, listening to someone cough up half a lung in the background.

I look up at him, and can't even find a smile. While I had to stay strong for Connie and Sophie, I managed it – but now I am running on empty.

"How is he, really?" he asks, holding my hands in his.

"Not good," I reply, shaking my head. "Pretty sure it's meningitis, though we don't know what kind yet. If it's bacterial, and it spreads, then... Oh God, then so much could go wrong. He could lose limbs. He could be left with hearing loss, or seizures, or kidney issues... He could die, Jake!"

Saying it out loud makes it true, and I am swamped with terror. I can't stop blinking, and the sounds and sights around me are blurred and dream-like. A cartoon version of reality.

Jake tries to take me in his arms, but I move out of his reach. I don't want to be comforted or consoled. I don't deserve it. I cannot accept it.

"This isn't your fault," he says quietly. "You did everything you could."

"Everything I could apart from actually be there! If I'd heard the walkie, or if I'd been where I was supposed to have been when Sophie came for me, then we could have been here hours ago – and every second counts in a case like this. I let him down."

"You didn't. You got him here. And you don't know how this will turn out – he's young and healthy, you can't assume the worst..."

I let out a bitter laugh, and move further away. This isn't Jake's fault either, but I am too raw, too wired, too anxious to let myself off the hook that easily. Being here, dealing with this, is sickeningly familiar, and I know I can't cope if I don't focus. If I refuse to let myself be distracted.

"That's the thing, Jake," I say, staring past him at the man who has finally retrieved a Mars Bar from the vending machine, "I've been trying so hard not to assume the worst, about everything. I've been trying so hard to be positive, to not expect everything that can go wrong will go wrong. Yet here we are –

facing the worst. Look, this isn't the time or the place for a conversation – and I'm in no state to have one. Thank you for your help, but you should go home now. There's nothing more you can do here."

I see the flicker of hurt that crosses his face before he manages to control it, and I hear the effort in his voice as he replies: "I can stay. For you."

"No," I answer, softening my tone, "that won't help. Not right now. I'm tired and stressed, and it's going to be a long day, and I don't have anything to spare at the moment. Go home, Jake – I'll call you later, I promise."

I can tell that he doesn't want to leave, note the reluctance in his body language as he turns to walk away. He wants to stay, to make me feel better at a time when I know nothing can, not even him. He wants to reassure me, to try and convince me that things will be okay in the end.

That's easy to believe when you're sitting on the beach at Starshine Cove, watching the tides. But here, in this place, in territory I know so well, it seems like an impossible dream.

I turn to walk back to A&E, tripping over my own shoelace and barely managing to stay upright. I have lost my balance, in every possible way.

Chapter Thirty

Sophie goes home after a couple of hours, promising to feed and walk Larry, and fill in George and Archie. Connie gives her the world's biggest hug before she leaves, brushing strands of blonde hair back from her face and kissing her exuberantly before she finally releases her. It's the kind of gesture that would make teenagers cringe at any normal time, but this is far from a normal time.

I probably shouldn't still be here either, but I suspect the registrar has figured out it would be a lot more trouble to try and make me leave than to deliberately ignore my presence.

The tests have come back, and Dan has been diagnosed with meningococcal meningitis. He is receiving targeted treatment now, and has had a CT scan, which was blessedly clear. The nurses have set up a fan next to his bed, and his temperature is coming down. The next two days will be vital, and Dan will be watched by several hawks, including myself, to see what happens next.

I explain all of this to Connie in clear layman's terms, avoiding any of the long-term risk factors that I know exist but would completely freak her out before it's even remotely necessary. Naturally enough, I can't extend the same courtesy to myself, and I am tortured by visions of Dan facing a lifetime of disability. Of missing out on medical school, of his whole future being stolen, or at least radically changed. Of Dan not making it.

I'm not quite illogical enough to think all of this is my fault – these illnesses are out there, they happen, and I couldn't control that. I did not invent meningitis. But I'm not sure I'll ever quite forgive myself for the delay in getting him here, either.

We develop a routine, Connie and I, of sitting together, and of giving each other breaks while we seek out too-hot coffee from machines, visit the cafeteria, or take walks outside in air that smells of fuel and cigarette smoke. It is intense, being in a hospital – the strange combination of boredom and adrenaline, the way you get to know the staff by sight, overhear conversations about other people, lose track of time without your natural rhythms. I have worked in them, and now I am at the bedside of a patient, and it is challenging on both sides of the curtain.

The morning visiting hours bring, predictably enough, the arrival of George. I'd spoken to him on the phone and advised him to stay away while his own health status is still in question, but obviously he ignored me. Meningitis isn't excessively contagious, but as a precaution the hospital pharmacy has issued antibiotics for the people who have had extensive close contact with Dan – Connie, Sophie, and a couple of friends he'd had a sleepover with. George will probably be fine, and he is wearing his mask, but I am still concerned.

He silences me with one hand held up in front of my face, and announces: "I'm here, love, and I'm staying. Don't waste your breath."

He looks tired, and Connie looks haggard despite her attempts at humour, and I wonder how hard this must be for them – not only to have Dan so sick, but to be back in the hospital that has so many associations for them. That must remind them of the day they lost Simon and Sandy.

I am surrounded by pain – theirs, my own, the suffering of the people around us. The young man who was admitted after a bicycle crash who I know is in a bad way; the daughter of the elderly man with terminal lung cancer; the junior doctor who looks exhausted and on the point of breakdown by dealing with it all. The pain is everywhere; it is a virus, it is airborne – and it is poisoning me with every breath I take.

It is suddenly all too much for me, and I feel like I need to scream. To yell, to cry, to tear off this mask and suck in the oxygen that I feel starved of. To run from the smell of disinfectant and hospital food, the sound of the machines, the constant ringing of the phone. I need to escape before it all smothers me, before it ruins me and renders me useless.

It is a familiar feeling, one that I had every single day of my working life in hospital, and one that I know will overwhelm me if I don't pay attention to its demands.

I fake the need for a coffee, politely extricate myself from the room, and dash to the lifts. My heart rate is rising, and my palms are clammy, and each inhale I try to take seems to choke me. I literally run for the automatic doors, hitting a wall of rain outside as I almost collide with a man wheeling a toddler in a buggy.

I hastily apologise, and keep moving, heading for a nearby bench. I sit down, ignoring the puddle that soaks my backside, and pull off my mask. I turn my face up to the sky, and let the raindrops splatter across my skin, hitting closed eyelids and rolling down my cheeks. They hide the tears that I feel joining them, that I know I've been storing up until I was alone. I grab hold of the bench I am sitting upon, grip it so hard I feel a fingernail break.

You are okay, I tell myself. You can do this. You can do this, you can do this, you can do this...except, I don't think I can. I don't think I can even let go of this bench, never mind go back inside.

My solitude doesn't last nearly long enough. I hear someone approach, and glance up to see Jake. He looks alarmed, and whips off his rain jacket, tucking it around my shoulders. It is too kind a gesture for me right now, and I find myself hiding from his gaze. I don't want him to see me like this. I don't want him to see the pain and the anger and defeat that I know will show in my eyes. It's not fair to impose myself on him in this state. He won't understand, and he shouldn't have to try. I am not fit for public consumption.

"Are you okay?" he asks, crouching down so we are face-to-face. "Is Dan okay?"

The rain is lashing down, flattening his hair, running in rivulets across his forehead. I force myself to meet his eyes, to take it all in, to confront the man who not so long ago I thought I was falling in love with. Now, when I look at him, I am blinded by regret. I know it makes no sense at all, but I can't separate him – us – from what has happened to Dan. And being here, in this place, has opened up so many wounds I fear I might bleed out. I thought I was strong enough to move on, to put my past behind me – but I was wrong.

Now, I just want him to leave – it is all too messy. Too complicated. Too hard. He will never understand, and I don't have the reserves of emotional energy to even try to explain. I am alone in this, and that is the only way for me to be.

"Dan's okay so far," I say, seeing but not feeling his hands on my knees. "We'll just have to wait and see. You're getting very wet."

He smiles gently, and replies: "That doesn't matter. How are you, though, Ella? I know this must be hard for you..."

I move his hands away and stand up. "Yes. But not as hard as it is for Connie and Dan."

He climbs to his feet, but keeps his distance. You can only push someone away so many times before they get the message.

"Why don't you come home?" he asks. "Have a shower, get some sleep, something to eat. I can bring you back here in a few hours if you like."

The thought of those things gives me a fleeting sense of calm. I imagine being warm and cosy, tucked up in Jake's big bed, him beside me, allowing myself to relax in his arms.

The calm is only fleeting, though, because now, whenever I imagine myself there, I also imagine Connie, frantically calling me. The walkie unanswered in the other room. Dan, lying in his own bed as bacteria runs riot through his body. Me, failing them all.

"I don't think I can," I reply, my voice barely audible. "I should have been there for them, Jake. I should have been at home, not..."

"With me?" he finishes for me, obviously understanding my line of thinking even if he doesn't like it.

I nod, feel rain drip from my nose as I do it. He sighs, and I see him clench his eyes shut for a moment as he gathers his thoughts.

"You're allowed to be happy, Ella," he says simply. "You're allowed to have a life of your own."

Not so long ago I would have agreed – now, I'm just not sure that statement is true.

I stare at him, and see a stranger. Everyone is a stranger, really.

"I've got to get back," I answer, passing him his coat. "Be careful on the roads when you drive home."

I walk away, staggering across sodden grass, passing beneath a blocked drain that gurgles with rainwater and cigarette butts. I pull off the fingernail that I broke, seeing blood rise from the torn skin, the vivid red quickly washed away in the downpour.

I stand outside the doors, and stare inside. I don't want to go back in there. I don't want to face it all again.

I close my eyes, force myself to imagine Dan's face. Force myself to picture Connie, at his bedside. Force myself to walk through those doors.

Chapter Thirty-One

The breakthrough comes on the following evening. Dan has been regularly monitored, tested, poked and prodded, and so much blood taken that it's a miracle he has any left. I've also been sneakily doing my own checks, just to double up. Throughout it all, he's been patchy – drifting in and out of consciousness, not making a lot of sense when he's been awake, restless when he's been asleep.

Connie and I are both slumped in our chairs when he comes to. The nurses found us one recliner, and we have been swapping in and out of it – I am currently in the uncomfortable plastic seat, and haven't felt any sensation in my rear end for over an hour. I am trying to do one of Connie's crossword puzzles while she snoozes, but finding it impossible to concentrate. The letters and the grid and the shades of black and white have all blurred in front of my tired eyes, swimming like monochrome alphabet soup.

I don't even notice Dan is awake until he speaks in a croaky but lucid voice.

"Hey," he says, struggling up into a sitting position. "You look like crap. What happened?"

He is rubbing his arm, which is undoubtedly sore from all the blood draws, and looking suspiciously at the IV.

Connie snaps into full alertness at the sound of his words, and we both jump up and go to his side. Connie kisses him and I check his temperature. We both have our own ways of showing affection, I suppose.

He tolerates her for a few moments, then bats her away with a floppy hand, telling her to leave him alone before he pukes in her hair.

"Aaah, he's back!" she announces delightedly, clapping her palms together. "He's being a twat, he must feel better!"

I see the hint of a grin play across his cracked lips, and decide she is right – he is most definitely feeling better. This doesn't mean he's out of the woods, but it is a very encouraging sign.

"How are you?" I ask. "How much do you remember?"

"Umm...not a lot. Being ill at home, feeling so bad I couldn't even play Xbox. A few bits and pieces from being here. You talking to me like you were prepping me for an exam."

I laugh, and the sound feels alien to me – there hasn't been a lot to laugh about recently.

"Yes, well, I hope you were paying attention – if you were, you'll have superb first-hand experience of IV insertion and lumbar punctures."

"Ouch," he replies, pulling a face. He is quiet for a moment, and asks: "What's up with me anyway? And do you think it'll count as work experience?"

This is greeted with far more hilarity than it deserves, and I know that we're not just laughing because he's funny – we're laughing because we are relieved. Because he could have died. Because we have been sitting at his side for a very long time, lost in fear.

"You have meningitis," I explain. "Bacterial. You've been on some super-duper drugs and it looks like they're working.

There'll be more tests, and I wouldn't book in any mountain climbing in the near future, but it looks like you'll be okay."

At this point the doctor arrives, obviously alerted by the sudden eruption of giggles in a usually silent room. He smiles at the sight of Dan up and talking, asks him a few questions, and then sends in a nurse to do more observations. She finishes up by looking at him critically, and declaring that it's time for a wash.

Dan is, by this point, definitely feeling well enough to tell me and his mum to bugger off for a bit.

"If I'm going to be humiliated," he says, waving his hands towards the door, "then I don't want to do it in front of you."

I meet Connie's eyes, and see the sparkle of joy in them. She nods, and we reach an unspoken decision to leave him to it. We promise to be back soon, and make our way to the cafeteria.

We have both been here separately during our shifts, but naturally enough, I know nobody, and Connie seems to have made friends with all of the staff and a proportion of the customers.

"How's he doing?" the cashier asks us as she rings up our drinks. "Any change?"

"Yes!" Connie declares gleefully. "He basically just told me to get lost!"

"Aaah, that's wonderful news, love," the woman says, patting her on the hand. "Onwards and upwards, eh?"

We find ourselves a corner seat with a window, so we can enjoy our view of the ongoing rain, and Connie flops down with a huge sigh of relief. I know it's not just because of the view.

"How come these places are so tiring?" she asks, stirring sugar into her mug. "I mean, all we've been doing is sitting on our arses, but somehow I'm exhausted."

"I know. It's a weird effect hospitals can have. Somebody should probably do a study on it."

She says she's tired, and I can see that's true, but she is also newly energised, and buzzing to tell Sophie the good news. I listen to her half of the conversation, and she puts her phone away. She sips her coffee, stares through the window, then abruptly bursts into tears.

It comes from nowhere – one minute she is fine, better than fine in fact, and the next she is a soggy, squelching mess. I dash over to her side and put my arms around her, and she weeps into my chest for a solid five minutes. Around us, people ebb and flow, casting sympathetic glances in our direction as Connie heaves her heart out.

Eventually, the sobs that are wracking her body slow, and then subside, and she finally comes up for air. Her face is smeared with strands of hair and snot, and she's left a big damp patch on the front of my T-shirt. She points at it and laughs, and I roll my eyes.

"Look, it's like the Turin Shroud!"

"And I didn't think I could look any worse..." I mutter, as she dabs at me ineffectually with a napkin.

"You are a bit of a slob," she replies, wrinkling her nose.

"Well, if George hadn't brought you a change of clothes, you'd still be in your pink PJs wouldn't you? I'm just...fragrant!"

Admittedly, the fragrance is not one that would attract many celebrity endorsements – it is Eau de Hospital: the smell of a woman who hasn't changed her knickers in a few days combined with sleeping in a chair. My hair feels greasy to the touch, and I've been using sugar-free gum as dental hygiene. I am, to be frank, minging.

But bad as I look on the outside, I think internally, I look even worse. I have made myself stay, I have faked it until I made it. I have been here for them, to the best of my admittedly pretty crappy abilities – but now that it seems as though we might have turned a corner, I am already desperate to escape.

"Will he be all right?" she asks seriously, as she gives up dabbing.

"I can't say for sure, Connie, but I hope so. I think so. The staff here know what they're doing, and it seems like we caught it in time..."

We both pause after I say this, and then both try to speak at the same time. I gesture for her to go first, and she says: "Thank you, Ella. For everything. If you hadn't turned up when you did, I don't know what would have happened."

I stare at her in astonishment, because I was going to say exactly the opposite.

"No, Connie," I reply, "please don't thank me. I should have been there earlier. I should have come round to check on him, even if you thought he was okay. I should have answered your calls, and answered the walkie, and been there for you... I wasn't, and we're lucky that we're sitting here talking like this, because it could so easily have ended very badly. I messed up, and I'm sorry."

I have rarely seen Connie lost for words, but this is one of those occasions. She frowns at me, and screws up her eyes, and in the end answers: "Ella, you only have one thing to apologise for."

She pauses for dramatic effect, and forces me to respond: "Okay. What?"

"The fact that you didn't tell me about Jake. That's where you were, isn't it? With him? What's going on?"

Everything, I think, and maybe nothing. Now I have been away from him, spent so much time here surrounded by my own demons, I am struggling to make sense of it all. I yearn for him, but I also dread seeing him – feel swamped by the complexity of a new life that just a few days ago felt so simple. I should have known better – there is always a booby trap, a buried landmine to step on, a tree root to stumble over. Something always goes wrong.

I paste a smile on my face, and say: "That's a story for another time."

Chapter Thirty-Two

I stay with Connie and Dan for two more days, fortified by George dropping off some clean clothes, and on one visit, Larry, who greets me in the car park with such ferocious enthusiasm that it makes me cry. He has been fine, George tells me, living the *vida loca* with Lottie – but he has missed me, that much is obvious. He stares at me from the rear window as George drives him away, and I feel my heart crack. I wave, as though he can understand such a concept.

On the second day, we have a meeting with the same doctor who admitted us, who tells us that Dan is making a great recovery, and should be able to go home soon. I know they'll keep an eye on him, but ask anyway, receiving all the right answers about follow-up care and check-ups. I am beginning to suspect that Dr Malik is a little bit afraid of me, which isn't necessarily a bad thing.

Dan himself is feeling much better, well enough to roll his eyes at his mum, call me a control freak when I check his notes, and start to complain about the fact that he gets lime jelly for pudding with each meal. Every single complaint he makes, every petulant accusation that leaves his lips, feels like a victory – a step in the right direction. Proof that he will be okay.

That afternoon, I tell Connie that I'm leaving, that everything is going well enough for me not to be needed here any more. She hugs me, and thanks me, and warns me she will be expecting to hear all about my romance with Pub Daddy as soon as Dan is discharged. I make the right noises, let her think that will happen, and get a taxi back to Starshine Cove. I cannot engage with the driver's cheerful chatter; I can barely engage with myself. I need to be alone, but I know I have hurdles to leap before that happens.

I keep up my 'everything's fine' persona while I collect a very happy Larry from George's cottage, while I chat to Archie as he weeds the flower bed around the green, while I update the Betties. They are all interested, and thankful, and full of plans to celebrate when Dan gets home. I think I fake it well enough, but I can't fool myself – a distance has opened up between me and these people, this place. A distance that I welcome, a distance that I can hide behind.

Maybe it's what happened with Dan. Maybe it's spending too long in a hospital, which was like living in a horror film flashback sequence for me. Maybe I'm just finally waking up from the dream that has been my time in Starshine, and realising that I can't maintain it. That this isn't me, much as I'd like it to be. I am a fraud, even if it's only me who recognises that.

I let myself into the attic, and am relieved to finally stop pretending. Relieved that I don't have to smile, or make small talk, or be touched by anyone else. Relieved to be alone again.

Larry rushes ahead of me, sniffing around and pawing at corners just to make sure nobody has invaded his territory while he's been gone. There is still a used coffee mug in the sink, crumbs around the toaster from breakfast the last time I was here. My pyjamas are folded on the corner of the sofa bed, and another couple of Thomas Hardy paperbacks are piled on the table. In the bathroom, my make-up is scattered on the shelf below the mirror, left over from a lifetime ago when I was getting ready to meet Jake.

It looks exactly as it did when I left it, but it feels completely different. I can see the physical signs of the life I was leading, but it doesn't feel like it belongs to me now. I am numb, removed, taking it all in through alien eyes – watching myself here, but not feeling anything at all.

I take a shower, dry my hair, dress in fresh clothes that still smell of fabric conditioner, and make myself a coffee – black, because the milk has gone sour. On auto-pilot, I clear up, empty the dishwasher, pack my belongings. As I've discovered in recent months, it is surprisingly easy to load your whole life into a suitcase once you make that decision. I am becoming the mistress of the moonlight flit – except that it's the middle of the day.

I feel brittle and frail, as though I have aged a hundred years over the last few days. Every movement I have made since I climbed out of the taxi has been measured and controlled; every item I have packed, every dish I washed, every surface I wiped, felt like an insurmountable challenge.

I look around at my little attic room, at the place that once felt like a haven, and say: "Goodbye, hobbit hole."

I load my bags into the back of the car as quickly as I can, because I don't want to have to lie to anyone, or even worse, tell them the truth. The truth is that I am broken, I am damaged, and I am of no use to this village, or these people, or even myself. I can't live like this, slipping in and out of normality, getting closer and closer to a community that I might one day let down. This time, it was Dan – and this time, it didn't end in disaster.

It was close enough, though, to shake the real me free – the me that isn't ready for this. The me that is worried that next time, it won't end so well. What if Miranda has complications with her pregnancy, or her labour? What if George's skin cancer is serious? What if one of the women I talk into attending the mobile breast screening unit gets bad news?

Even thinking about it takes me to the edge of panic – rapid heartbeat, shallow breathing, a churning stomach. I know the signs well enough; I've lived with them as well as treated them. I am a wreck in human form, and I can no longer ignore that. The last few days have opened my eyes, shown me who I really am – not just who I want to be. I've been living in a fairy tale, one that ends with happy never after.

What am I, after all? I'm a doctor who can't cope with stress, who can't cope with caring, who can't cope with life-threatening situations. A doctor who can't even control her own mental health, never mind her patients'. I'm a doctor who is scared of hospitals. That makes me no doctor at all, and the people who live here deserve more than that. More than I can give. They'll be better off without me.

I walk briskly around the green, Larry trotting happily by my side. He is blissfully unaware of all my turmoil, and I am thankful to at least be taking something positive from this whole experience. I might not have found my happy place, but I did find a dog.

I pause outside the inn, and consider messaging Priya. I reject the idea – it would be unfair to seek solace, to look for help, to find support. I need to do this alone, and I need to do what is right for everyone.

I see Jake behind the bar at the inn, chatting to Matt. They both look up when I walk in, and Jake's face breaks into a smile of welcome. It doesn't take long for that to change – he knows me too well; he can tell that I'm not here for a Starshine Special and a fond reunion. He tells Matt he'll be back soon, and follows me across the room – right to the little snug where we sat and talked, on my very first night here.

Part of me didn't want to do this. I gave some serious consideration to just driving away, avoiding the pain of it. But I'm not that ruthless, and knew I had to see him face-to-face. He has been left before, and I know his wife told him she was going in a text message, while he was with his dying mother. He carries scars, as we all do, and although what I am about to do will hurt him, I can at least give him the honesty and respect that he deserves.

He sits across from me, runs his hands through his thick dark hair, and sighs. He is still the most handsome man in the world, which doesn't make any of this easier.

"You're leaving, aren't you?" he says simply, a muscle in his jaw twitching as he waits for my answer.

"I am," I reply. "And I'm sorry. Everything that's happened – it just showed me that this isn't right for me. Not yet. Maybe never. It's not your fault, Jake, I want you to know that..."

"Right," he says, smiling sadly. "It's not me, it's you?"

"That's about the size of it. I know it sounds like an excuse, but it's true. You've been nothing but good for me, Jake – but I can't stay here, like this. I'm just no use to anyone at the moment. I fell to pieces when people needed me the most, and I can't do that again. I can't go through that again. I know that makes me weak, I know that makes me a coward – but maybe that's what I am. Maybe that's what I'll always be."

"You're not a coward," he says firmly. "And you're not weak...and even if you were, is that such a terrible thing? Aren't we all allowed to be weak sometimes?"

"Not like this. Not when you're responsible for other people. The longer I stay, the more they'll start to get used to having me around. The more they'll depend on me – and I'm just not feeling very dependable. It wouldn't be fair to stay, to carry on like this, knowing that I could crack just when someone needed me most – it'd be like you renting out a property to someone, knowing the roof could fall in at any moment."

"I think," he says slowly, gazing out of the window, "that

maybe what I'd do is try to fix the roof before I condemned the whole property."

I nod, but stay silent. He is hurt, and maybe he is angry, and he has every right to those feelings. The best I can do is acknowledge them.

"I'm sorry," I say again, reaching out to place my hand over his on the table top.

He wraps his fingers into mine, and says: "I didn't expect any of this, you know. When you walked in that first day, I thought wow, she's pretty, because I'm a male and I have eyes. Then I talked to you, and thought wow, she's clever and funny as well. Then I...well, then I really got to know you, Ella. No, that's not quite right – I didn't just get to know you. I fell in love with you. If you're going to leave, then I have to say that out loud, instead of skirting around it in my own mind. I love you. And now, seeing you here like this, knowing that you're calm on the outside but falling apart on the inside, I don't know whether loving you means I should be fighting for you to stay, or letting you go."

His fingers stroke the skin of my palm, and his eyes roam my face, and I feel the full impact of it all. Of his touch, his look, his words. His honesty and his bravery and his love. I wish it changed things, but it doesn't – I feel like a ship that is about to sink, and I don't want to take him down with me.

I lean across the table, kiss him lightly on the lips, and pull away.

"I love you too, Jake. But you have to let me go."

Chapter Thirty-Three

Larry looks at me from his spot on the sofa with a deep level of betrayal in his eyes. Maybe embarrassment, I'm not sure.

He is on Priya's couch in her home in a leafy suburb of Birmingham. He has been a huge hit with her two little girls, and once he got used to a new place and new smells, the feeling was entirely mutual. Which is probably why he allowed them to comb out the long hair on the top of his head and tie it up in miniature pink scrunchies. He now has two furry ponytails sticking straight up into the sky like space rockets, and looks sad about it. I scratch behind his ears and tell him he's handsome.

It is after 10pm, and Priya has finally got the girls to sleep. Her husband, Martin, is on a night shift, and we are making a dent in a bottle of wine. I have been here for three days, and am grateful for the respite – but this particular conversation with my friend is fast becoming something I am not enjoying at all.

Over the last few days, I have told her everything. About Mark and Kim, about Lizzie, about Starshine and Jake. About the way that being back in a hospital made me feel. She has listened, and questioned, and understood. She has not judged, or tried to fix me, or given me her opinion – until now. Now, she is in full flow. I blame the wine.

"Do you have any idea how many NHS staff developed mental health problems after the pandemic?" she asks, waving her glass in the air.

"A lot?" I say quietly, knowing she's going to tell me.

"Yes, a lot! There've been all kinds of studies about it since, including one by the British Medical Association, by the Government, organisations all over the world. Everything went up – anxiety, depression, PTSD. It was hell, and for a lot of people it still is – but I also know a lot of people like you, who just ignore it, just try and pretend none of it matters any more. Who try to just forget the things they've seen, the things they've experienced. Who just think they can do a yoga class or burn a scented candle and tell themselves everything is all right."

That one hits home, as I remember my frustratingly ineffective meditation classes, my failed attempts at self-care.

"Well, that stuff can work, can't it?" I say.

"It can help, yes, for some. All kinds of things can help – but what's struck me in recent years has been how bloody awful doctors are at looking after themselves. How they'll do everything they can to take away the stigma of mental health issues for other people, but gloss over their own. If you had a patient with the same symptoms as you, would you send them away and tell them to go for a long walk and perhaps to buy a colouring book?"

"Maybe," I snap defensively, knowing that I most definitely wouldn't, "maybe that would be enough. And anyway, I don't have symptoms – I'm not sick!"

She shakes her head, smiles sadly, and pours me another glass of wine. I haven't seen her in the flesh for years, and she looks older but still gorgeous: laughter lines around her huge brown eyes, her hair cut into a stylish bob.

"I beg to differ," she replies, more gently. "Even from what you've told me, I can tell that you are. You've lost a baby, and never had time to deal with that. You've lost your long-term partner. You've lost any sense of control over your life, and your response has been to shut down. Panic attacks, anxiety, social isolation...leaving behind your work, your friends, the things that make you *you*. None of that is a sign of a healthy mind, my love."

"Priya," I reply firmly, "I know you're a psychiatrist and this is an occupational hazard, but please stop trying to...*shrink* me!"

She sips her wine, looks at me sadly, and replies: "Shrink you? Honestly, Ella, I don't think I could make you any smaller than you are now."

Her tone is kind, but her words are like poison darts. I am almost 40. I have no home, no nearby family, possibly no career. I have nothing apart from a stray dog.

I curl my arms around my knees, and bite my lip. I want to cry, but I think that if I do, I might never stop. I know she is saying these things for my own benefit, I know she is trying to help, not to be cruel – but it still hurts. Everything hurts. I am one big human-shaped sore spot.

"You know," she says, sitting beside me and leaning into my side, "that this isn't a sustainable way of life, don't you? What do you think might happen next? You're welcome to stay here for as long as you like, but it won't change anything. You can run as much as you like, but you'll still be you. The answer isn't to try and live in a sensory deprivation tank, Ella – you need to open up, not close down. It's the only way."

"I could do something different," I reply, "I could retrain. Do a job that doesn't matter so much."

"Yes, you could," she says, stroking my hair back from my face. "People do, and sometimes that's the right thing for them. But for you? I don't think so. Even when we were young, you were always the most committed of all of us. Even when we had that holiday, after medical school, I remember you still being switched on...like that time we met those cute boys in that nightclub in Paris, and you tried to diagnose one of them with diabetes because he kept going to the loo..."

"Yeah. I think maybe he was just snorting cocaine, with hindsight."

"Me too," she says, laughing at the memory, "but that's who you are. Your issue has never been that you don't care enough – you care too much. From what you've told me, the way you've been living for the last few years, you've been doing your best to remove that part of yourself, exorcising it like it's a malignant tumour. But it's not, it's an essential part of you. Even now, I've seen you sneaking away on your phone. I'm going to take a wild guess here and say you've been checking up on your patients."

I stay silent, but she is right. I told the GP practice partners that I was on sick leave, rather than simply resigning, so I still have access to the system. I have seen that Dan has been given a clean bill of health and gone home with an after-care action plan in place; I have seen that George's mole was low-grade and no further treatment is required. I have seen that Miranda has been attending her pre-natal sessions. I felt sneaky as I checked, like some kind of voyeur.

"I have," I reply eventually. "But I don't think I've been doing that because I'm a great person, Priya – I've been doing that to clear my conscience. To make myself feel better about leaving them."

She gives me a little thump on the arm, and says: "You see? Even now, you're trying to find the worst in yourself, trying to prove you don't deserve anything good in your life. This man, Jake?"

I nod, and feel myself tense. I haven't spoken to Jake since we left, and even hearing his name feels painful.

"Jake, who by the way is quite clearly the hottest dude in Dorset..."

"Possibly the world," I reply.

"Possibly the world. Anyway, Jake – what kind of person is he? Is he an idiot? Is he reckless and compulsive? Does he have a disastrous life based on poor decision-making, drug use, low self-esteem? Or is he just, you know, a bit stupid?"

"No!" I bleat defensively. "He's not like that at all. He's kind, and measured, and thoughtful. He's a successful business-man. He's a million miles away from stupid!"

She grins at me like she's proved her point, and continues: "Right. So, would a man like that fall in love with you if you were as much of a wreck as you think?"

"I see what you're doing here, Priya, and I'm not buying it. I just think maybe he doesn't really know me, not all the bad stuff, not the things that are lurking beneath the surface..."

"But you say you were close, that you shared everything with him. Why don't you trust his judgement?"

Jeez. She is relentless, and I have a flash of pity for her patients.

"Okay, you win," I finally say. "I don't trust my own judge-ment. Is that what you want to hear?"

"I want to hear that you'll get some help, babe," she answers. "I want to hear that you'll let me help you, or let someone else help you. I want to hear that you're not going to give up on yourself."

I am desperate for this conversation to end, to go to my bed in her spare room, to escape. Except knowing Priya, she may well follow me in and talk to me while I'm asleep as well.

"What would that look like?" I ask, hoping to shut her up. "Getting help?"

"I don't know. We can figure that out. I have resources, colleagues, things I could suggest. You could even see my therapist."

"You have a therapist?" I ask in astonishment. "But your life is perfect!"

"Nobody's life is perfect, and yes, I have a therapist – and let me tell you, I am an absolutely horrible patient. I personally think my therapist hates me, but that doesn't matter – she's not my friend, she's part of my support system. As is Martin, and the girls, and my book club, and the occasional glass of wine. We all need help sometimes, my love, it's as simple as that. The tricky part for you will be accepting it."

Chapter Thirty-Four

I wake up the next morning with a hangover, and the feeling that I can't breathe – that all the oxygen is being forced out of my body.

I blink open my eyes, shake my head to clear the fug, and see that Priya's three-year-old daughter, Zara, is kneeling on my chest. She is holding a lipstick, and I suspect that I am now the proud owner of a clown face. Lower down, Kiara, her older sister, seems to be painting my toenails. What is it about me that makes little girls want to give me a make-over? I see, as I smile and gently move Zara to one side, that Larry is keeping well out of it all on the opposite side of the room. Coward.

"Auntie Ella's awake!" screeches Kiara, leaping off the bed and running out of the door, followed by her sister. "She's finally awake! She wants Coco Pops for breakfast!"

Larry runs after them, suddenly interested.

I rub the back of my hand over my mouth, and it comes away smeared with a bright shade of deep red that would look fantastic on Priya but is awful on me. I lift my feet up, kicking off the duvet, and see that each toenail is a different colour. Nice.

I put one hand on my chest as I stare at the ceiling, realising that even though the miniature succubus has gone in search of sugary cereals, I still feel short of breath. Still feel somehow crushed, as though there is an unseen pressure physically pushing down on me.

I take my own pulse, and reassure myself that I am not on the verge of a heart attack – I just feel dreadful. As in, literally full of dread.

I stay still, close my eyes again, and do some deep breathing, mentally counting in and out, in an attempt to set myself right.

I am unsurprised that I am not greeting my new day with joy, because even by my low standards I really did not sleep well. Partly because of the wine, but mainly because of the conversation I'd had with Priya. This tough love business is, well, tough. It was the emotional equivalent of being run over by a steamroller.

I get up, pull on a fleece over my pyjamas, and head downstairs into the kitchen. Priya is up and dressed, showing no signs of last night's indulgence as she leans against the island sipping coffee.

"Nice look," she says, "are you auditioning for the lead role in *It*?"

I grab a sheet of kitchen roll and start to clean myself up, as she asks: "And did you really say you wanted Coco Pops for breakfast?"

Kiara looks at me imploringly behind her back, eyes huge and hands held together as though she is saying her prayers. Impossible to resist.

"I did," I reply. "I bloody love Coco Pops."

Priya gives me a face that tells me she knows exactly what is going on here, but plays along anyway.

She pours me a mug of coffee, and I silently watch as she pulls bowls out of the dishwasher and grabs cereal from the cupboard. The girls have taken Larry into the garden, and I soon hear them shrieking in horror as he does 'a massive stinky poop!' That's my boy.

As she adds milk to the cereal, Priya looks up at me, and meets my eyes.

"Are you okay?" she asks simply.

"No," I reply, putting down my coffee with trembling hands. "I'm not okay, and you were right last night. I've not been okay for a very long time. Priya, I...I think I do need help."

Part Four

Happy Ending?

Chapter Thirty Five

It takes about three hours to drive from Priya's house to Starshine Cove. I spend a lot of that journey dealing with a low-level sense of anxiety, but also excitement. I am returning to a place where I am unsure of my welcome, unsure of the outcome. That, I tell myself, is okay – it is natural to feel some concern, to feel unsteady, to simply feel. I am allowed to be nervous, because I am not superhuman.

I have techniques to better cope with this kind of thing now, and most importantly, I am able to recognise and accept the fact that this is challenging.

The last month has not been easy, but it has been necessary. I have had countless sessions with a therapist, I have joined a peer mentoring service run by other doctors, and I have laid myself bare like never before.

There have been a lot of tears, and a lot of frustrations, but also a lot of laughter and some moments of almost euphoric joy. I am not, by any means, 'fixed' – again, because I am not super-human. I am flawed, and I will always be flawed, and that is all right. Everyone else is, too.

I am, though, now brutally honest with myself – and I find

that I don't really mind it. That the monsters under the bed disappear a lot quicker once you drag them into the light. Priya was, of course, right – the one person I could never run away from was me. Once I got to grips with the idea that I was stuck with myself, the only option was to try and make that a better place to be.

I followed her advice, and carried that honesty through into other areas of my life. I went out for dinner with Mark, and we talked about losing Lizzie in a way that neither of us had been able to before. I contacted my parents, and came clean about my issues. I picked up the phone and spoke to the GP practice, and explained why I needed a leave of absence. These were all small and positive steps, but now I feel ready to take the big ones. The ones that have led me back here, to Starshine, and to the life I left behind.

I have no real idea what will happen next, which is terrifying – but I do at least now have an understanding of what went wrong in the first place. I have exchanged messages with Connie and Dan, briefly spoken to George on the phone. All of them reacted with kindness and understanding, which doesn't surprise me given the kinds of people they are, but still leaves me grateful.

Jake has only been in touch once, a one-line message asking me to let him know I was safe. I told him I was, and left it at that. I needed the time and the space to figure out what I really wanted, and being in close contact with him would make that impossible.

And now, I have had some of that time and that space. Now, I am here, driving these familiar curving roads, making the steep descent down the hill and towards the coast. Larry has been going frantic in the backseat for the last few minutes, spinning in circles, pawing at the window, yapping in excitement. He, at least, seems happy to be home.

By the time I park the car at the back of the inn, it is dusk on a cold November day. I clamber out, and look around me as Larry gallops to the nearest pee point. The lights are shining from the mullioned windows, and I can picture the scene inside, imagining the logs on the fireplace, the lively chatter, the red velvet booths.

I glance towards the green, see the familiar circle of cottages and homes, the Pixieland flag in George's front garden flapping and fluttering in the breeze. I see Trevor closing up his emporium for the day, and hear a deep, solitary woof. Larry's ears go up, and I suspect Lottie knows we are here before anyone else does.

I let my eyes wander the village, spotting all the subtle seasonal changes – different flowers coming into bloom, a scattering of frost on the grass, fairy lights strung along the buildings twinkling in the fast-darkening gloom. It is the same, but different – just like me.

It feels strange, being back here – strange but not bad, I decide. When I first arrived, it all seemed almost alarmingly perfect – the way it looked, the way the people acted. Now I know differently. It still looks perfect, but I know what lies beneath – I know that the people here have lived, have suffered, have struggled, just like people everywhere. Some of them, in fact, have experienced almost unimaginable tragedy.

Their lives are not perfect, the village is not perfect, but it is a place like nowhere else. When these people are in pain, they don't just support each other – they allow themselves to be supported. They're not immune to hardship; they just help each other through it. That sounds so simple, but I know that it is not – I know that opening yourself up, to the good as well as the bad, is never easy. It's not the caves that makes Starshine so special, or the views, or even the cake – it is the people. The humanity of it all, the sometimes-scary sea of fellowship that they all seem to sail together.

I tell myself not to give in to being scared, and I push open the door to the inn. I take a deep breath to prepare myself, and my gaze goes immediately to the bar. I have imagined this moment so many times: planned what I might say, prepared myself for what I might feel. Now that it's here, I realise that no amount of prep would have helped. I am stepping into the unknown.

I remind myself that I need to do this. That I cannot run, because it simply doesn't work. That even though I won't be able to control how Jake reacts, I can focus on how I react. I need to find a little faith, and then leap into it.

In the end, I needn't have worried – because Jake isn't there. Matt is behind the bar, along with a now much rounder Miranda. They both look up when I walk in, and I see the look of surprise on their faces.

"Ella!" Matt exclaims. "You look fantastic! Can I tempt you to a taster of this new stout I've got in – a hint of plum, a touch of chocolate..."

"That sounds delicious, but no. I still have nightmares about last time. Miranda, how are you? Where's your usual T-shirt gone?"

She gestures down at herself and pats her belly.

"I got too fat for my I'm-not-fat T-shirts," she replies, grinning. "Bit of a design flaw. Are you...staying?"

Ah, I think, now there's a question.

"I have no idea, to be honest," I say, shrugging. "Umm...is Jake around?"

"It's his afternoon off," she explains, looking apologetic, as though it is somehow her fault. "Sorry."

I brush it off, and stand there, feeling vaguely embarrassed. I have spent the whole drive building up to seeing Jake again, and now this feels like a huge anti-climax. He could be anywhere – maybe he's gone to London for a meeting; maybe he's visiting his dad; maybe he's in Dorchester on a date. Apart from that one brief message, I haven't been in touch – anything could have happened in his life. It's been a month, and things could have changed, moved on, evolved. He could have met someone else, or hate me so much he has a picture of my face on a dart board.

"I think he maybe mentioned something about going for a run down at the beach?" Matt offers, interrupting my thoughts. I smile and thank him, and have a quiet word with myself for allowing my mind to go on a mini-rampage. Just because I know what I shouldn't be doing doesn't mean I always manage to avoid doing it.

I make my farewells, and go back to the car. There is a deep chill to the air now, and I retrieve a fleece from the boot. I pull it on, and briefly run my fingers across the pendant that Jake gave to me on my birthday. I never wore it much while I was here; it was kept hidden and secret, like our relationship. While I've been away, though, I've had it around my neck every single day. It's become a touchstone, a mantra given physical form. A reminder of why I'm worth fighting for – living proof that you need to let in the light to make things shine.

Larry dashes ahead, thrilled to be back, trotting down the steps and immediately rolling around on the sand as though he's trying to coat every inch of his body in the stuff.

I pause as I reach the beach, sighing as I stare out at the view. The moon is full tonight, hanging fat and yellow over the water, and the stars are perfect jewels of light in the black velvet of the sky. I have missed this, I realise – the way this place, these sights, the sound of the waves, lift my spirits. I had almost forgotten quite how beautiful it is.

There is no sign of Jake, either on a run or a walk or simply sitting on the beach, but as Larry suddenly sniffs the air and hurtles off along the shoreline, I start to realise where he might be.

I follow him, knowing that my dog is about to spoil any element of surprise here – I won't be making a dramatic entrance. This, I think, is no bad thing – Jake deserves a moment to clear his head, and I slow down deliberately.

By the time I reach the caves and make my way inside, Larry is on Jake's lap, little legs kicking in the air as Jake rubs his belly. A small torch is on the floor beside him, casting a singular beam against the shimmer of the cave walls. It is beautiful, as usual – but for me, there is only Jake. I look at him, and feel a physical thud inside my chest, followed by the flutter of a thousand butterflies.

I stare, and drink him in – his hair is slightly longer, and his trainers look new, but the smile is the same. The smile is still one that can make my knees wobble. I examine it closely, looking for signs that it isn't real – that he is just being polite.

When I don't find them, I smile back, and we are both still and silent for a few moments, lost in each other's eyes.

"Ella," he says finally, as Larry scoots off to explore. "You're back..."

I sit next to him, close enough to touch but not touching, much as I want to.

"I am," I reply. "It's so good to see you, Jake. I've missed you so much."

He quirks one eyebrow, and answers: "I'm glad. Where have you been?"

I let out a breath, and know I have a lot to explain. A lot to apologise for. A lot to make up to him. That I can't expect everything to just go back to the way it was; he is a human being, not a museum exhibit, and his life might look different now.

"I've been staying with a friend," I say. "I've been trying to fix the roof."

"Oh. And...how has that worked out?"

I laugh, and decide on honesty: "Well, it's still a bit leaky to be honest – but a lot better than it was. It'll definitely cope with a light shower, but I might need to do a bit more work if there's one of those storms-with-names coming up. Maybe I'll need some new tiles, or some patching-up, or maybe a bit of a repair on the guttering..."

I trail off, and he says: "Ready to give up on the whole roof analogy?"

"God yes! I don't know enough about roofs to carry on. Anyway. You get the picture. I'm so sorry, Jake, about the way I left. About shutting you out. About all of it – but it was necessary. If I hadn't left, then I wouldn't have been able to come back."

He nods, but doesn't respond. I start to feel a rush of desperation, of hurt, of need, and tell myself to breathe. That I have had time to prepare for this moment, and he hasn't. I can't expect too much, it wouldn't be fair.

"How have you been?" I ask, longing to take his hand, to touch his too-long hair, to bridge the gap between us.

"I've been...busy," he finally says. "After you left, it was rough. I'd forgotten how it feels, living with that kind of pain. I woke up in the morning still expecting you to be there. You left a hairbrush in my room that I couldn't even throw away. I missed you so, so much. So I did what I usually do to cope..."

"Did you finally buy Jupiter?"

"No," he says, grinning, "but I did decorate my apartment, and install a home gym, and help out with Miranda's new place. Her lease ran out and she had nowhere to go, so the gods of Starshine – by which I mean Connie and George obviously – decided to step in. We converted one of Trevor's stock rooms for her. There were chainsaws and claw hammers involved; it was very exciting...are you staying?"

The last question comes out in a rush, disconnected from the rest of his comments, as though it snuck up and ambushed him.

"I could," I reply, risking a touch to his arm. "I've done a lot of work, and I've done a lot of thinking, and I'm trying really hard to make some changes. I'd like to stay. I'd like to come home, be back here with everyone. Be back here with you. But I know I can't just waltz back in here and witter on about my new roof and expect you to—"

"Shut up," he says abruptly, his tone firm. "And come here."

I blink in surprise, and do as I am told. He runs his hands through my hair, holds my face between his palms, and kisses me. I melt into him, throwing my arms around his neck, trying to show him how much I love him in the simplest way possible.

When we finally move apart, I am breathless, and flushed, and also crying. He wipes away the tears, frowning, and says: "That's not the response I was hoping for..."

"No, it's okay," I reply, laughing, holding his hands tightly. "It's the good kind of crying. The kind that keeps the roof patched up. Jake, I love you, and I want to try and make this work. But I have to be honest. I'm not perfect, and I don't know how this will all turn out..."

"And that's scary," he says, completing my thought. "Yeah. For me too. The worst thing about it all, after you'd gone, was that I felt stupid – like I'd imagined the whole thing was more than it was. That if you didn't trust me when times got hard, then I couldn't be as important to you as you were to me."

"That's not true," I reassure him. "It really isn't. I just... couldn't reach out to you, no matter how much I wanted to. I was too messed up. I might still be, sometimes, but at least now, I'm willing to try, to really try...if you are. I know I'm asking you to take a chance, and I completely understand if you don't want to..."

He nods, and keeps hold of my hands, and gazes out towards the dark entrance of the cave.

"I do want to," he replies eventually. "And I have a feeling, you know, that things will actually turn out just fine. I think the signs are all there."

"Signs?" I say, as he pulls me next to him, puts his arm

around my shoulder and holds me close. "What signs? You're not the sort of person who believes in signs!"

"Maybe you're not the only one who's changed. Just wait for a minute, and then you'll see what I mean. I've been waiting here for an hour to see this, and I thought I'd be doing it alone. Do you remember when I first brought you here, and I told you that on some nights, when the angle of the moon was right and the stars were aligned, that this place came alive?"

I nod, and my eyes follow the finger he points towards mouth of the cave. At first, it is just the edge – a perfect slice of moonlight silvering its way inside. Then, moment by moment, inch by inch, it appears – the huge perfect circle of the moon, hanging right before our eyes.

I gasp out loud as it happens, as the whole cave is flooded with natural radiance, as the walls and the roof burst into full, glorious colour.

"You see," says Jake, his face alive with joy as we sit and stare in wonder, "signs."

He's right, I think, nestling deeper into his arms. It is a sign – and everything looks better in the light.

Epilogue

"Are you sure you want to do this?" Jake whispers, his face close to mine. "Neither of us has done this before. You don't have to, if you're not ready."

I kiss him quickly on the cheek, biting down my nerves, and shake my head.

"No, it's okay," I reply. "There's a first time for everything, right? Just be gentle with me..."

"I can't promise that," he answers, grinning as he walks away from me. I watch him go, chewing my lip, listening to the cheers and cries around me. They're all here, of course, fringing the village green – Connie and George, Dan and Sophie, the Betties, Trevor, Miranda, Archie and the girls, as well as familiar faces from the homes on the hillside. Everyone has come out to see this.

I glance up at a perfect blue sky, wishing for a sudden downpour to come along and end this. It is the last Sunday in November, but the weather is stubbornly refusing to cooperate.

I take a deep breath, and steady myself. I grip the bat firmly in my hands, hearing Connie's loud whoop-whooping noise as

Jake makes it to the big wooden barrel. He reaches in, pulls something out.

"Knock him for six!" yells George, as Jake takes a run-up. Even from this distance I can see the smile on his face as he bowls.

I see it hurtling towards me, have no idea what I'm doing, but take a mighty swing, whacking it as hard as I can. I am amazed when the bat actually connects.

I hear a dull thud, see it disintegrate, and feel cold, wet blobs spray all over me. They hit my face, land in my hair, splatter all over my jumper. I look down, see that I am now multi-coloured, and burst out laughing.

Within seconds, I hear the cry, as everyone stands up on the patio, arms waving in the air as they all yell: "Jelly Bomb!"

A Letter from the Author

Dear reader,

Huge thanks for reading Escape to Starshine Cove, I hope you were hooked on Ella's journey. If you want to join other readers in hearing all about my new releases and bonus content, you can sign up for my newsletter – it's totally free, I won't send so many your inbox hates me, and I promise it will be fun!

www.stormpublishing.co/debbie-johnson

If you enjoyed this book and could spare a few moments to leave a review that would be hugely appreciated. Even a short review can make all the difference in encouraging a reader to discover my books for the first time. Thank you so much!

I hope you enjoyed your escape to Starshine Cove, and being part of Ella's world. Like many of us, I lead a busy life, full of joys and challenges, and finding the time to read is such a delight. I know that without the magic of books, the power of stories, and the pixie-dust that a good tale can sprinkle over your mind, I'd be lost.

I created Starshine Cove because for me, it represents so much that is good about the world – it's not just a beautiful place, it's a place that is rich in a sense of community. People support and accept each other, help their friends and family through the darker times. It's also a place where people laugh a lot – and isn't that what gets us all through in the end?

Nobody's existence is free from problems, but as the old saying doesn't go, a problem laughed at is a problem halved!

By the end of this book, I felt like all of the inhabitants of Starshine Cove were real and special. I felt like I could pop into the Cove Café for a coffee, or taste one of the Betties' cakes, and feel the sand of the bay beneath my toes. They became friends to me, and I really hope you feel the same.

I have lots more adventures planned for Starshine Cove, and I'd be so excited if you went on them with me!

Thanks again for being part of this amazing journey with me and I hope you'll stay in touch!

Debbie

facebook.com/debbiejohnsonauthor

x.com/debbiemjohnson

Acknowledgements

Creating Starshine Cove has been an exciting new venture for me, and I couldn't have done it without a whole load of people – it does indeed take a village!

On the professional front, thanks to my agent, Hayley Steed, to Elinor Davies, and the whole team at the Madeleine Milburn Agency. It's been a rollercoaster of a year, and I hugely appreciate your support. Thank you also to the team at Storm Publishing – my editor, Kathryn Taussig, MD Oliver Rhodes and Melissa Boyce-Hurd. It's hugely exciting to be along for the ride, and thanks for finding such a lovely home for Starshine Cove.

Personally, as ever, my heartfelt thanks go out to all my long-suffering pals – Milly Johnson most of all. That woman deserves a medal for listening to me moan so much. Also, big hurrahs to Catherine Isaac, Miranda Dickinson, Laura Kemp, Rachael Tinniswood and so many other fab authors. Not authors, but just as fab are Sandra Shennan, Pam Hoey, Paula Woosey, Ade Blackburn and my comrades at the pub quiz. I would be even less sane without you.

Pats on the back to my family for putting up with me – Dom, Keir, Dan and Louisa, as well as the Newton clan. Daniel, my middle child (he would add 'and best' here, but as a mother of three, I must remain impartial), was the first person to read a synopsis of this book, and made all the right sounds at a time I needed encouragement. He has personally requested that I point out how marvellous this makes him, and who am I to argue?

Printed in Great Britain
by Amazon